The Case Files of Henri Davenforth

Case File 4

Honor Raconteur

BREAKING AND ENTERING 101

What is that cackling?
That's Jamie.

What? I love a good heist!

Published by Raconteur House
Plymouth, MI

THE CASE FILES OF HENRI DAVENFORTH: Breaking and Entering
101 Case Files 4

A Raconteur House book/ published by arrangement with the author
Copyright © 2020 by Honor Raconteur
Cover by Katie Griffin
Clockwork spare parts by donatas1205/Shutterstock; *male man toilet WC* by
yougifted/Shutterstock; *old locomotive at night* by nikifor todorov/
Shutterstock

Report 01: A Royal Break-in

I leaned back for a moment, easing the tension in my lower spine. I'd been leaning over the table for several hours, conducting an experiment with sheep's blood in an effort to determine cause of death in a case. I was beyond tired, running into the realm of exhausted, but had no real time to properly rest. Ever since Sanderson had been fired, I'd been carrying his workload. Granted, I'd more or less carried half his workload from the beginning, but now I had *all* of it and was struggling to keep my head afloat. I'd taken precious time every few days to go through resumes and interviews in an effort to find someone to replace him. To no avail, sadly. Worse, the person whom I knew without a doubt could do the job, I wasn't allowed to extend an interview to.

If something didn't change soon, I might well stage a protest. I couldn't keep up with this insane workload much longer.

Sherard Seaton burst through my workroom's door like a damsel from some dramatic play. He didn't even pause at the doorway, just threw himself upon my worktable without any further ado, his head buried against the surface. And considering what I'd just done on this table, that wasn't at all advisable.

"Seaton, really," I chided him in exasperation. "I just conducted an experiment with sheep's blood two minutes ago."

He immediately jerked his head up but didn't leave off with his lamenting. He even looked the part of the damsel in distress, the dark liner around his eyes running and giving him raccoon eyes, an unshaved collection of stubble aging him. "Davenforth, you must help me!"

"Only if you cease with the dramatics and start being sensible." I knew this man could be practical if he so chose. I didn't know what to make of his theatrics. Either he was having a joke at my expense, or something had sent him teetering into this state.

Seaton gave me a hopeful look. "You promise to aid me?"

"You've come to my aid often enough, I do believe it's my turn to return the favor," I pointed out patiently. It was even true. The most notable account that leapt to mind was the insanity barely two months ago, when Sanderson had burst in here and attacked me. Seaton hadn't actually needed to do much but stand there and look threatening, but he'd dropped everything to come to my aid, and I appreciated it beyond measure. Of course I'd help him in return.

This assurance seemed to settle him, and he stopped draping himself across my table as if he were ready to perish on the spot. "We've got a problem at the palace—" He abruptly stopped and looked suspiciously at my open door. "How well does sound carry here?"

"Too well if the door's open."

Seaton immediately leapt from his stool, closed the door with hard finality, then retreated to his spot once more. Then, for added measure, he cast a silencing spell against the door. This time, the capable royal mage and magical genius faced me as he laid out the facts with a moue of distaste. "We've got a problem with security at the palace. Someone is routinely breaching the walls and strolling about not only on the grounds, but inside the palace itself."

My eyebrows shot into my hairline. Dear me, I did understand now why he was so utterly alarmed. The security measures and wards on the palace grounds were no laughing matter. It took the consistent work of three royal mages to keep them operational. The wards were the product of generations of royal mages' designs and ingenuity. Defeating them was no easy matter, nor should be. "How many breaches in total?"

"We've caught him twice," Seaton answered sourly. "I'm actually quite sure he's done it more often than that, but smart lad that he is, he's not admitting to anything we can't prove."

"You say 'lad.' How old is he? Magical?"

"Not a magical fiber in his being, and he's fifteen."

My jaw dropped and dangled near the floor for a moment. Fifteen?! And non-magical to boot. The idea of someone thwarting all the magical safeguards was far-fetched, of course, but I'd briefly entertained it as possible. Thanks to our last case with a locked-room murder mystery that featured a retired royal mage, I'd learned not to make assumptions when magic was at play. But non-magical? A teenager? "How is he getting in?"

"Blast it, that's the very thing we don't know! I've asked, of course, and the thing of it is, he'll tell you. He'll outline exactly how he's done it, but to him the magical ward was just this pretty, sparkly golden dome that encased the palace—it wasn't a hindrance. He said he climbed up onto the wall—"

I made a choking sound. The wards actually covered the walls on the *outside*—that move alone shouldn't have been possible.

Seaton gave me a grim, humorless smile in agreement. "—and walked along the top of it for a time, then saw a window on the ground floor he thought was open. He hopped off, investigated, and found it was indeed unlatched. Then he just popped in and went exploring."

"How long was he in before he was discovered?"

"A week, he says."

For the first time in my professional career, I was perfectly speechless.

Well able to read the expression on my face, Seaton grunted. "I unfortunately believe him. He hid up the chimneys during the day, or behind furniture, and moved about quite handily. Because he was up chimneys, though, he was smeared with a great deal of soot. It left marks wherever he was. We can confirm he sat on the throne, read through some of the books in the royal library, ate in the palace kitchens, and even slept under the queen's settee in her personal study."

I shuddered at that list. The thought of an assassin having that kind of free rein inside the palace filled me with dread. Queen Regina was one of the best monarchs in living memory, and we as a nation did not want to lose her. I was unaccountably grateful we were dealing with a teenager instead of a hardened criminal, even if this did promise to give me a migraine.

"You see my problem," Seaton concluded, giving me a hopeful look once more.

"I do see the problem, but I'm not sure how you expect me to help."

Seaton lifted two fingers. "On two points I think you are the right man to conscript. First, this is clearly not a case where more magical power can somehow fix the problem. You are not a man who relies on magic—quite the reverse. You rely on intelligence and forward-thinking to solve a problem, using magic only as a handy tool to aid you. I need that thinking right now."

Ah. Now this made more sense. That was exactly how I operated. It was a point of pride for me that despite my lack of magical power, I could still stand toe to toe with him. (It was also immensely flattering to my ego that he acknowledged such. I tried to not let it go to my head.) "And your second point?"

"You're a kingsmen consultant, so I can pull you in safely for this without having to do a great deal of paperwork first. You are, in fact, the perfect man for the job." His expression crumbled and he looked utterly done in as he begged, "Please help me figure this out. I've literally done everything I can think of, and even after we turned him out and fined him for the first entry, he did it again not two weeks later!"

Oh dear. "Twice in a month? Seaton, that's…"

"I know," he groaned, flopping on my table again before remembering that was ill-advised and popping back up.

"Wait," I advised him, holding up a hand. "Let's bring Jamie into this. She'll need to know, regardless, if I'm to help you, since I won't be available to her. And she might have some insight to offer."

"I would have already brought her in, but she wasn't at her desk."

"Ah." And who knew where she'd be. My partner was not one to sit about. She preferred to be up and in motion if at all possible. I picked up my texting pad from nearby and scrawled onto it: *Jamie, can you come to my workroom? Seaton has a problem.*

After a moment, her answer came through in neat script: *Be right there.*

"She's coming," I assured him before setting the pad aside again. I looked at my friend, so utterly distraught, and felt charitable for a moment. "Need some chocolate?"

He gave me a look so hopeful it would put any dog's puppy eyes to shame. "Do you have any of the peppermint ones?"

I really should just stock up on chocolate at the rate my friends ate through it. Why I kept buying a box at a time was beyond me. Without a word, I fetched the box and offered it to him, which he took with a sigh, nimbly opening the lid and plucking two of the sticks out.

The door opened and Jamie sailed through, taking

in the scene with a pursed mouth and a calculating eye. "If Henri's sharing his chocolate, it *must* be bad. Is the zombie apocalypse coming?"

"Hardly," I drawled to her, pleased I knew this reference. "Shut the door, please. This shouldn't get out."

She did so, curiosity rising, and snagged two pieces of chocolate on her way to a stool. "To fortify myself," she explained cheerfully as she took a seat next to Seaton.

"Of course," I deadpanned, as dry as any desert. "Seaton will have to give us particulars, but the gist of it is this: A fifteen-year-old boy is routinely breaking through palace security and roaming about the grounds at will. No one has been able to prevent his entry. He's been caught twice in the past month."

Jamie's hand stayed itself in the act of popping a piece of chocolate into her mouth. She slowly lowered the hand, eyes darting between my face and Seaton's, as if suspecting us of pranking her. "Wait, are you serious?"

Seaton nodded forlornly and reached back into the chocolate box.

"How's he getting in?" she demanded, voice rising in pitch.

"He *says* he climbs the outer wall, walks along it until he spies an unlatched window, and makes his way in from there," Seaton answered glumly. "I can't prove otherwise. The wards don't show any signs of being countered or broken."

Jamie whistled low before popping the chocolate into her mouth.

Something about this account bothered me. I pulled a journal out from the shelf behind me, something to take notes down on, and flipped to a blank page. "You said the wards show no signs of disturbance. Why did the guards not see him on top of the wall?"

"He mostly enters at night, or near dawn, I think. And really, the guards don't focus on the walls or walk the perimeter. The only points of weakness in the wards are on the entrances, so that's where they focus their attention."

It made sense, of course. With the wards preventing any entrance along the walls, why bother wasting manpower there? With four entrances into the palace grounds, they had quite enough to guard, and it was better placement to focus on the entrance points.

Except in this case.

"And the ground floor windows aren't locked?" Jamie inquired, following this closely.

"We didn't see a point of enforcing that level of security before this," Seaton explained. He rubbed at his shoulder and neck, as if the tension there was building to uncomfortable levels. "Why should we? Any visitor allowed in was either already approved or under escort from the guards both in and out."

Jamie nodded slowly, that intelligent mind of hers going at full throttle. "Are the wards like any other set of wards? Under the same rules?"

"Ours are more stringent, I believe, than the ones you normally see. They protect against outside attack, of course, and will rebuff any strong elemental force— say, a typhoon. But we couldn't regulate them in any way where people are concerned." Seaton's hands spread in a helpless manner. "We have so many who come through on legitimate business, but there's no way to predict who's coming or who might need access in the future. We set it so anyone escorted by the guards at the gates can come through."

"And the kid obviously didn't have an escort, if he's just hopping the wall. What's his name?"

"Eddy Jameson."

I stopped scribbling as an idea occurred to me. "Seaton, may I assume the wards don't have a list of those who have permissions?"

"Correct." He nodded sharply with his confirmation. "The spellwork on the wards is hideously complex as it is—if we had to add and remove names from it, it would become even more complex and likely jumbled in the process."

"Like constantly amending security software," Jamie muttered to herself in a rhetorical fashion, staring sightlessly forward. "The coding would get screwed up beyond repair, I betcha. So, wait, how do the wards recognize who's got permission to stroll through?"

"A symbol is applied to personnel, just below the nape of the neck. The wards recognize it," Seaton answered with strained patience.

"Like a magical tattoo?"

"You can think of it as such, yes. It's applied and removed with a spell."

"And it's not something someone can lose or have stolen, which was my next question. Eddy didn't hack the wards by stealing a badge or something. Hmm." She sat back and thought some more.

I made another note to include this new information when the obvious occurred to me. "Seaton. The conditions of the wards are something like 'any without permission or with ill intent cannot pass,' correct?"

Seaton's smile was strangely proud and triumphant even while staying grim. "I knew you'd pinpoint the weakness instantly once I explained. That's exactly the problem, that wording."

Jamie's head snapped around to stare at him. "Wait. Because Eddy doesn't have any ill intentions, the wards don't consider him a threat, so it's letting him in?"

"Essentially, yes. Or at least that's the only thing that makes sense to me. Technically, even without the ill intent, he shouldn't be able to just waltz in. Somehow, he's found a loophole around the permissions. Jameson claims he's just curious about the inner workings of the palace, that he only wants to watch. I believe him. He isn't stealing anything or doing any damage. The wards don't consider that a threat, so he can just waltz in as he pleases. It's enough to give everyone a migraine, myself included."

"Celebrity stalker, much?" Jamie muttered. "But if that's the case...wait, does that mean anyone without ill intentions could just walk in?"

Seaton lifted a finger to his lips. "Shhh. We do not want people thinking that. Technically, they shouldn't be able to without permission. The wards have varying levels of security. Most of the time, it operates at its lowest mode of protection. At its highest, it won't let anyone in or out. The problem is that we changed it to a higher setting once we knew of Jameson's entrance, and he *still* walked right through it. According to the settings of the ward, he should not have been able to."

"Yeah, I can see why your panties are in a twist now. What should have happened when he walked through?"

"At the lowest setting, you're simply repelled," I answered, making a face. "At the highest, you're incapacitated until someone retrieves you."

"Huh. So, you can't really alter the rules completely because people who should have entrance might be either kept out, or knocked out, depending on the security level of the wards." Jamie tipped back in her chair, staring at the ceiling in blank thought. "How do you change the wards to keep him out, but still keep it flexible enough to let people in?"

Seaton gave her a sage nod. "That, my friend, is the question."

Henri's Additional Report 1.5

Seaton and I spent a full week on the wards without any improvement to the situation. It took me a full day just to get up to speed on matters, as of course I was hardly an expert on the wards, and then we had to nitpick them apart.

Changing the source of power was out. Altering the way they were anchored to the buildings and walls surrounding the palace grounds was truly out, as none of that would help our cause. That left us with somehow altering the way they functioned.

I lay sprawled on the carpeted floor in Seaton's study. My back screamed after being bent over the worktable for nearly a full day straight. The hard surface was exactly what my protesting muscles needed in that moment. Seaton lay similarly sprawled on the couch nearby, his head the opposite direction from mine. A fine pair we made.

"Change the way the wards anchor to the gates," Seaton offered, not even lifting his head.

"We tried that."

"No, I mean change it so no one can go in willy-nilly."

"We tried that too, remember? It's an on-off clause. You can either enter through there or not. It's why gate guards are on those points."

"But if we turn it to off—"

"We turn the palace grounds into a very pretty prison. I doubt Her Majesty would be pleased."

"We can change it from an on-off clause," Seaton bit out stubbornly.

"Of course we can. And then we'll have to find and alter every single clause that deals with a gate or side door and hope we don't miss one. Otherwise, the whole design fails in a spectacular cascade with no possibility of redemption."

"Love is dead and never existed. All you did was betray me as I lay sick and festering. You are the definition of dread."

"What are you on about?"

"You're being mean."

"Because I keep disabusing you of your half-baked notions?"

"You're supposed to be supportive," Seaton whined at me, head flopping to the side so he could glare.

"If you want to try it, go ahead," I riposted mildly.

"That's exactly the tone Jamie uses on Clint when he's about to do something stupid."

I shot him a toothy grin. "How observant of you."

Seaton subsided with a dark mutter. "You're quick to shoot me down, but what solution is there to this?"

"If I only knew."

Really? We're doing Henri Additional Reports now?

I deemed it appropriate since you've taken over my notes completely. And I hardly felt like rehashing the entirety of what we've tried. Doing it once was exhausting enough.

So, did you think of something good?

Sadly not. uh-oh

That about covers it.

Report 02: Queen on a Warpath

I am a woman on a mission, wooooah ♫

"Jamie."

I looked up from the paperwork on my desk and broke out into a smile. Gibson was one of my favorite people in the world, the big brother I always wanted growing up, and the biggest teddy bear. It was always fun to see him. I popped up to give him a hug, which he returned, dwarfing me in the process. I'd believe him part werebear, really, if not for the fact that he was ash-blond with pale skin. If we were on Earth, I'd suspect him descended from Vikings. He had the right look for it.

"Gibs. Are you here for business or pleasure?"

"Now, that's a tricky question," he answered with a grin, dropping into my visitor's chair next to my desk. "It's always a pleasure working with you. But I'm definitely here to enlist you on a case. We could use a fresh perspective on this one."

It must be a doozy if he was here to fetch me in person. "Alright, I'm all ears. Wait, should we fetch Henri first?"

"He's at the palace right now. Passed him and Seaton on the way out."

"Ah, right, the palace wards." It wasn't a good sign that even a week after Sherard had brought this problem to Henri, they hadn't found a solution. The teenager hadn't broken in again, so there was that at least, but the problem was still in want of a solution. "I can't actually tell if they're having fun or not. I know it's stressing them out on one level, but every time I ask how things are going, they get this excited air about them as they explain things to me."

Gibson nodded in understanding, expression wry. "I've seen what you're referencing. In truth, those two are peas in a pod. I think they like tackling magical puzzles together.

It's probably rare for them to meet someone else who can intellectually keep up."

"So, they're enjoying the chance to play with each other." It was true the other royal mages were appointed because of their power, not necessarily their brains. Sherard and Henri's grades in school had been practically neck and neck, they were so close. Registered geniuses. I'd seen them like this before, where they were neck deep in a puzzle and having too much fun to quit. It was why I wasn't really worried about them at this point. When they forgot to eat or sleep, that was when I would need to step in. "Okay, so you're still here to fetch me even when you know Henri's on palace grounds. Why?"

"Had a very interesting case occur last week." Gibson planted an elbow on my desk and leaned in, dropping his voice to a more confidential rumble. "We've kept it quiet, so you probably haven't heard, but a train was robbed on its way to Bristol. Specifically, the guarded gold in the shipping cart was stolen. About three hundred thousand crowns in gold, to be specific."

I whistled low. That was a lot of money for this world. About the equivalent of seventy-five thousand dollars in US currency, or at least that was my rough estimate. Figuring out how much things cost, and what all my salary could cover, had been not so much fun the first few months on my own. When I'd first found out my salary was two thousand crowns a year, I'd about hit the floor. No matter how I tried, I couldn't do a straight crowns-to-dollars conversion and get the math to work out in my favor. Then I did an analysis and realized how little things actually cost. Turned out, I was actually making decent money for the economy. When a loaf of bread basically cost, like, five cents, the money went a lot further.

"Yikes. How?"

"That's the question, right there." Gibson nodded sagely. "We have no clue. They did it so smoothly we're not sure how they got in, got out, or even how many were involved. No real suspects either. I've been staring at this case for five days, and my brain's about as active as a dead hamster."

"I now understand why you want a second opinion. But for this, I really want Henri too. He's got a knack for asking the right questions."

"Oh, I've requested both of you. I know better than to separate you two." He wagged his eyebrows mischievously.

I rolled mine and refused to rise to the bait.

Gibson kept giving me these nudges. Like now. Why, I wasn't quite sure. He liked Henri, I knew that much. He trusted the man with me. Apparently, he thought we were a good match, too, hence these nudges.

I put that aside. I wasn't ready to talk about it yet, and this definitely wasn't the place. Rumors flew through the bullpen and didn't even need a spark to start them half the time. I didn't want something like this noised about. It would embarrass Henri half to death, for one.

"Alright, so getting back to this train theft—I assume kingsmen have jurisdiction of this because it goes outside two city limits?"

"Correct."

I hadn't been on many train rides since my arrival. Maybe a half dozen. I had a feeling that to figure this out, multiple trips would be in order. "Alright, let's go fetch Henri. No, wait, let me pass this on to Penny first."

He looked down at the paperwork on my desk. It was a personal landmark for me that I could now fill out basic paperwork without needing help. I'd conquered that much of the vocab, at least. I still didn't know enough to be able to comfortably read a full novel, but I was getting there. I'd now been on this world for two and a half years, and if the language wasn't so hideously complex—and if the translating spell on me didn't hamper learning a language by 'cheating'—I would have gotten a better grasp on it faster. Oh well.

Lifting the form, I waved it a little. "It's okay, I'm basically done with the case. I just need to submit the final forms for processing my suspect. Penny can wrap up for me. She was working the case with me anyway."

"You're still mentoring her?"

I shook my head. "No, she's a detective now. Officially one since last week, actually. She just worked this one with me because Henri was severely backed up with lab work."

"They still haven't hired someone to replace Sanderson?"

Remembering all the interviews Henri had sat in on, I snorted. "Yeah, that would be a big fat no. Henri insisted on helping with the interviews."

Gibson stood as I did, eyeing me. "This will be good, I can tell. Alright, Henri insisted on helping with the interviews. And?"

"He asks five questions—he firmly maintains they're basic questions—and hands them two different projects to test. Something he sees often from the field. They have to answer all questions correctly and get the correct result for the tests. Not do the tests the way he would, mind, but just get the right answer."

Gibson's jaw dropped a little, voice rising with every word. "And you're telling me not even one candidate can manage it? How many people have interviewed for the position?"

"I've honestly lost count. The captain's been frustrated, but as Henri pointed out, hiring someone who can't even do the basics won't do any of us good. That just means botched evidence. What's further frustrating him is that women are not allowed to apply for the position."

Gibson fell into step with me as we walked to Penny's desk. She wasn't in the bullpen with the rest of us—there wasn't any room for her. Instead she was in the new annex building, which, honestly, meant nicer working conditions. The newer building had better ventilation and more windows. Not to mention the prototype for air conditioning, which made absolutely everything better. No one in the building would need it in another month or so, as we were sliding into fall now, but still. Great to have. I was a little jealous.

"I find it very strange a woman would be barred from applying," Gibson said, visibly perplexed.

"The rationale, or so I've been told, was that the commissioner felt it was too emotionally strenuous for a woman to handle." My voice was dry as a martini as I relayed this because, really, the stupidity of that thinking amazed me. Women handled childbirth, poop, vomit, all the blood and broken bones a child suffers growing up, and were often nurses and doctors who saw horrendous diseases and mutilations. But something from a crime scene might be too much for her? Really?

"Your friend is a very progressive thinker. I can see why this would bother him."

"Mmm," I said in mixed agreement. "It's partially that. Partially because he knows of a very good candidate. A woman he went to school with. She's been struggling to find steady work, which infuriates Henri, as she's quite intelligent. But her study focus was the same as his, and there's not a lot of positions for that specialty to begin with."

"Add in rules like this, that bars a woman from even applying, and..." Gibson trailed off with a grimace. "Can't he get it overruled?"

"We're trying. Gregson's on board with the plan. It's the commissioner who's fighting it. He's got very backward opinions about females, and he's running scared right now because of the whole Sanderson scandal. He doesn't want to kick over any woodpiles."

Gibson went two steps ahead to open the annex door for me, an evil smile on his face. "You know, if our good queen knew about this rule, she'd have a fit."

I sent an evil smile back at him. "I knoooow. It's tempting, isn't it?"

"I don't think it should just tempt you."

Stepping through the doorway, I paused a beat so he could join me. "You really think I should say something? Isn't that sort of an abuse of my relationship with her, though?"

"If you're helping this society make forward progress, can you really consider it any form of abuse?"

Now that was a good point. And food for thought.

"Alright, I'll think about it. Wait, did you think to tell Gregson you're nabbing me and Henri?"

"Did it first thing," Gibson promised.

"Good."

The annex building had more space to it—wider hallways, more individual rooms and offices, a larger jail cell for holding. It was, in essence, a newer, larger, brighter version of the precinct building next door instead of an extension of it. More than a few people were envious of the newer digs and wished to move over, but the move would be too much of an interruption in daily affairs. It was easier to stick the new people into the new building than shift it all around.

Penny's desk was near the hallway, in the corner of the bullpen and oriented to face the back door. She spied us as we came in and her head came up, cocked in curiosity. It was still a little strange to see her in a three-piece suit instead of an officer's uniform, but it was a good look on her. She wore a navy-blue pinstripe today, blonde hair up in a bun, and more than a few people who passed her gave her an intrigued look. Not that she seemed to notice.

"Hey, Penny," I greeted. "As you can see, Gibs is here to fetch me and Henri. Can you wrap up the case? I've got about half the paperwork done for my side."

"Sure," she agreed easily, holding out a hand for the forms. "Is it a murder again?"

"Theft this time," Gibson informed her as I passed the papers over. "It's a doozy. Also outside of city jurisdiction, so it falls to us to solve it. You might not get them back anytime soon."

"We'll survive," Penny drawled in return. "Good luck?"

"Oh, trust me," Gibson sighed as he turned back toward the door. "We'll need it."

When we arrived at the East Gate to the palace, I performed a quick experiment. After Belladonna's alterations on me, most magic had no effect. But 'most' still left some that could impact me. Wards were on a grey boundary. Most wards didn't have much effect—I could feel them, but they couldn't stop me. I wanted to see if the palace wards fell into that bracket.

In an obscure, mostly out-of-sight corner of the wall, I tried to put a hand on it, see if I could climb up. I was rebuffed immediately and without any hesitation. It felt like a mild electric shock, enough to make me tingle but not hurt. Huh. These wards were better designed than most, then, and thought to include those magically altered. I'd have to pass that along to Henri and Sherard.

Changing directions, Gibson led me to the nearest gate and walked me through the wards without issue. We'd swung by my apartment to fetch Clint, as I had a feeling he'd come in handy for this investigation. He sat on my shoulder as we headed for Henri, pleased as punch to be included in another case.

The normal foot traffic of guards, palace staff, and visitors all went about their own business on the different sidewalks and one-lane roads inside the grounds. But intermixed I saw additional guards pulled from the city guard. The black uniforms stood out among all the red. I eyed the heightened security with interest. This time, they also had people walking the perimeter, and I knew precisely why.

As we walked toward the Royal Mages' Building, I asked Gibson in a low tone, "Has anyone else managed to find the same loophole and get in?"

"No. But every person we've caught trying had a nefarious purpose—the wards automatically rejected them. It's not gotten out how the teenager defeated the wards, thankfully, and they're still keeping the ne'er-do-wells at bay." Gibson walked another few steps before relaying, "Rumors are flying about that the wards are failing slowly because of their age. That this is a sign they need to be taken down and redone again from the ground up."

I imagined the work that would entail and whistled low. I bet that made a lot of people unhappy. "Well. I hadn't heard about that. How're Henri and Sherard taking that idea?"

"They both claimed it was a rumor, that it didn't bother them." Gibson snorted at the memory. "They were also swearing up and down quite vilely, though, so take that with a grain of salt."

"Yeah, sounds like them." I wasn't even a magician and this was giving me a headache. I didn't want to be in their shoes and actually have to solve the problem. I spied a familiar head of dark hair ahead of us on the sidewalk and paused at the four-way to greet the queen and her entourage of secretary and kingsman. "Your Majesty. How are you today?"

"Vexed," Queen Regina answered bluntly and with a pointed look at the kingsman hovering right behind her. "Not that I don't love you, Marshall, but all this shadowing of my person is growing tiresome."

Marshall's narrow face unbent to give his queen a rueful smile. I knew the man well; he was one of the kingsmen who had helped straighten out the whole Belladonna mess after my arrival. We'd become close friends during that time. He was a good one to put with Regina during this time. He had great situational awareness and a large store of patience. "Sorry, Your Majesty. Until they figure out the wards, we can't take chances."

Regina let out a vexed growl. She was decked out today in a light blue day suit, the lacing at the skirt and around her collar giving her the appearance of a woman about to leisurely sit down for tea and cookies. It completely jarred with the expression on her face. She looked ready to bite someone. "Jamie, tell me you're here to aid me."

"I'm actually here to snag Henri," I said apologetically. "Gibs wants my take on a case."

"Oh, the gold theft?" Regina looked to Gibson with approval. "That also needs to be figured out quickly. I have things that must be shipped to the coast, and if the trains are compromised, I need to know soon. Although I do wish you would leave Henri where he is. He and Sherard work well together. I have high hopes they'll come up with a solution."

I'd anticipated this very thing and soothed her with, "I will give him back soon, I promise. But I want his take on things. And it might be good to take him away now, give him a breather. He's been staring at this problem for a week. He needs a break from it."

She reluctantly nodded, sighing heavily. "Oh, very well. But don't keep him long. I want this resolved."

"I absolutely promise we'll solve it as quickly as we can." I eyed her, evaluating. Regina looked like a woman at the end of her patience. She was sitting between two problems that irritated her, but she didn't have the ability to solve them herself. I judged she would probably appreciate a problem she *could* solve, something that would give the satisfaction of helping, even in a sideways fashion. "Actually, Your Majesty, there is a way you can help. With the wards, I mean."

Her eyebrows lifted in surprise. "Whatever do you mean?"

"Do you have time to walk with us, talk to Henri?"

"I do, as it happens. I'm out for a stroll. It was too stuffy inside the palace." Her pointed look at Marshall indicated the source of all the stuffiness. Marshall gave her a sheepish grin in return.

"Excellent." I indicated the path toward the Royal Mages' Building not far from us, and she fell into step beside me. "Here's the gist. Henri's overworked. Seriously, truly, overworked. Ever since his co-worker was fired, they've not been able to find a good replacement. And they were short on magical examiners even before Sanderson was fired."

Regina listened carefully. "How can I help with that?"

"The thing is, there's a particular woman Henri knows who he feels will be perfect for the position. She's got the same training he does, and he's very vocal about her intelligence. But she's not allowed to apply for the position because she's, well, female."

Regina stopped dead in her tracks. I could literally see her rage meter edge toward the red zone. "I made it quite clear two—no, almost three—years ago now that women were not to be barred from any position in the workforce. *Any* position. On what grounds is this woman being denied?"

"The police commissioner took that command to mean he had to let women be officers and detectives, but in his words—I'm roughly paraphrasing—forensics is too emotionally difficult for a woman to handle."

The rage meter edged a little closer toward boiling point. "This is outrageous! The man can't interpret my words as he likes. Alright, I understand why you've brought this up. I'll straighten it out personally. Poor Dr. Davenforth, I didn't realize how much work he was juggling."

"It's part of the reason why I said something." Internally, I was relieved I was able to sic her on this problem. For everyone's sake, this was a good solution. "He's basically worked sixty-hour weeks for the past month. It's gotten worse since Sherard came to him for help. Not that he's complaining, but I don't see how he's thinking straight when he's so exhausted."

"And it's all perfectly avoidable," Regina fumed, stalking forward. "I'll get the name of this candidate from him and appoint her myself. I won't put up with this nonsense."

Oh dear. I might have put her on the warpath. Sorry, not sorry.

Clint, perched on my shoulder, chose that moment to give us the appropriate soundtrack. "R-E-S-P-E-C-T ~ find out what it means to me ~ R-E-S-P-E-C-T ~ take care, yeah!"

Queen Regina was at first startled, then her face lit up in a gamine grin and she held out a hand to him. "I couldn't agree more."

Without batting an eye, Clint hi-fived her, looking immensely smug.

Who needed a radio? I had a Clint.

We entered the building and went up. The Royal Mages'

Building was not like most standard office buildings. To start with, it looked very much like an ancient wizard tower plopped into the palace courtyard, with aging grey stone walls and elaborate stained glass in each window. It rose three levels, each floor belonging to a different mage. The floors connected via staircases, but since none of the royal mages liked each other much, they didn't interact until absolutely necessary. Sherard, as the youngest and newly appointed of the three, had the top floor. I slung Clint down and into my arms to make it easier to climb the stairs. Otherwise he'd dig his claws into my shoulder. No, thank you.

It was never more obvious that Sherard liked red than when you came into his space. The walls were red, the carpet was red and gold, and generally if there was a surface available, it was red. It kinda looked like a brothel in search of patrons, but the look didn't gel with the many, many books and scrolls, or the blackboard covered in magical theory. And by that, I mean the blackboard was turned to lay flat, nothing more than a projection surface for a cool, magical hologram-looking outline of numbers, symbols, and other things that went straight over my head. I'd have mistaken it for Dr. Strange's lab if I hadn't known better.

A table sat squarely in the middle of the space—it was new, I'd not seen it before—with a whirlwind of papers scattered about the two extra chairs, carpet, and table surface. If this space was anything to judge by, the research for the project had definitely gotten out of hand.

In fact, Sherard and Henri both looked rough. Red-rimmed eyes from lack of sleep, shirt sleeves rolled up, shirt hems untucked at the back, their black hair mussed and standing in all directions. If I didn't know better, I'd say they were on some binger of illegal narcotics, that's how out of it they looked.

Both men seated at the table looked up at our entrance, then scrambled to their feet to greet their monarch.

Regina returned their bows with an acknowledging nod, then focused on Henri. "Dr. Davenforth. I understand a policy in place among my policemen prevents females from applying or holding certain positions in the forensic division."

That was obviously not a question. Henri blinked, mentally switching tracks before answering, "You're correct, Your Majesty."

"Jamie's read me into the situation." Regina inclined her head toward me. "I'm quite miffed. I thought such restrictions lifted years ago, upon Our royal command."

Henri's expression turned slightly evil as he heard that royal 'our.' "Indeed, Your Majesty, I'm equally irritated by the attitude. My female colleagues have proven quite capable in every area. I'm blessed to work with them. That I'm denied future working relationships because of a person's gender vexes me sorely."

"Well said, sir. Well said indeed. Now that I'm aware of the problem, I will fix it immediately. I understand you are shorthanded at the precinct and are overworking yourself in order to heed Our call of distress. I wish to thank you for doing so without complaint. I will speak personally with your police commissioner—"

Oh, to be a fly on the wall for THAT conversation.

"—and deal with him appropriately." There might have been chains and hooks and lye in the queen's tone with that promise. "But I wish to aid you personally. I understand there is a woman you wish to put forth as a candidate for the open position of magical examiner?"

"There is," Henri agreed hopefully. "She'll be stunning at it, I have no doubt."

"Give me her name," the queen commanded regally. "I'll appoint her myself."

That was far, far exceeding her authority into everyday matters, but would we tell her that? Not on your life.

"Colette Harper." Henri practically bounced with happiness, the widest smile on his face. "I believe she's currently freelancing with the Kingston University as a laboratory assistant."

"And this woman has the same education as you?"

Regina's expression turned wrathful. "Shameful to waste that intellect. I'll attend to this immediately. Gentlemen, Jamie, I will solve this problem. You solve mine."

"We'll do our best," I promised firmly.

It's truly remarkable how severly you wound her up. Let's just say I'm glad our good queen is all for women's equality. Otherwise you'd have started a revolution.

Aw, Henri, you say such sweet things.

Report 03: Gold Heist

I watched the queen stalk out, a woman on a mission, and wondered at it. Just what had Jamie *said*? I had no doubt she'd couched the information to get a rise out of Queen Regina. She must have, to get that severe a reaction.

Seaton seemed to have the same thought. He stared at Jamie suspiciously. "What did you do?"

"I didn't actually have to say much." Jamie grinned back at us, the naughty child who had successfully raided the cookie jar. "I told her how overworked Henri is. Why he's overworked. That he's probably not thinking straight because he's so tired. Then I dropped in the fact that women still aren't allowed to hold positions in her police force. She's already irritated because of the heightened security measures. She was happy to have something to direct her temper at, something she could immediately solve. It settles the feeling of frustration a little."

Seaton rounded the table and hugged her. "You devious woman. I love your mind. I am sorry I'll miss the show, however."

"You're not the only one," Jamie assured him, still sporting that evil smile. "I did a quick test for you guys, and the wards rebuffed me immediately. I couldn't climb over the wall."

I grimaced. "I expected that outcome. Thank you for trying."

"You're welcome, but I didn't come just for that. Henri, we've got a case."

"The gold theft off the train?" I hazarded. In fact,

I'd heard something about it. The kingsmen seemed to talk of nothing else but that and the dicey security the wards currently offered.

Gibson gave me a nod of confirmation. "The very one. Sorry, I know you're in up to your neck with work, but we could use another set of eyes on this one. We're quite puzzled and without any leads. I thought Jamie would be a good one to pull in, and of course she refuses to go without you."

That pleased me enormously, not that I'd ever likely admit to such aloud. I loved working with my partner. It made my heart happy she felt the same way about me.

Still, the situation wasn't ideal for me to leave. Seaton and I were no closer to a solution to this problem than we'd been the first day I'd been brought on board. I bit the interior of my cheek and turned to look at him. "What do you think, Seaton?"

"Go," he encouraged me with a heavy sigh. "I think you could use the mental break. And maybe being out and thinking of something else will give some fresh perspective on your return."

I didn't see how sitting in this room going round and round in circles would be of any benefit whatsoever. I had to agree with his assessment. "Very well. I'll come back as soon as I am able. Gibson, I'm familiar with the gist of the case, but all I've heard are rumors."

"Grab your suit coat," Gibson encouraged. "I'll brief you on the way to the station."

Jamie dropped a hand into the voluminous bag she preferred to cart about, brought a comb out, and took my head in hand without a by-your-leave. I grimaced in understanding as she dragged the comb through my rambunctious locks. "I look disheveled, don't I?"

"I think Queen Regina took your appearance as confirmation of the state of things," she soothed me with a wink. "It's alright. I just know if anyone else saw you like this, you'd be embarrassed to death. The back of your shirt's untucked, by the way."

"Bless you, yes." I hastily rectified this, and only then did I realize Clint balanced on Jamie's shoulder. Oh dear, I really was out of sorts if I'd missed his presence. "Clint, you'll accompany us?"

He nodded seriously. Clint adored working on cases, and truly, it was in his nature to want to work. He was made to be a magician's familiar, after all. This role wasn't what his creator intended for him, but no one could cast disparagements upon his contributions. Clint was often able to access places we could not, and his viewpoint helped us ask the right questions.

Truly, acquiring him for Jamie was one of the smarter decisions I'd ever made.

I settled my clothing back to rights so I looked respectable instead of something Clint had dragged in. We bid Seaton good luck and exited the building. Truthfully, I felt the better for it. Just breathing in fresh air helped clear the cobwebs from my mind. I hadn't realized how stale my thinking had become until I exited the room.

Gibson escorted us off palace grounds and into one of the stand-at-ready vehicles issued for kingsmen use. We climbed in with Gibson (thankfully) driving. The car had a closed top, which muted the street traffic from the other vehicles around us, allowing for easier conversation. I settled into the back, as the front could more easily accommodate Jamie's longer legs.

As we puttered along, Gibson inquired, "Davenforth, you've heard something of the case?"

"Yes, the kingsmen talk of little else. That and the wards, I should say. I don't have any particulars, however, just that a great deal of gold has been stolen, and there's no trace of how it was accomplished, or by whom."

Jamie turned in the front seat to sit sideways,

making it easier to converse with all of us. "It was three hundred thousand crowns in gold stolen."

I whistled low. That was quite the sum. "Ingots or coins?"

"Mix of both," Gibson informed me. "Six ingots and three boxes of gold coins. You can see the logistical challenge."

"I can indeed. That's a great deal of weight to shift."

"And they did it somewhere between the Kingston and Bristol stations," Gibson threw in sourly.

I took in the news with a blink. As I rarely traveled outside the city, I wasn't sure how much that complicated matters. "How long of a ride was it between stations?"

"Start from the beginning," Jamie requested of Gibson before explaining to me, "He's not actually told me everything. We thought to wait on you to join us first."

Sensible. It saved the man from having to repeat himself. It was one of my pet peeves, so I did endeavor to save others from it.

"The gold shipment left Kingston six days ago, at six o'clock in the evening, and arrived in Bristol station at 6:40. It was then discovered the gold was missing."

I fetched a small notebook from my pocket and jotted down notes as he spoke. I was so overworked these days, I couldn't trust my mind to retain the details. And I had the feeling this case especially would revolve around the details.

"No other stops?" Jamie asked, also bent over a notebook and scribbling away.

"None." He shifted lanes to avoid a bumper collision ahead of us on the road. "Still, it's quite the question of how it was even pulled off. There's no sign of forced entry on any of the multiple locks. The security is quite complex too. There're two wall vaults surrounded by a padlocked gate. Each vault has three separate, lockable compartments inside, with each compartment able to hold multiple portable safes. In this case, the safes contained iron-banded wooden boxes with wax seals on the bands, to verify the contents are undisturbed. So, five layers of protection.

"When we arrived on scene, the safes containing the boxes of gold had actually been removed from the vaults and taken to the station office in preparation for handing them over to their owners. No one suspected anything was wrong until the iron bands were removed and the boxes opened to verify their contents for final delivery."

I whistled low. That was indeed impressive. "What was in the boxes? There must have been something, or the weight would have tipped off the handlers."

Gibson gave me an approving nod. "You're correct. They'd filled the boxes with lead shot. Now, to further add to the complexity of this, the weight was a perfect match for the gold."

"How do you know that?" Jamie interrupted.

"It's one of the security measures. Any gold shipped is put into the box, sealed, then weighed. The weight's recorded and sent with the inventory checklist. On arrival, before the box is opened, it's weighed again. Only if the weight matches do they take it to the claim area."

"So, whoever did this not only knew of a way to get around all the many locks," I said, mostly thinking aloud, "but knew precisely the weight of the boxes. Enough to bring the correct amount of lead shot to substitute it with. How would they know that?"

Jamie made an inquiring noise in the back of her throat. "Doesn't that mean this has to be an inside job? How else would you know all that, otherwise?"

Gibson shrugged as he added, "That was my first thought too. Except they didn't take all the gold."

I blinked, staring at the back of the man's head.

"Excuse me? How much was left?"

"Two ingots, which equates to roughly sixty-three thousand crowns. I would think if this truly was an inside job, they would have been better prepared to take the lot of it."

True, thieves were not inclined to leave loot behind. And sixty-three thousand crowns was a great deal of money. Although it begged the question: Why leave those two ingots behind? Surely two ingots didn't present that much of a logistical challenge?

Jamie uttered a noise that meant she didn't wholly agree, a doubtful frown pulling her brows together. "I don't think we should be so quick to leap to conclusions on this. Think about it. You and Henri were both impressed they were able to shift three hundred thousand crowns' worth of gold in a short period of time. You're not sure how they managed even that. What if that was the upper range of what they *could* feasibly move? What if three hundred and sixty-three was just too much? They could have sensibly chosen to take what they could and not been stupid and greedy."

Gibson shrugged again. "Possibly. Thought's crossed my mind. Practically every possibility's crossed my mind at this point."

"I personally prefer stupid, greedy thieves," I threw in sourly. "They're easier to catch that way."

Jamie held out a fist, knuckles toward me. "Totally agree."

I bumped knuckles with her. I still found this an odd mannerism, but I enjoyed the way she grinned at me every time I played along. It was as if we were sharing a secret, just the two of us. My inner child approved.

Gibson turned as the train yard came into sight. The station itself was a long, rectangular building off to the side with some parking along the front so passengers could be dropped off. It was busy, of course, with people entering or departing the city. Behind it sprawled the three warehouses that housed the train cars, along with the repair and maintenance service stations. I'd only been on a case in there once— an accidental death of a train worker that had looked suspicious. One of the best adjustments in recent law was to make the working conditions of the train yards safer. Casualties had dropped by forty-eight percent since the measures were put into place.

It was a noisy atmosphere, noxious with all the fumes from the engines, and if one wasn't quick on their feet, they were liable to be run over. Gibson parked behind the train station, in an area more dirt than paved lot, but even here many people came and went. I stayed close to Jamie and Gibson's sides as we made our way across the multitude of crisscrossing tracks in an effort not to be separated from them.

Over the noise, Gibson explained in a loud voice, "They set the luggage car aside for us. It's been untouched except by kingsmen's hands since the theft was discovered."

That was good news. The case might be coming to us rather cold, but if the car was untouched, we had a good chance of seeing something others had missed. Gibson had high hopes for that, I knew, otherwise he'd not have gone to the trouble to fetch us.

Unlike passenger trains, with their many windows lining the car on both sides, baggage cars had nothing in the way of natural light. There were precisely four doors in—one on the front and back of the car, so people could go through, a wide cargo door on the side, and a smaller door on the other side to allow employees on and off. This one was even more secure than most baggage cars, as it only had the cargo and employee door. The doors on either end of the car were missing on this model. For security purposes, I assumed.

It did have ventilation running along the top in a raised arch along the roof. Considering some of the chemicals that were shipped routinely along this route, the ventilation was likely another safety measure. The car was otherwise unadorned, its blank brown face deceptively unremarkable. One wouldn't think by looking at it that one of the greatest train robberies in history had occurred inside.

Three hundred thousand crowns. Good heavens, I was still mentally reeling from that.

The cargo door was bolted, but the employee door was not. At least, not with a physical lock. Gibson did away with the magical seal on it and opened the door, waving us through.

Inside the narrow confines of the interior, we barely had room to maneuver around each other. The vaults—I assumed the two large metal blocks at the far end of the train were the vaults in question— dominated a good third of the car's length and made for tight quarters. Just in front of them stood a padlocked crisscross wood pattern stretching from floor to ceiling that blocked anyone from casually brushing up against the vaults. The rest of the train car was lined with metal shelves bolted into floor and walls, respectively.

Personal luggage had been claimed, as the shelves lining the car on either side were empty. I had enough room to walk down the middle of the car without my shoulders brushing up against the shelves, but not much more than that. It was stale in here. The car had not been visited recently, but it didn't smell in any way odd.

Jamie went right to the vaults, pulling on gloves as she moved. "Six days of people coming and going, likely not able to get any usable prints here. But still, I should dust for them anyway." She bent a look at Gibson. "You did wear gloves, correct?"

"Of course I did," Gibson responded with a wounded

hand over his heart. "You'd skewer me otherwise. Anyone investigating wore gloves."

"Good. Cuts down on the number of prints to parse through and throw out. I'll start in on that after we're done with the initial sweep."

Pulling free a wand from my bag, I lined up a catch-all sheet and row of small jars. "I'll do a diagnostic of the area as well. Just in case there's traces of saliva, hair, or some such we can use for evidence later."

Gibson leaned in a little to watch as I ran the diagnostic spell, collecting trace evidence. It was something I'd refined after partnering up with Jamie. It certainly was more comprehensive now than it had been before her influence. A little too much, truth be told. I stared at the list of things found, then at my samples lined up neatly along my feet, and groaned.

Also leaning over my shoulder, Jamie took a look and snorted. "That's too much evidence. It'll take you forever to get through all that, and you're not even sure what's helpful at this stage. Any of that could belong to our thieves."

"Unfortunately correct. I'll label and store this for now. It'll be better to use it as corroborative evidence after the fact, I think." Finishing the sweep, I ended the spell and then carefully stoppered up the bottles and hit the rest with a preservation hex. "Alright, free to move."

Jamie patted the feline perched on her shoulder. "Clint, get on top of the safes for me. See if there's anything strange up there."

"Okay," the feline said happily, immediately bouncing off her shoulder, using her as a springboard to get to the top in one elegant leap. It never ceased to amaze me the lengths he could jump.

"Gibs, walk me through this," Jamie requested.

"Right, so this was how it was explained to me." Gibson put his shoulders to one of the walls, getting

comfortable and allowing us room to maneuver at the same time. "When gold is brought in for shipment, it's brought in with a listed inventory of everything going. Then it's packed into a wooden crate which is then bound with iron bands and wax seals impressed over the bands as an added measurement to prove the gold stays untouched during shipment. Probably to keep some guard from sneaking a few coins, tell you the truth."

I made more notes, flipping pages as I ran out of room. "The guards have keys, then?"

"One set, yes. There're two sets of keys in total. But I'll get to that." Waving a hand to the vault, Gibson continued. "Boxes are weighed, as I said before, and put into a safe; then they're brought in here. See how there're different compartments in each vault? Those each have separate locks. Because they have enough gold shipments coming through here from different people, they can't put just one person's gold in each safe. Not enough room for that nonsense."

"And then there's this padlocked area here that locks to keep anyone from approaching the vaults. It looks kinda like a castle gate. You can get a hand through these—" Jamie stopped abruptly and squinted at it. "Henri, is there a spell on this thing?"

"Yes, but it's more of a deterrence spell," I explained. A glance was enough to identify it. "An encouragement for people not to get too close. It will give you a mild jolt if you really do put your hand inside."

"Ah. There's a warning written here, that's what caught my attention."

With her immunity to spells, it didn't surprise me the spell on the wood had no effect upon her.

Undeterred, Jamie continued, "Okay, so Gibs, the guard has a key to this outer padlock?"

"Correct. He's the only one with a key."

"And was he in the car during the trip?"

"No. When the train's in motion, he's anywhere inside. He seems to move throughout the train, multiple people spotted him, although no one could vouch for him for more than a few minutes at a time."

Jamie stared at the padlock a bit longer. "Priors?"

"Not with him. Clean as a whistle. I interviewed him myself and he was highly distressed about the whole thing. Says he's afraid he'll lose his job over this. It could have been an act, but he says he didn't see anything untoward."

I made a note of that. It wasn't that we believed someone automatically innocent if they had no prior trouble with the law. But we did move them further down the suspect list, because it was far less likely they were involved.

"I still want backgrounds on everyone working the train yard that day. And alibis. We'll need them to parse through possible suspects. And there was absolutely nothing hinky about the bands?" Jamie still examined the doors carefully.

"Actually, there was. The bands themselves looked fine, but the imprint of the wax seals was different. It didn't quite match the emblem of the business." Gibson splayed a hand. "No one noticed until they brought the boxes into the claiming area. But that doesn't surprise me. They came in at almost seven o'clock, after all. The train yard's too dim to be able to see much. Easy to overlook. But that's the other reason why I doubt this was an inside job."

"They'd have been able to duplicate any seal used by the companies ahead of time and have them on hand," I concurred aloud. It did make sense. Especially as there were only a few companies that dealt with gold and shipped it on a regular basis. Perhaps a dozen altogether. It would be easy enough to copy those seals and have them on hand.

I looked around the car again, this time using

my magical sight more. There was nothing here that looked odd to me, and yet...some sixth sense tingled. All was not right here.

Perhaps something of this showed on my face. Jamie turned to me, head canted in question. "What, Henri?"

"I see no signs of spells cast—" I paused and looked to Gibson for confirmation. Most of the kingsmen were magicians themselves, so I had no doubt they'd checked for this. He gave me a nod in affirmation. "And yet there is magic here. We have a silencing charm pasted on this wall. Why?"

"I asked the same question," Gibson informed us, tone a touch wry. "I'm told silencing charms are common on trains. The rattle and creak of the rails gets monotonous after a while so they block it."

My doubt doubled hearing this. "But inside a baggage car?"

"Guard claims when he does have to be in here—the company apparently requires it sometimes, depending on what's being shipped—he puts up a silencing charm. Helps him."

That still didn't quite sit right with me. As tiresome as the noise no doubt became, wouldn't he need to hear it if something was awry outside the car?

I put the question aside for now. "The other thing that bothers me is—Clint?"

The Felix was on his back legs, one paw lightly balanced against the outside door of one of the vaults, his nose nearly buried in the lock. His whiskers twitched before he tilted his head toward me and reported, "Tickly grass."

Suspicions raised, I went straight for him, slipping sideways past Jamie to enter the area. Then I knelt, fetching my wand as I did so. I angled the notebook to be directly under the lock and used the tip of my wand to coax out the sprig of greenish-brown I could barely detect a peek of.

"Duuuude," Jamie drawled out, leaning over my back. "Good nose, Clint! I thought I smelled something magical, but I put it down to being the silencing charm thingy."

The Felix sat back on his haunches, entirely pleased with himself.

As he should be. It only took a glance of the withered herb on the white pages of my notebook for me to recognize it. "Raskovnik."

Jamie and Gibson hissed in recognition. The first case I'd worked with Jamie had involved the magical herb that could unlock anything once a sprig of it was applied. I say herb but it had the same thick vines as clover, and the richness of the green appeared blue at certain angles. Although this sample of the specimen curled brown around the edges.

"Clint," I informed him gratefully, "you might very well have given us the first break we needed to solve this. Well done indeed."

Purring, he arched against my arm. I put my wand down to give him well deserved scratches behind his ears, which made him purr all the louder.

"I missed that," Gibson hissed in frustration. "We checked for anti-locking spells, of course, but the Raskovnik isn't well known. Or easy to acquire. We don't normally check for it. Confound it, I should have."

"The very reason you called us was to get a different perspective," Jamie told him with a sympathetic look. "Don't beat yourself up, man. Thanks to Clint, we now have an interesting lead to follow. Okay, so they used Raskovnik to get through the vaults, at least. What about the compartments and safes?"

"No hint of anything magical on them. I did check that thoroughly." Gibson ran a hand through his hair. "Although I'll check again to be safe."

Jamie accepted this with a nod. "Whether they

did or didn't with the safes, they still had to have the Raskovnik for the vaults. That hints they couldn't unlock it themselves. I would think if it was an inside job, they'd have keys to all the locks."

Gibson grunted sourly, still not over missing a vital clue. "You see why I'm not so quick to point fingers."

"Yeah, there's enough wiggle room for doubt. Although it still begs the question of how they knew it was on *this* baggage car, on *this* train, on *that* particular night. Surely they didn't just luck into it coincidentally. Henri, Gibs, what's your take on this? Are these magical thieves or more garden variety?"

"That," Gibson said with a decade's worth of sighs, "is the other question I really want an answer to."

"Alright, let me do a sweep for fingerprints, and then I want to take a look at the safes and boxes."

"Certainly," Gibson agreed, still sighing. "I'll help."

The more I learned, the more baffling it became. Just what kind of thieves were we dealing with? And how, under the vast blue skies, had they done this?

Report 04: Tools of the Trade

Gibson had taken custody of the safes and boxes, along with everything else found with them. It meant retreating to kingsmen territory—more precisely, their Evidence Locker.

It was not nearly the size of the one at the precinct, of course. They didn't really delve into crimes that much here. Still, they'd encountered some murders, theft, and the like over the years that required a holding room of some sort be established. It was attached directly to the red brick building that served as their office building. Really, it wasn't much larger than a single room addition. I hadn't been in here before—Henri hadn't either, judging by the way he studied the place curiously—and I had to say, it wasn't impressive at first glance. Just shelves, one long table in the center, and a log nailed to the wall for when evidence was brought in or taken out. Hardly hi-tech, even for them.

The safes and crates and bags of lead shot were lined up against one shelf, with a neatly pinned card slid into a glass holder on the bottom of the metal bracket that read: *Train Gold Heist evidence.*

My cat chose to perch on the edge of the table and attend to his right ear as we worked. I pulled on gloves again before pulling the first safe off the shelf and moving it to the table. "Let me pull fingerprints from these first. Henri?"

He put the bag down nearby and pulled out the brush, dust, and tape I needed. "Here. While you do that, I want a closer look at the bands. Those metal bands look sturdy, certainly something that can't be easily bent with bare hands. Gibson, when you arrived, were the boxes open?"

"Yes. At first they weren't aware anything was wrong, not until the first box was opened. Then they opened all of them to determine just how much had been stolen." Gibson made a face. "Which I don't blame them for, but I wish they'd left at least one intact until we arrived on scene."

Henri made a face. "I must agree. Still, I think we can salvage a bit of evidence from this. The bands, while broken, still have some of the wax seals attached to them. If we're clever, we might be able to piece it together."

I didn't look up from the fingerprint I carefully levered tape over. "You think the seal might tell us something?"

"I find it curious they didn't try to replicate the seals of the gold companies," Henri answered, even as he moved the bands over to the table carefully, trying not to jostle the wax still clinging to them. "There's only a handful of companies. Seals are small and take little space and weight. Why not forge something? Why take the chance of someone noticing something off while the safes were still on the train?"

I pursed my lips in thought. He had a good point there. "Gibs, are the safes moved to the clerks' office? Or are the boxes taken out of the safes and brought in?"

"I understand the safes are taken out, usually. The boxes stay in the safes until someone claims them."

"So, even in a bright office, no one noticed the difference? You said the theft wasn't discovered until the boxes were opened. Clearly, the clerks are not observant."

"Man makes a good point," I observed to Gibson. "So, Henri, you think...what? The thieves just felt it unnecessary to go to that much trouble to forge a seal?"

"Or perhaps none of them had the required skills to do so. It would take some effort and expense to have one made, and that assumes you know how to contact a forger. If you don't, you'll have to come up with a very good reason to request a legitimate artisan to do the work for you."

"Which would still raise questions, considering it's a gold company's seal. Huh. Yeah, you're on to something there. But that begs the question, where did this seal come from?"

"We can only know"—Henri paused as he concentrated on sliding a fine blade under the wax, lifting it carefully off the iron band—"once we have an idea of what this looks like."

"I'll leave the delicate work to you."

Gibson grabbed the other safe and started lifting fingerprints too, once I showed him how to do it. It meant we ran out of powder rather quickly, but it was alright. I only found partial and smudged prints, with very few clear ones that would make any sort of sense when compared. By the time we covered the safes and the boxes, Henri had lifted off every possible wax imprint he could, and I was able to dust the iron bands, too.

It was quiet as we worked, which was likely why it sounded so loud when Henri straightened with a groan of satisfaction. "There. That's what it looked like."

I stopped dusting and leaned over to get a better look. The mellow light cast funky angles on things sometimes. The seal looked... "Generic. I think that's the word I'm looking for. That circle and swoopy thing could belong to several companies."

"Yes, I can think of nine companies off-hand with a logo based on a similar design. And not all of them gold. Their choice in grabbing this makes more sense now. It's rather versatile, isn't it?" Henri flipped open his notebook to a blank page and started sketching out the seal.

"We'll need to track down how many stores you can buy that in later." I went over the last of the bands but didn't find anything useful. I was also on the dregs of my powder, so it was just as well. "I think I'm done here. Those bands are wicked, though, that's not something you can bend with just hands. Tools definitely got involved here. And these locks are no joke, either, from the looks of it."

"Yes indeed," Henri agreed, still sketching. "Gibson, is it possible to take one of the safes back to my lab? I want to run some experiments on it."

"Of course."

I had a feeling I knew what kind of experiments. "You want to know how easy it is to make a mold of the lock, make a key to fit it?"

"That's one of them, yes. And how easy it is to pick it."

"I would imagine not very, but I do want to test that." I had a feeling we should try someone who didn't know the first thing about making molds in order to perform that experiment. After all, we weren't sure who our thieves were. Were these professionals who somehow slipped in? Employees of the station who saw a good chance to get rich quick and took it? I could really flip a coin at this point. But if we were talking employees, then odds were they didn't have a thief's skillset. Which meant they had to figure out basics, like making molds.

Henri started putting tools back into the bag. "I think I'm done here for the moment. Where to next?"

"Maybe the gold company?" I offered. "I'm not entirely sure what all they do, to tell you the truth, and I need more info."

"They're a distributor more than anything," Gibson informed me, carefully replacing safes and boxes back onto the shelves. "They've got a mining facility outside the city, but they refine and forge everything here in Kingston into either coins or ingots. It's then shipped out from here."

Interesting. "All the gold companies operate like this, or just this one?"

"All of them, I believe." Henri closed the bag with a snap. "Gibson, should I come back for the safe?"

"No, I can have someone deliver it for you. Don't worry about it now."

"Splendid. Then let's go interview the gold company employees."

We might as well. There were a lot of interviews to do and really, I wanted to knock them out all at once. Sadly, we didn't have that kind of time before work stopped for the day. This was definitely a case where you had to pace yourself. The first order of business was details. I had a feeling the devil would be in the details, and right now Henri and I didn't have enough of them.

We trooped over to Gold Limited, the business that had just lost a huge chunk of change. It looked like a mercantile store from the front, maybe with a mix of a pawn store thrown in. Painted gold scales adorned the front windows, along with the name of the company in an arch over the top. Friendly enough, except for the iron bars lurking on the other side of the glass.

I leaned into Gibson's side as we approached the bright red front door. "You've interviewed these guys, right?"

"Yes. They confirmed shipment of the gold for us, and I questioned the shipping clerks. I don't suspect any of them." Gibson gave a one-shoulder shrug before checking both ways to make sure the street was clear, then headed off across the pavement. "I've got solid alibis for all of them. I don't think they were involved."

"Even as informants?"

"The possibility's there. I just have a gut feeling they're not part of this."

Sometimes that gut feeling was correct. Often, in fact, but sometimes even a veteran detective could be fooled. Gibson was right to listen to his gut but get alibis for them anyway. And we'd keep them on the suspect list until we got firm answers. Right now, I wanted answers more than anything.

The red door's shop bell chimed as we stepped through. The front receptionist looked up with a professional smile that turned hopeful seeing Gibson's red uniform. "Kingsman Gibson! Any breaks in the case?"

"Yes and no. Yes, as in very capable colleagues have joined me, and we've unraveled a bit more of how things were done. We've more questions of your shipping clerks, if you don't mind."

"Of course not. Mr. Elwood left explicit instructions to aid you in whatever way we can. Please, come with me." She did give Clint, who rode on my shoulder, an odd look, but was too well trained in customer service to say anything.

I assumed Elwood was their boss. We followed the perky receptionist down a very short hallway into the back room. It was brightly lit, the rectangular shape of the room crammed with packing supplies, scales, a wall safe that took up most of the opposite side of the room, and a loading dock door that was currently locked and closed.

Four clerks looked up at our entrance and flocked to Gibson with keen interest. I assumed them to be invested in the gold heist and wanted an update. They did double takes seeing Clint, though, with one of them actually reaching out a hand toward him before thinking better of it.

My eyes roved over them: an elderly gentleman probably on the verge of retirement, a very pregnant werebadger, and two younger gentlemen who had to be related. Brothers, cousins, something of that ilk. The ginger hair and dusky freckles were a dead giveaway. Not to mention those jug ears.

"Kingsman Gibson," the elderly man spoke in a slow drawl, his dark, craggy skin lighting up hopefully. "A break in the case?"

"Yes and no," Gibson answered again. "I've called in colleagues who are more experienced with theft than I am, and they've found some interesting evidence. They also have questions for all of you. Everyone, this is Dr. Davenforth. He's a magical examiner with the Kingston PD. And this is his partner, Detective Edwards."

Henri gave them a genteel smile. "Pleasure. If you don't mind, we're trying to get an exact sense of both the weight and the timing of all this."

"Of course," Old Man assured us, gesturing toward a row of barstools nearby. "Here, sit, ask all you want. I'll talk with you."

Everyone else got back to work, although I could tell they kept one ear trained on us as we took the offered stools.

"Kingsman Gibson asked about the schedule before," Old Man said ruminatively. "What happens is, we get a shipment of unrefined gold in from our suppliers, and we spend some time in shop applying our mark to things, double-checking quality, and such. Then, when we get an order in, we package it into the crates and weigh it all, create our own invoice that goes with the shipment. We only ship it out on the evening train, as it has no stops and is more secure that way. We time it so the gold goes to the train yard fifteen minutes before the evening train leaves—less time for a would-be thief to lay hands on it, you see. Not that it did us any good this last time."

I wrote this down in a leather book as he talked—in English. I was still faster in it than Velars. "Doesn't that make it tight, to get it on the train?"

"It does," he allowed amiably. "But they expect us, too. We've got it worked out to a science. They normally have it in the safes and on board about five minutes before the train departs."

That was extremely tight. If the thieves didn't even know if the gold would be on board until five minutes prior to departure—in this day and age it wasn't like they could text that information to someone. So how had they known? "What are the odds this was a competitor's work? Stealing from you, I mean."

He shook his head before I could get the full question trotted out. "A competitor wouldn't wait for it to be shipped. With our mark on the ingots and coins, it becomes that much harder to sell without the provenance paperwork. A competitor would know this and strike here, at the company."

Good point.

"We've taken precautions here in the shop, too," Old Man continued without prompting. "We're not allowed to step outside the room an hour before or after the shipment goes out. Just in case. I can vouch that no one had a chance to call or alert anyone on this stolen shipment."

I stole a glance at Gibson. The reason why he didn't really suspect anyone here? Probably. They wouldn't be very good informants if they couldn't alert their group. "Thank you, sir. That's all very good to know."

"I've heard over three hundred thousand crowns was stolen," Henri prompted, his own notebook in hand. "But how much weight is that? Gold coins and ingots separately."

"Ah. Well, ingots are four hundred troy ounces—"

I blinked at him. Troy ounce? "I'm sorry, a what?"

"It's a unit of measurement for precious metals like gold," Henri explained. "Slightly less than a regular ounce. An ingot is about twenty-five pounds."

Old Man nodded peaceably. "Twenty-seven-point-four-three, to be exact. We lost six ingots and three boxes of gold coins."

"How are the coins packaged?"

"Coins are sectioned off in bags of one hundred coins each, five bags per box. That makes each box five hundred troy ounces—a little over thirty-four pounds. That's standard industry practice. Makes it easier on all of us if we use the same weights and packaging. The ingots are the same, where it's two ingots a box. Always two ingots a box—the weight gets to be too much to easily carry otherwise."

I scribbled numbers like mad. "That also industry standard?"

He nodded several times. "It is."

"And how well known is this knowledge outside of your industry?"

"I wouldn't think it common knowledge. But not hard to find out, either."

It did amaze me that even without Google, people seemed to be able to lay their hands on the right answer. Or maybe I was just conditioned to Google everything. I shared a speaking glance with Gibson. We'd wondered how the thieves knew how much weight to bring and put in each box—but if the boxes held a standard weight, then the thieves would know just by the contents. They could easily make the swap, gold for lead, without a scale being necessary. "So, the total weight of everything?"

"Between the weight of the ingots and the gold coins, it came up to just over two hundred sixty-seven pounds. At least, the portion stolen is that much."

I whistled low. That was a lot of weight to shift in a hurry.

"So, whoever stole this had to carry two hundred sixty-seven pounds of lead shot on, then carry the same weight back off. That's a lot to cart about."

"That it is. And the bands, the metal ones around the crates, we have special tools for those. Not something many people can manhandle themselves." Old Man tipped his head down and gave me a pointed look. "You're looking for some mighty strong people, Detective."

Dryly, I answered, "I think we guessed that, sir."

We ended up at Miss Amelia's Bakery because, frankly, we could all use sugar and caffeine after taking a look at the situation. Gibson looked done, just utterly done, but then, he'd been banging his head against this particular problem for a full week without getting any closer to an answer. That had to be frustrating. Even more frustrating that my cat had found a clue he'd missed despite going over the car three times.

Henri, of course, was just tired from life in general. He downed a cup of tea before his cinnamon roll arrived, then ordered another, but didn't look any better despite the caffeine now in his system. I really had to find a way to get him to go home and sleep tonight instead of pulling overtime at the precinct. Again.

I absently petted the purring cat in my lap. Clint was sprawled out like some woman's fur stole across my thighs, vibrating with his purrs. It was incredibly cute, which was partially why I indulged him, despite the purple fur he left all over my black pants. He was beyond pleased with himself to have been so useful today, and he'd probably be unbearably smug about it for the next week. For today, though, he definitely deserved all the pets.

Taking a bite out of my cinnamon roll, I enjoyed the flavor and sugar and felt my mood lift. It was hard to eat good food and feel bad at the same time. As I ate, I thought about the mechanics of the theft. "Two hundred and sixty-seven pounds of gold. That's a lot of weight for one person to shift. Even two people. Most people can't carry a hundred pounds any real distance."

Henri's head came up. I could see that intelligent mind crunching data. "Were all the bags in the compartment accounted for after the theft?"

"Yes," Gibson confirmed. "Nothing missing."

"So, they didn't hide their loot into one of the suitcases and get it out that way," I mused aloud. "They had to carry it out themselves. Seriously, I don't see how they managed with just two people. I think we're looking for at least four people to pull this off."

"Between sixty and seventy pounds each." Henri's mouth pursed. "Yes, that should be doable. Sixty pounds can be obscured in pockets, in briefcases, and the like easily. The coins could go into pockets, at least, not the ingots. They might clink a bit when they walk, but it wouldn't be enough to draw someone's attention."

"And they'd have to move in a hurry," Gibson agreed. He was slowly coming out of his moroseness as he cottoned onto our words. "We closed down the train yard pretty quickly after the theft was discovered. I'd say within fifteen minutes of the train's arrival at Bristol, the theft was reported. We had them lock everything down, and constables were on scene in less than five. Of course, it took us longer, but no one was allowed to leave before we arrived and checked them ourselves."

That likely had made a lot of people unhappy. Especially since it didn't yield an arrest. "And there was no place for them to hide the gold or tools while waiting to be searched?"

"No, we made quite sure of it. And we searched the premises too."

I figured they had, but it didn't hurt to double-check. "Okay, then that just verifies it for me. It had to be at least four people. No way for them to move out quickly otherwise."

"And someone had to get rid of all the tools," Henri said slowly, staring blindly ahead as he reached for his tea. "They must have had quite a few tools."

Gibson shifted in his seat, facing Henri more directly. "I've got my own list of possible items used for this job, but I'm curious what you think."

"Hmm, I'll have to ponder this more carefully, but off the top of my head, I'd say the Raskovnik, silencing charm— they had no guarantee the guard would apply one, so they'd bring their own. Whatever keys they managed to copy, or a skeleton key for the outer locks. A torch, small handsaw, fix-it charms—"

I interrupted this list because some of it I didn't follow. "Wait, why the saw?"

"Only way to get through the wooden boxes without damaging the iron bands," he said, then stopped dead. "Curse it. The wax seal was different. That meant the bands *were* changed."

Oh dear. He really was tired if he was forgetting details like that. "Yeah, so they must have had some tools to deal with the bands."

"Probably not welding tools, as the bands weren't welded," he muttered, to his cinnamon roll more than to us. "But pliers, duplicate bands, wax, and stamps at the very least. Then, of course, the lead shot. We still have the question of how they weighed the shot, so perhaps a scale? And something to clean the mess up with. Undoing the wax seals, reapplying them, shifting gold and lead about, they were sure to have made some mess. But the area was perfectly clean, wasn't it?"

Gibson nodded confirmation. "That it was. I suppose that should have been someone's first hint, really. What train baggage car has a cleanly swept floor that late in the evening?"

Truly. And I still wasn't convinced the guard wasn't somehow involved. If it was his job to patrol the baggage area, then how did the thieves off-load all the gold? How did they get past this man who was supposedly on duty? Was he just incompetent at his job, or were they that good? I leaned more toward the theory they'd somehow paid him off.

"I think we might need to do a dry run of this ourselves in order to get an idea of timing and tools. Something might occur to us that way. And I'd like to go into Bristol and talk with people there, too."

"I'm game for that." Gibson sank back with a tired sigh. "I'm so glad I fetched you two. This really isn't our element in some ways. We're not used to this kind of crime. Magical incidents, scandals, security for the royal family—that's our forte."

"Oh, come on, you helped us a lot during that city epidemic," I refuted.

"Sure, because you and Davenforth took lead. You basically told us what to do. This is exactly why Queen Regina wanted you two on board. You think differently. You're trained to think differently. We need that sometimes."

Okay, that was fair. "Tell you what, Gibs. Let's stop here for the day. We've got a lot to think about, a lot to do, but I've got a feeling we need to stop in at the precinct tomorrow and properly report in how much time we'll need to tackle this one. That and help Henri's friend get started."

Henri blinked at me owlishly. "You think she'll have already fetched Colette and dragged her to the precinct?"

I stared back at him with an arch look. "You've got a sister and mother, Henri. Have you ever seen them drag their feet when they've decided something needed to get done?"

His eyes crinkled up at the corners. "You make an excellent point."

A thought struck and I turned to Gibson. "You can probably lay hands on this information faster than we can. See what sources there are for Raskovnik in the city."

He nodded as he stood. "I can request the information tonight. Can I expect you at the train station in the morning?"

"Sure thing," I promised him.

Henri waffled a hand back and forth. "I might not be able to get in quite that quickly if Colette really was hired today. I'll send you a message about when to expect me."

"That's fine. I hope for your sake she has been. See you tomorrow."

We finished off our snacks, I hefted a cat onto my shoulder, and we left the bakery. Since it wasn't that far of a walk to our apartment building, we chose to not snag a taxi. Frankly, Henri could use the exercise. He'd been bent over a magical problem in one form or another for weeks now. His whole body was going to freeze in that position if he didn't stretch it some.

I walked at his side, looking at his serious case of panda eyes, and felt bad I'd so quickly accepted this case. Not that we had much choice, but still. He was already overloaded as it was. "Henri, how about this. Let me do the initial legwork on this. When I feel like I need you, I'll call you in. You're juggling too many irons in the fire right now."

He gave me a grateful look. "I am, and thank you. But I still want to be part of the investigation and keep track of everything. I might not be able to help as much, but at least once a day I want to come in and check with you. Perhaps sit and be a sounding board for whatever theories you have."

"Sounds fair. And I'll help with your ward problem, as I can."

"Thank you. We'll likely need it. We're not having a great deal of luck in that regard." He sighed, the sound full of stress and tension, and rolled his head back and forth. "Just having someone capable as a third magical examiner would do much to ease the workload I'm currently carrying."

I crossed my fingers and mentally prayed Regina really had found Colette and appointed her. It was too soon to check on that yet, though, and that was fine. We were at the end of the work day anyway. "I'm for a bubble bath as soon as I get home."

Henri sighed, both relief and weariness in the slump of his shoulders. "Sounds heavenly. I might well do the same."

A good night of rest was what the doctor ordered. Curled around a furball, I more or less got it, although a panic dream did wake me up once in the night. Fortunately, Clint pulled me out of it quickly, and I was able to settle enough to go back to sleep afterward.

Henri certainly looked better with a full night of rest in him. We walked to work, stopping for pastries and coffee on the way, talking as we normally did. These early morning chats were some of my favorite times with him. It had been weeks since we'd been able to, what with him swamped in the lab. Lately, he went in two hours ahead of me to get a jump start on the lab work. I was glad he hadn't chosen to do that this morning.

The precinct looked as busy as usual, people coming in and out of the main doors, sometimes in handcuffs, sometimes with that look of distress that meant trouble. Henri held open the door for one woman with a toddler in her arms, and she gave him a grateful look as she sailed through. I went ahead as well, planning in my head all the things to be done today. Let's see, talk to Gregson first and give him a proper idea of how long this job would likely take so he knew not to assign us cases. And then ask about…oh?

A woman I didn't recognize stood just outside of the captain's door, talking to Gregson in a low tone. She looked unbearably excited and trying to hide it behind a professional demeanor. As we entered the bullpen, she noticed us, and her face lit up in a smile. "Henri!"

My normally reserved partner looked just as giddy and returned the greeting. "Colette! Thank all the stars." He beelined for her, taking hold of both arms to kiss her on either cheek. She had to bend down a little to allow this, as she stood a good head taller.

I took in this woman with curiosity. I'd heard about Colette, of course—Henri had talked about her often enough—but this was the first time I'd seen her. She wasn't a traditional beauty, but she gave off the impression of someone really fun to know. She reminded me of an Amazonian warrior—tall and broad like a linebacker, with thighs that could probably crush someone. Her hair was neatly pulled back into a two-tiered bun, the wiry black hair held further in check by a multitude of tiny braids.

Judging from her general look and that ebony dark skin, I'd say she was from Ciparis. She looked like that nationality, at least. Henri had never mentioned where she was from, just that she'd gone to school with him. I loved her smile—it was joyous and fetching, and I found myself smiling at her without really meaning to.

"Queen Regina marched her into the precinct herself, informed me she was now one of my magical examiners, and that if anyone else tried to block me from hiring the right people, I was to inform her directly," Gregson reported. Well, he might have cackled mid-statement, but then not one of us blamed him for that.

Heck, I was cackling. "Really now. No, I'm not surprised. She was mad as a striped hornet yesterday when I told her."

Colette looked at me with interest. There was a charming lilt to her words, making it clear Velars was a second language to her. "I'm sorry, you are...?"

Henri belatedly did the introductions. "Forgive me, where are my manners? Jamie, this is Colette Harper. Colette, Detective Jamie Edwards. My friend and partner. She's also the one who advocated to the queen yesterday about women being allowed to work as magical examiners."

Colette stuck out a hand, and I shook it, pleased with the strength. I hated limp-fish handshakes. "Welcome to the madhouse, Dr. Harper."

"Colette," she corrected me firmly with a wide smile. "And I owe you dinner, I think, for sticking up for us women. I'd never have gotten hired otherwise. And you, Henri, I understand the recommendation came directly from you and with strong urging." Her dark brown eyes were a touch bright with unshed tears, happy ones. "Thank you both, truly. I thought I'd never get a chance to really work."

"Oh, there's work to be had," I said, dry as a martini. "Trust me on that. You'll shortly be drowning in it."

"Captain, I'll run her through the procedures and get her caught up to speed as I can," Henri volunteered. "Her new hire paperwork is complete?"

"Barely begun," Gregson denied with a shake of the head. "But if you're working both the kingsmen case and the palace wards, I know you're not going to be at the precinct much in the next few weeks. I can do the paperwork with her later. Take her."

"Thank you." Henri cast a glance at me that silently asked me to come along. I almost didn't—a lot of what he would discuss with Colette would go right over my head—but I second-guessed that assumption. If Colette would be at crime scenes, she'd need some self-defense training hammered into her. And I'd have to school her on modern forensics too. Not to mention she was now one of six women working in the precinct. It would be good to get her introduced to all the girls.

Yeah, okay, Henri had a point about me tagging along. I followed him as we wound back toward his lab, him pointing out where things were as they walked. Colette listened carefully, asking questions, and I hoped for her sake she was a quick learner. She was about to get thrown into the deep end.

We reached the lab and settled around Henri's worktable. As I took a seat, Henri explained seriously, "You'll be put in the lab next to mine, so when I am here, do feel free to pop in with questions. I'll give you one of our pads so you can text me questions as well. I'm afraid the captain is right, I'll be out and about for the foreseeable future, but I don't wish for you to flounder because you weren't properly introduced to the work here."

"I'll try to catch up quickly," Colette promised. "Tell me the procedures—I'm sure there're rules for handling evidence—and I'll stick to them."

"I'll do so. First, allow Jamie to fill you in on some of the basics." Turning to me, Henri added, "It will take hours to get Colette sorted enough here to even begin work. I don't wish to keep you tied here for all that time. You're still to meet Gibson at the station."

I nodded, as that was fair. "Colette, there's a few things you should be aware of, some advancements in forensics. I'll walk you through the most important ones now. But before I do that, a few things. First, you're now one of six women to work here at the precinct. Us girls get together every other week, as the insanity permits, and go out to dinner. We meet up regularly for self-defense training and sparring with the girls from the other stations, too. I'd really like it if you joined us. They're fun ladies to know, and it's a fast way to make some friends here at work."

Colette looked touched by the offer, a hand pressed over her ample chest. "Jamie, that's kindly offered. Thank you, I'd love that. But do I need defensive training too?"

"You'll be called regularly out to crime scenes, and those aren't always safe," I explained patiently. "And sometimes, we stumble into situations just on our way home. Best to be prepared, right?"

She looked a little doubtful. "Frankly, Detective, looking at you I know you have the skills to take a man down. But I'm not very fast on my feet. You think I can?"

"I can take down anyone I wish." I arched an eyebrow at her in challenge. "And anyone I train can do the same."

The light in her eyes told me the challenge was accepted. "Then I accept the offer. Thank you."

"Good! Alright, back to forensics. Let me start with fingerprints."

Colette was an excellent listener. She took notes, asked questions, and Henri pulled examples from other cases so she could get a good visual on what I explained. She absorbed it all like a sponge. I wasn't sure if she was a genius, but I'd bet she was darn close to that level. This woman had intellectual prowess, alright. I now completely understood why Henri had been so adamant about having her hired.

It took about two hours for me to explain all the basics and set up training times for her. We walked her through how to use the texting pad too, and she was like a kid with a new toy on that one. By the time I left them to discuss all the magical things, I felt like I'd gained another excellent colleague. Time would tell if she became a friend or not. I rather hoped she would.

I bid them good luck and left them to it. I was halfway to the train station to meet Gibson when an idea struck and I pulled out my pad, jotting off a note to Ophelia, Henri's mother.

Ophelia adored the pad beyond words. It helped her keep track of her child, so she usually had it on hand. As usual, she was quick to respond to my greeting. *Hello, Jamie! What good news?*

Colette Harper's been hired as a magical examiner at the precinct today, I responded.

No! Oh excellent, Henri was so advocating for that. I should throw a dinner party to celebrate it.

And that's exactly why I'd contacted her. *Would you?* I wrote. *Henri and I have a kingsmen case we were just handed, otherwise I'd do it.*

Oh really? You must give me the particulars when I see you. But no, dear, don't worry about the dinner, I'd love to host it. Give me a few good dates you and Henri would be available.

I loved how she now trusted that I knew Henri's schedule as well as my own. Not that she was wrong, mind you. I carried on the conversation as I walked, smile growing as my feet covered the pavement.

One problem down, two to go.

I've earned my 'panda eyes' by working every day.
I'd like to point that out.

growing up is stupid

I have no counter argument.

Report 05: Trial by Fire

Colette watched Jamie leave, eyebrows arched a little, nose scrunched. It was her thinking face.

"What, Colette?" I prompted.

"She's not at all what I mentally pictured," Colette said, still staring at the closed door as if she could see through it. "You described her to me as this formidable woman. I thought she'd be a giantess. But she's quite pretty."

"The women of my acquaintance are typically both lovely and formidable," I drawled, amused at her observation. "Take yourself, for instance."

She let out a rolling laugh, her head thrown back. "You smooth talker!"

Colette knew very well she wasn't my type. We'd tried kissing exactly once—it had felt so much like kissing a sibling that we'd sworn to never do it again. Our relationship allowed me to give her such compliments without her thinking too much of it. Although I did wish she would at least believe me. I wasn't entirely jesting with her. She was a very attractive woman in her own way.

Laughter subsiding, Colette asked, "Did she really mean it? My joining the other women for dinner and such."

"She truly did." I understood the hesitation. Colette adored Kingston more than her home country, which was why she stayed, but she'd found it difficult to make female friendships here. I wasn't entirely sure why. "Colette, in truth, you have far more in common with Jamie than you might realize. You do know she's sometimes called the Shinigami Detective?"

Colette blinked at me, her expression perfectly blank for a moment. Then she slammed her hand against the table, making everything on it jump. "That's it! Heavens above, I knew I'd recognized her from somewhere, I just couldn't place it. She was in the papers for weeks a few years ago."

"Yes, so she was. She's also not from Kingston. It's fascinating, hearing her talk about her homeland. But the point I'm attempting to make is that she's just as displaced sometimes in Kingston as you are. You'll find her to be a good listener. I'm not sure if you two will choose to be friends—that's of course entirely up to you. But give her a chance, Colette."

"I'm inclined to do that just because you like her," Colette answered in her usual forthright manner.

"Good." I mentally crossed fingers and wished them the best. I'd dearly love it if they were friends. "Now, back to task. The workroom you'll take over used to be Sanderson's."

Colette made a face, like she'd sucked a rotten lemon. "I had a feeling. What can I trust in there, anything?"

"Highly doubtful. He almost destroyed this whole part of the building due to his carelessness at one point. When the renovation was complete, I put proper safety and preventive hexes throughout the room, but odds are he tampered with them afterward. The man was slapdash even on the best of days. His records are also a complete mess. For now, until I can help you sort that room, feel free to use mine. Most of the work is piled up in here anyway."

"But what if you come back to the precinct?" Colette cocked her head at me. "Or do you not anticipate that happening?"

"I might, in theory, have enough time to do so. If I do, it'll be to help you settle in here. We're..." I trailed off, running a hand over my face. Gods above, I was tired. I could feel the exhaustion in my bones, weighing like an anchor on my mind, dragging me inexorably toward dark, inky depths. Last night's rest had done much to restore me, but it wasn't enough to make up for the dearth of rest I'd failed to acquire over the last month. I could cheerfully sleep another two days, truth be told.

At least I had the option of sleep in my foreseeable future. The extra effort of catching Colette up to speed was well worth it.

"Henri," Colette said, her bluntness dulled by concern, "I think you've taken on too much."

"I wouldn't have, if not for that bastard, Sanderson. This should have been more or less manageable." I rubbed at my temples, the dull headache threatening to become more poignant. I might have to take a headache reliever potion if it didn't subside soon. "And with you now here, it will become that. Alright, let me run you through procedures."

The rules were simple enough, really. Put up magical barricades around each project to protect against cross-contamination. Keep a detailed list of what came in, what went out, and what tests were run. Flag priorities in colors ranging from red to green— green being a cold case that was being re-examined. Although I did warn her nothing should be in the lab more than thirty days. Law was slow, yes, but it *did* move.

Colette jotted down notes in her spidery handwriting, and I felt a wave of nostalgia. It was like being back in our student years, working together on labs. I was of course heartened for her sake that she now had gainful employment that made proper use of her training and intelligence. But I was selfishly, utterly glad she was my colleague here. It was always better to work with a friend.

I glanced at the table, saw three different pieces of submitted evidence tagged Red: Urgent, and sighed. Well, it was good to do something with Colette anyway, walk her through it in practice instead of just theory. "Colette, those three must be done right away. You technically can't handle anything on your own just yet—your paperwork must be completed first—but would you like to accompany me?"

"Set 'em up," she ordered, already standing and reaching for the nearest one.

The sheet attached to the front of the thin wooden box had familiar handwriting, and I cocked my head sideways to read it better. "Ah, that's Gerring. He's a beat cop who's working on becoming a detective. Also one of Jamie's ducklings. He'll have handled that with gloves, so do the same."

"The fingerprints thing she told me about?" Colette looked at the evidence with keen interest. "That really works on helping to solve cases?"

"Usually it's evidence for after the fact, a way to prove the criminal was indeed on scene. It's foolproof, though. No two humans have the same fingerprints."

"Crickey. No kidding? I'll need to set her down and ask more questions about it. I get the feeling she just handed me the gist." Colette's dark eyes turned sharp and penetrating. "This something from her country?"

"It is. She knows a great deal and graciously teaches us. We're slowly incorporating it into practice here." I set the small barricades, little more than magical walls that reached from table to ceiling, readying a form nearby, and gave her a nod.

According to Gerring's report, the charm submitted was one thought to be faulty, something that started a fire instead of preventing it. I had my doubts just because the charm was perfectly intact. If it was the cause of a blaze, shouldn't it also be in ashes by now?

Frowning in concentration, Colette performed a

diagnostic on the charm, her wand slowly panning over the surface of the paper and ink. It was simple in design, a perfect square paper with the red, stylized flame and black written instruction wrapping around the paper like a border. Then her frown grew deeper, brows needled together. "Henri. The charm looks fine. I don't see anything wrong with its design or quality, but there's a sticky residue on top of it."

I blinked at her, then sat up to see over her shoulder. Indeed, there was—a light residue, as if from tape. It was visible only because some lint had gotten stuck to it. "Well now. Perhaps the owner unwisely covered the charm?"

"Looks that way to me. If you cover any part of the design, it makes this pretty much useless. I don't think this is a case of charm-causing-arson. More like stupidity on someone's part." She looked to me for an opinion.

"Indeed, it does. You'll find most cases are like this—carelessness, stupidity, or negligence causes a great deal of the trouble in this city. Well spotted, my friend. I'll jot that down and we'll put it in that bin there, near the door for Gerring to retrieve at his convenience."

It was only the work of a moment before she had it back in its box with my report attached to the top. Then she turned to me with a curious tilt of her head. "That's a spell even a first-year student can manage. Are you telling me that of all the candidates, none could do something like this?"

"Oh, they could normally do the diagnostic test. But they couldn't examine a charm as you just did and see it properly. They couldn't diagnose something and come up with any observations. That's what frustrated me. They were incapable of critical thinking."

Shaking her head, she returned to the table. "Their loss is my gain, I suppose. Alright, what's next?"

I'd known she would be good at this.

We completed the three things demanding an answer, then one more because it had been sitting on my table for at least a fortnight, which I deemed unacceptable. The rules stated under thirty days, but anything over fourteen, and hives threatened to break out on my skin. I had no wish for a case to grow cold because the evidence came back too slowly to be of any use.

Colette picked up things quickly, and by the last task, I was nothing more than an observer. Almost everything on the table was simple enough that even a third-year student should be able to manage, so I had no doubt she would do swimmingly. Still, I impressed upon her to ask me questions if she had any doubt whatsoever.

I took a taxi toward the palace, as I still had wards to somehow fix. On the way, I belatedly realized my mother had tried to reach me earlier. I picked up the pad and hit the phone spell button, typing her name in the box at the top.

My mother's voice came through a moment later, and I had to lean away from the pad, her excited soprano filling the cab. *"Henri, I heard Colette's been hired! I wish to throw a celebration dinner party for all of you. Jamie says you're free this Rest Day. Do ask Colette if she's able to come or if I need to choose a different day."*

Jamie says, eh? No guesses on the source of her information. Still, it pleased me Jamie would go out of her way to make Colette welcome. "I believe Rest Day will be fine, Mother. You can ask Colette directly. She now has a pad of her own."

"Excellent! I'll do so immediately."

"Thank you." After we ended the call, I put the pad aside and closed my eyes for a moment. Tired but elated summed up my state of being perfectly. Mayhap if I got proper rest, my mind would start functioning again at optimum levels and I'd finally be able to conceive of a way to either augment or alter the palace wards. Sleep, and not being forced to focus on a dozen other tasks, would surely do the ticket.

One problem down, two to go.

You know, that's precisely what I said?

You two are rubbing off on each other, I've noticed. You're starting to use each other's phrases and mannerisms. It's actually quite hilarious.

Well, you know what they say about great minds thinking alike.

Report 06: Hot Mess Express

Gibson and I met up at the train station for our meeting with the shift manager, the affable Mrs. Watts—a werewolf with the most pristine white fur I'd ever seen. She'd dyed the patch right over her eye in a blue swatch, which I assumed was some sort of fashion statement. She looked like a goth kid to me, being cool, which tickled my funny bone.

She sat behind her desk, in her rather cramped office that overflowed with portraits of family and knickknacks, and gave us a professional smile. "Kingsman Gibson, Detective Edwards, welcome. Thank you so much for taking this case seriously. I don't mind telling you it's alarmed our CEO thoroughly, and of course everyone who works the line. I'm personally quite affronted we had thieves slip through our guard so easily. If you have suggestions on how to tighten security to prevent this from happening again, I will listen with gratitude."

Well, she just made my life a whole lot easier. "I have a few, in fact, but we'll review those with you a bit later. We'd like to ask some questions first, get a better handle on matters."

"Of course. Do be seated." She waved us to the two leather armchairs bracketing each other.

I sat and immediately wanted a chair just like it in my apartment. It was way comfy. Settling, I flipped open my small notebook and got ready to jot things down. "First question. How often do gold shipments come through here?"

"They're not on any regular schedule," she answered steadily, already pulling a report and handing it over to Gibson. "On average, we have perhaps two or three a month. Sometimes they all come on the same day. Sometimes they're a week apart."

Made sense, I suppose. Gold shipments would be all about supply and demand.

Gibson flipped through the report with a slight frown. "How are you notified a shipment's coming in?"

"We're not, typically. A courier comes in with the shipment and brings it to our clerks' office, does the necessary paperwork to ship it. Much like any other thing we ship."

Huh. Now that was interesting. "You aren't given any head's up at all? I would think so with a shipment that valuable."

She shook her head with a long exhale that set her whiskers quivering. "We did so at first but soon discovered it caused trouble. We were essentially notifying the thieves we had something of value coming. We lost one out of five packages on a routine basis. After two months, we switched to this method. No advance notifications. We also don't put any sort of special packaging around the gold. Many things are boxed in wooden crates with iron bands—chemicals, for instance. Medicines. Sensitive post."

My curiosity climbed steadily as she listed this out. Of course, it made sense. If you kept the gold in an incognito package, the thieves wouldn't be able to tell what was really inside. It was a great deterrent. "So, really, the only indication it's important or pricey is when it gets put into the vaults in the baggage car."

She nodded, fur bristling along the nape of her neck and top of her head in renewed aggravation. "That is correct."

"Who's responsible for that?"

"Our shipping clerks. They're overseen by the train guard. He has to know what's on board to properly safeguard it."

So, we were back to him. Gibson had interviewed the clerks and guard before we came onto the case, and I'd reviewed his interview notes. No one had stepped out of the office until they loaded the baggage car. No way to alert someone with everyone watching each other.

"We absolutely had to offer some safeguard, of course,

which was why we devised that system," Mrs. Watts continued. "We've had shipments go through for nearly eight months without issue. I'm quite wroth it failed so spectacularly."

Gibson made reassuring noises. I was too busy thinking to do any of that.

If there was no advanced notification, and if most of the employees here at the station didn't even know what was in the boxes until they were put in a safe, then how in the wide green world did the thieves figure it out? How did they know to hit *that* shipment? Blind luck? Surely not. This heist was far too well planned for such a slapdash approach.

I pulled my mind back into the present to leave the office with Mrs. Watts, and we walked the line of baggage cars behind the station. It was noisy down here, the smog thick and irritating in my throat, and I had to clear it consistently. Really glad I didn't work in this area. The smoke would kill me eventually.

As we climbed into one of the cars, Mrs. Watts shifted her skirt out of the way so Gibson didn't accidentally tread on it, then asked me directly, "Is this an inside job, Detective?"

I hoisted myself into the car to face her. "We don't know. Really, right now I can debate it either way. Certain aspects make me think it is—like knowing there was gold on board that night. Who else would know but an employee? But in other ways, it doesn't seem so. If it *was* an inside job, they would have been able to lay hands on all the necessary keys. We know for a fact they had to use other means to open some of the locks."

An aggravated growl caught in the back of her throat. "That's vexing. I don't know whether to trust my employees or not."

"I understand the frustration, believe me. I'm not sure if I can trust them either. We'll be looking into them very closely until we get some answers. I need a full list of the employees working the day of the heist."

"Yes, of course, I'll prepare that for you and get it to you by end of business day," Mrs. Watts promised.

"Right now, the best suggestion we can give you is to put at least two guards in the baggage cars every night. Whether or not gold is in here, or anything valuable." Gibson gave the compartment a wave of the hand. "It'll throw thieves off the scent some, but also it's harder to bribe two people. If you can manage three guards on every line, that's even better."

Mrs. Watts eyed him sideways. "That sounds, Kingsman, as if you're quite sure one of my employees was bribed."

"As Detective Edwards said, you can make an argument either way." Gibson paused, mouth working, then admitted sourly, "But in truth, I'm leaning that direction. I know they didn't have all the keys, but we're assuming they had three. How did they get all those keys if they didn't have any inside source at all? How did they know what to prepare to get through all the safety measures without some insider knowledge?"

Now those were two excellent questions. I didn't have an answer for either of them.

Mrs. Watts' face fell. "Oh dear. That's a very good point. Alright, I'll take your suggestions to heart. I'll aim for two guards, although I'm not sure if I can manage that with my current resources. I might have to hire some more to augment my guards."

"I'd suggest it, yes. Also, can you verify for me if it's just your employees handling security on the train? None of the gold companies have security ride with it?"

"That's correct. Their security is responsible for delivering and receiving the gold at the stations. They're not part of the security during shipment." Mrs. Watts grimaced, her nose wrinkling up to show a lot of very sharp canine teeth. "More's the pity. This might have been prevented otherwise. I'll definitely have to hire on additional help, just to help prevent a repeat of this occurrence."

Remembering Henri's suggestion this morning, I pitched in, "And if you could, put a special magical barrier over the doors. Something that will alert you if there's something magical breaching the doorway. That way you know if someone's trying something sneaky."

She magicked out her own notebook from a voluminous pocket in her dark skirt and wrote things down with a pencil. "Sound suggestions, all of them. Thank you. Who do you recommend to do the barriers?"

"I've a short list of people I use for that," Gibson informed her. "I'll send their contact information to you later this afternoon."

"I would appreciate it, Kingsman."

"We'd also like to do a dry run with one of the cars. The timing of this is so tight I feel we'd gain some insight if we take a run ourselves. Is that possible?"

Mrs. Watts looked off into space for a moment, brow furrowing in thought. "I think it's doable. Not during the weekend, we're usually quite busy during that time. Perhaps in the mid-afternoon—there's a bit of a lull then. I can arrange for an engine and baggage car to take you on the same run to Bristol. It will take me a few days to arrange. Is that alright?"

"Completely. Thanks very much."

Gibson turned in place, looking the baggage car over with squinted eyes. I had no idea what he was doing, but it made me think. If there was no notification ahead of time, even with an inside source, it didn't give the thieves much of a head's up. The gold was put into the vault a few minutes before the train left the station. A few minutes wasn't much time to get the word out and get the right people on board.

My friend turned and caught my eye, and I could tell we were both thinking the same thing. In near unison we both said, "Passenger list."

Mrs. Watts blinked at us in bemusement. "I beg your pardon?"

Gibson waved me to do the honors so I explained, "The only trains the gold goes out on is the evening express. No stops that way, more security. We'll need a passenger list. Not for just that night, but for…hmmm…about two weeks prior. Every train that went out from this station. I think the only way our thieves could reliably know they were on the right train—and get here in time—was by riding the trains consistently until they could verify *this* was the train with gold on board."

Her golden eyes narrowed. "Yes. Yes, that would be the only way, wouldn't it? I'll get you the list. It might take a day or two to get it all copied over, but I'll have it delivered to you." She looked about the train car with open dismay. "And could you both sign off on a report stating we weren't negligent? The insurance company guaranteeing this shipment is screaming at me that we didn't take proper precautions."

"I'd be happy to," Gibson assured her gently. "You did everything possible, really. We're just dealing with some very, very clever people."

Her lips peeled back from her teeth in a snarl. "May their cleverness hang them."

I grinned at her. "I can get behind that."

We drove away from the station with Gibson at the wheel because, for some reason, he didn't trust my driving either. Although unlike Henri, at least he didn't grab at imaginary handles and try to slam his foot down on nonexistent brakes when I drove "recklessly." I didn't really mind today. The traffic getting in and out of the station was horrendous. We were crawling at the moment.

"Those lists are going to be not so fun to compile," I pointed out to Gibson. "And we need to run a lot of background checks on the employees. I feel the urge to draw in a junior and make him help with grunt work."

"It'll be good for his soul," Gibson agreed blandly. "And not every name we come up with from that list is really a possible suspect. I'm sure more than a few people use the trains to commute to and from work. A few neighboring towns are bedroom communities for Kingston."

"Yeah, I'm aware, but it'll give us a starting point. And maybe some of those people won't have a good reason to board the same train back and forth." I knew I was reaching a bit, but we had no suspects and not much else to go on. "After this, want to see if we can track down the source of the Raskovnik?"

"Might as well. The person I set on it hasn't found anything missing. You have a place to check?"

"I do. I also want to see if we can track down the emboss seal they used to redo the wax stamp. I know it was rather generic looking, but…."

"Doesn't hurt at this point." Gibson cast me a glance before trying to horn in on the next lane so he could make our turn. "Davenforth going to join us at some point?"

"Maybe not this week. We've had good news, though. Queen Regina appointed a new magical examiner. Henri's over the moon Colette's finally here. He spent this morning catching her up to speed. I don't think she'll need much hand-holding, but there're procedures she doesn't know, and he's got to walk her through those before she accidentally contaminates evidence."

"I'm glad for everyone involved he's got someone else shouldering the load now. Once this woman—what's her name?"

"Colette Harper."

"Once Harper's caught up to speed, you think he'll join in?"

"He hopes to. He's basically darting between lab and palace, but he did say he wants us to keep him abreast of what's going on. I think he's actually miffed he's missing the fun, although of course he didn't say it that way. For all his protests that he's not a detective, he actually enjoys the intellectual challenge of it."

"He certainly agreed to be a kingsmen consultant readily enough." Gibson gave me that arch look again that spoke volumes. "Although I think he did so because of you."

I shrugged in agreement. He wasn't wrong. "He refuses

to let me have all the fun."

Gibson snorted disbelief and chuckled. "You keep telling yourself that, Jamie."

"I will, thank you. Alright, Raskovnik?"

"Yes, let's get that question sorted if we can. I did do some inquiry. That's a very controlled substance. A contact gave me the name of the main company that deals with it. Shall we go talk to them?"

"With pleasure." I only knew of my university contact—Master Gardener Pam Pousson—who grew it, but she did so for exhibition and testing purposes more than anything. I doubted anyone would be able to buy anything off her. She was too sharp for that.

Gibson drove us a little further out than I expected, toward the north of the city. We weren't in the retail part, but more in the distribution side, where warehouses and docks abounded. I guessed us near the channel most of the larger corporations used for shipping purposes, as I could smell the water.

At a large, two-story red brick building, he parked next to a dinged metal door and hopped out. I followed suit, reading the sign as I did so: Magical Items Imports. A straightforward enough name.

No bell chimed as we stepped into the narrow confines of the dingy office. In fact, no one sat at the single desk in the room, and there was only one chair for visitors. Clearly, this place existed for business operations and nothing else.

Another door led further into the warehouse, and Gibson opened it and stuck his head through before calling, "Hello!"

"Be right with you!" a husky voice called back.

It didn't take more than a minute before a stout woman wearing pants and a leather apron came in. She pushed goggles up to her forehead as she moved, removing a leather glove that went straight up past her elbow. She'd obviously been working on something. She took in Gibson's red uniform with a blink, then me, and her thin eyebrows nearly got lost in her dark hair. "Can I help you?"

"Kingsman Gibson. This is Detective Edwards," Gibson said with a wave. "We're here with questions about Raskovnik."

"Uh-oh," the lady said with a grin. "That's never a good question. Means something's been stolen. I'm Hettie, boss of the warehouse. Here, take a seat. Tell me what's up and I'll help as I can."

She hauled a barstool out from under the desk and passed it around, which Gibson took and perched on, leaving me the chair. I sat, pulling out my notebook. "First, you do carry Raskovnik?"

"Not often, no. Usually there's not much demand for it. I've had two shipments in this year, I want to say, but I can check my records and verify that."

"We might need you to. Anything this month?"

Hettie shook her head no. "Not as recent as that. Beginning of summer was the latest shipment. Not much call for it, like I said. What's your time frame for this?"

"Past two weeks," Gibson supplied.

"Hmm. Definitely not something from us. And we only sell to the University, registered magicians, and the like. But I can give you the name of three other companies that handle the stuff as well, if that'll help? I can't speak for whether they'll have had some this past month, but you can ask."

"I'll be happy to ask," I assured her, glad we weren't leaving completely empty-handed. "Names and addresses, if you would."

"Sure." Hettie rattled it all off. She fetched her books as she did so, letting Gibson take a look so he could verify with his own eyes what the record showed. She was so non-plussed about this that I had to wonder how many policemen had come with this very question? Or something similar, at any rate.

We thanked her for the time and information and left, Gibson once again behind the wheel. He pulled away from the curb with a low purr of the motor, swinging us around to head back toward town center.

"Well, that was something of a bust, but at least we

have a lead on who else to ask." I kept the notebook out in case we needed it. "I guess go to—" A beep sounded on my magical pad and I dug it out of my pocket. It was Sherard, his scrawled handwriting more scrawly than usual. It took a second longer to make out what he was saying. Then I groaned. "Gibs, change of plans. Go to the palace."

In a rhetorical fashion, the big man said, "I'm not going to like this. Right. What happened?"

"The teenager got inside the wards again." I squinted as I tried to read the rest of it. It looked like Sherard had written the message with one hand while running downstairs, which was likely what had happened. "Looks like they didn't catch him until he was in the library."

"Knew I wouldn't like it." Gibson took a hard right, cutting someone off in the process. The maneuver set off a chorus of blared horns and swearing that he ignored. For once, he put on the speed, driving more like I did. "Have they got him in custody?"

I wrote an answer back as I replied, "Yeah. I think we got called in for moral support. Before, you know, the two of them lose their minds."

"I don't think that would take much right now."

"Sadly, I suspect you're correct."

We hauled rubber into the side palace gate, which was basically a kingsmen entrance. I'd never seen anyone else use it, at least. Gibson parked, catching my arm. "I'm going to follow up on the next Raskovnik source. You don't need me for this."

"True enough. Okay, go." I lost no time getting out of the car and hoofing it to the location Sherard had given me. It was one of the smaller, round guard houses that dotted the road. Barely large enough to hold three people at a squeeze, the thing had its door wide open with both Sherard and Henri looming in from outside.

I jogged up. "Henri! Sherard!"

Both men turned with twin looks of relief on their faces. Why, I had no idea. It's not like I knew how to fix this hot mess express. Slowing, I came to stand between them, leaning in to see who was inside the little tower.

There, square in the middle of the floor with cuffs on his wrist, sat the troublemaker. Oddly, he didn't look like one. He wasn't ugly, wasn't beautiful, just this quirky fifteen-year-old with sandy brown hair and ears too big for his head. He'd likely grow into those. He looked bummed out and also nervous, staring at us with open trepidation.

I stared back because really, what were we supposed to do with him? We couldn't even prosecute him, as trespassing wasn't illegal here. Trespassing as a crime was rather a modern invention, and it hadn't caught on in Kingston yet. Although at the rate Eddy was going, it wouldn't be long.

"We need a tiebreaker," Henri said, visibly agitated. He kept shifting his weight from foot to foot and shooting glares at the kid. "I'm all for killing him. Seaton's of the opinion we can ship him off to sea."

I knew both men were joking, but they really didn't look it. The kid, at least, seemed to buy it. Swallowing hard, he looked at me pleadingly.

"You can't kill him," I chided Henri. Since he looked really stressed, I put a hand on his back, rubbing a soothing circle into it. He leaned into the contact, settling enough to stop fidgeting. "Killing doesn't solve all problems. And Sherard, stop kidding, you can't ship problems out to sea either. He's a kid—he doesn't understand fully the problem he's causing."

"I think he's old enough to understand," Sherard denied flatly.

Yeah, okay, at fifteen you should be able to. But had anyone actually explained it? I doubted that. I took a half step in, sank onto my heels, and looked the kid in the eye. "Do you know who I am?"

He shook his head a little from side to side, still eyeing me like I was either savior or executioner.

"I'm Detective Jamie Edwards, Kingston Police. The two men behind me are in charge of the palace wards. The one on my right is Dr. Henri Davenforth, Magical Examiner with the Kingston PD and also my partner. The one on the left is RM Sherard Seaton."

Eddy's eyes went so wide they consumed his face. He breathed out a cuss word I pretended not to hear.

"Kid, you're in hot water with them right now, make no mistake. You're seriously driving them nuts by sneaking through wards we thought were nigh impenetrable before your appearance. You understand that by coming in here, you're making everyone really nervous? That people are afraid someone else will figure out how to get in, like you have, and harm the royal family?"

He started to shake his head again, but the mannerism stuttered to a stop and he wet dry lips instead. "I don't—not hurt." He swallowed hard, trying again. "I don't want to hurt anyone. I was just curious the first time. I wanted to see."

He really had no idea what he was doing to us by waltzing in. My suspicion was right. No one had talked to him. "Okay. I believe that, as you didn't do any harm in here. What about the third time? This time?"

"This is, um, actually the fourth time I've come in," he admitted with a wince.

I heard a thump. I didn't look, but I suspected Sherard had just slammed his forehead against the stone exterior of the building.

Blowing out a breath, I rephrased and carefully kept my patience. "Okay, so why did you do it the next three times?"

"I wanted to read the books. I like the books here, they're pretty."

I was enough of a bookworm to empathize with this sentiment. He looked to be from a poor family. Everything on him was threadbare and fraying at the edges. He likely didn't have any chances to read a book, much less own one. Still....

Behind me, Henri muttered in despair, "He wanted to read the books."

"Stop," Sherard whimpered, the sound muffled. He probably still had his face planted against the stone. "Stop talking. I want to cry."

I ran a hand over my face. Good gravy, no wonder the guys were losing their marbles. I'd never seen a criminal with such innocent intentions before. "Okay. Eddy? Coming in here just to read the books is a very poor life decision. You understand that people here are spooked, and are quite willing to shoot anything that moves?"

He squeaked out, almost like an alarmed mouse, "They'd shoot me?!"

"Kid, there's a long line of people willing to shoot you. Trust me. In fact, I'm taking you home right now before someone does." I reached out, grabbed him by the arm, and hauled him up. "Come on. Quick, before someone loses their temper. Boys, go home. Seriously, that's enough for today. It's quitting time, and you both look cross-eyed."

Henri nodded wearily. "Meet up at the precinct in the morning to discuss what you discovered today?"

"Agreed. Sherard, you come too. I'll even bring sweets so you both have plenty of sugar. If you want an order, text it to me."

"Chocolate," Henri whimpered to me as I passed him.

I paused and gave him a quick kiss on the forehead. "Lots of chocolate just for you, I promise. I won't even snitch any. Come on, Eddy."

I have to say, breaking into a palace in order to read has to take the ultimate bookworm prize. I've done crazy stuff to read, but that takes the cake.

What's the craziest thing you've ever done?

Very bold of you to assume I've peaked.

Jamie's Additional Report 6.1

I kept a hand on Eddy as we walked. I trusted the kid about as far as I could throw him. He stayed under my hand, shoulders slumped, both hang-dog and nervous. As he should be. We waited outside for a taxi. Fortunately, with us being around the palace, there was no shortage of taxis driving about hoping for customers. I was able to pile him in very quickly, giving the driver the address.

"Where to?" I prompted Eddy.

He rattled out the address, loud enough for the driver to hear, but kept his eyes on his hands. I belatedly realized the cuffs were still on and used my key to take them off. Pocketing them, I eyed him as he retreated from me.

Eddy slumped in the corner of the cab, hugging the wall as much as possible, as if afraid I'd eat him or something else ridiculous. The silence was so taut I couldn't handle it after a while and my nerve broke. "So, the books. What books were you reading?"

He didn't look up as he answered in a bare whisper, "There was a picture book of foreign places I liked. It had stories for each picture. And a mystery novel."

"Ahh, mystery. Hard to put those down when you start them."

He didn't even nod, just sat there glumly.

Yeah, okay, that foray didn't pan out. Try another. "Eddy, how much trouble are you going to be in with your parents?"

"Lots," he whispered, somehow looking even more pitiful than before. "They're already mad at me."

"Well, you keep breaking into places you shouldn't. It's rather understandable. You've got a job, right? Can't you afford at least a library pass?"

Eddy shook his head miserably. "If I work, I can't get to the library before it closes."

"Ah. That would be a problem, alright." I didn't think he could afford to buy his own books either. Those weren't exactly cheap. The printing presses were slowly becoming more and more efficient, so each year the prices in books dropped a little, but they hadn't invented the paperback yet. It was still all leather and hardbound books. Durable, yes, but not cheap. For Eddy, buying a book would be a once-a-year treat. Anything more than that was a pipedream.

I understood the problem, but I had no solution to offer him.

"If you don't mind my asking, how are you getting in?"

"I just can."

"So you're, what, just waltzing in?"

"Not through the gates, not normally," he answered, still not looking up at me. "But I can spot places no one's watching, and I go through them. And there's usually a bottom floor window no one's locked that I can slip through. After that, it's easy."

Easy meaning he basically had the run of the palace. Ye little gods and pink elephants, was it really that simple for him? That he could just waltz in? "Do you feel anything from the wards?"

"Not really. It tingles a little."

Uh-oh. Yikes. Did I dare tell the guys that or not?

The cabbie pulled to a stop. I kept a hand on Eddy as I pulled him free and paid the driver. Eddy didn't try to run, but I wasn't sure about his reasons. Perhaps he felt like he might as well face the music? Or there was nowhere else for him to go that wouldn't land him in more trouble. That was likely it.

The apartment was one of those narrow townhomes that stood barely fifteen feet wide and connected directly into the ones on either side. It was built from clapboard, needed a coat of paint, a pressure wash, and someone with the energy to do something about the bedraggled flower boxes attached below the windows. I knocked on the weathered front door, hoping a parent opened it. At this time of the evening, surely at least one of them was home.

A tired, thin woman opened the door. She was not obviously kin to Eddy in looks—she was fair in skin and hair—but one look at her face as she looked down at her son removed all doubt. Without a word, she grabbed him by both shoulders and started shaking him.

Eddy winced but didn't fight the hold.

"What is WRONG with you?!" his mother screamed. "Gods strike me on the spot if I didn't raise you better than this!"

I didn't think her reaction was for show. She was on the point of tears, she was so mad. Poor lady, she was probably on the verge of trying to beat sense into him. "Ma'am? I'm Detective Edwards."

"Detective." She took in a deep breath, eyes closed, visibly pulling herself together. "Thank you for bringing him home. I don't want to ask where you found him."

Unfortunately, I had to tell her. "He broke into the palace. Again."

Her eyes slit open like a basilisk, and the voice emanating from her was the voice of Doom. "Eddy. Get inside the house. Now."

Eddy scurried past her, head down the entire time. Yeah, the kid was going to get it now. I'd have more faith about it sticking this time except he'd already been punished by his parents, and it clearly hadn't made much of a dent with him. "Ma'am, you should know everyone in charge of palace security is at their wit's end. They're talking about shipping your son off to sea. Or incarcerating him."

Her eyes sparked fire. When she spoke, her voice trembled with anger. "Is my son aware of that?"

"Yes, ma'am. I just wanted to tell you, as I'm sure he wouldn't relay any of that. But he's seriously pushed them past any sort of luck or favor. If you can't get it through his head that what he's doing is wrong, we're going to have to punish him rather drastically, I'm afraid. Please be aware of this."

"Thank you, Detective. You're very kind for giving us the warning and not just throwing my no-account son into a cell and throwing away the key. Frankly, I'm tempted to do it myself. I'll beat this into him if I have to. His father will certainly have some choice words to say when he gets home later."

I gave her a nod and extracted myself. "Yes, ma'am."

Stepping away from the door, I gave her every indication I was leaving. She closed the door behind me and immediately laid into her son. I crept back up the two stairs necessary to lean against the door and listen. Best technique of a detective: listening. The old adage said you never heard anything good while eavesdropping, but I'd found that to be patently untrue. Now, for instance. I learned all sorts of interesting things by eavesdropping. The least of which was just how far back Eddy's bad habits went.

Oh yeah. We'd definitely have trouble out of this kid again.

It *TINGLES?!*

You misread that. No tingles.

There better not be tingles!

Shh, no tingles. Get back on topic with me.

I feel like someone needs to routinely check in on this kid.

I'll do it!

By 'check in' I do **NOT** mean 'scar for life.' Just to be clear.

Report 07: So Many Theories

If you see me jogging, kill whatever is chasing me.

As promised, we retreated to the lab the next morning. Seaton couldn't stand to be on palace grounds a second longer, and I still endeavored to catch Colette up to speed. In fact, Seaton was so desperate for a diversion that he pitched in and helped us with the lab work. It was, of course, far below his position to do such tasks, but I certainly had no intention of deterring him.

As Jamie came inside, I paused her in the doorway so I could finish up the project on my side, then cleared it so she had room to set her goodies down. She waited patiently at the yellow line, accustomed to lab protocols. With the table clear and a barrier up to protect everything else on the surface from possible spills and crumbs, I waved her inside.

"Cinnamon rolls?" Seaton asked her hopefully.

"Two," Jamie answered with a wink at him. "Just for you. And sun tea, sugar, apple tarts, and chocolate covered cherries for Henri."

I descended upon the offerings with quick thanks and eager hands. The first bite was bliss. I sank into my stool with a sigh of pleasure, a sound Seaton echoed on the other side of the table.

"They wouldn't tell me the details," Colette stated as she helped herself to one of the teas. "Only that the troublemaker got in again."

Jamie sipped her own tea before grimacing. "Long and short of it is, the kid's a natural thief. Seriously, I think he's part cat. He's got an eye for finding the weakness in security, too much curiosity for his own good, and doesn't seem to have any common sense to keep him in check. You know the little voice in the back of your head that warns you when something's not a good idea? I think his is broken."

She'd clearly spent more time speaking with the boy than I had. Now that I had chocolate, I was more inclined to look directly at the problem. "Did you speak with his parents last night?"

"His mother, yeah. Dad was still at work." She took the stool next to mine, reaching for the box and selecting a tart. "He lives on East Side—in the poorer section, no less."

Oh dear. I saw the problem immediately. East Side was the poorest section of the city, with few areas rivalling it. Most people there had one legitimate occupation and one illegal occupation in order to make ends meet. If he'd grown up in that environment, his moral compass might very well be warped.

"Eddy's the eighth child of twelve, so resources are already tight in the family, and while he does have some education—his grandmother made sure every child went to school up until they were twelve—it got cut short. Parents can't feed every kid; they all need to work when they're old enough. Eddy supposedly has a job with the docks as one of their runners, but he keeps getting docked pay. He's too busy breaking into places, so he doesn't always work his shifts."

Seaton finally cleared his mouth of cinnamon roll long enough to get a question out. "I'm surprised you got all this from the mother."

"Eh." Jamie shrugged, a twinkle in her eye. "Not so much. I just delivered Eddy to his loving mother, reported what happened, then asked her to deal with her son. I stepped outside and lingered. Walls are thin. I could pretty much hear everything and make the necessary educated guesses. I mostly stayed to make sure she didn't beat him into an early grave, which she didn't, but the info was a bonus."

Colette sniggered. "Now that makes more sense. Where else has Eddy broken into?"

"I didn't get the full list, but Mrs. Jameson mentioned an art gallery, a judge's house, and—this is the kicker—the police commissioner's house."

I exchanged surprised looks with the others. "We would surely have heard about break-ins with some of those locations if the wards had been disturbed. I know for a fact they'd have wards."

"I don't doubt it. But the palace wards should have reacted too and didn't. I think Eddy's some kind of anomaly. He's got something about him that can squeak past even tough wards. And he likes the challenge of getting in. Maybe because he only wants to get in, not actually do anything, the wards don't recognize him as a threat? That's just a guess, but it seems he can come and go through them as he pleases, as long as he doesn't violate the restrictions of the wards. Even though the wards should be blocking him because he doesn't have permission to be there." Jamie cocked her head at me, expression sympathetic. "I think he's the antithesis to a burglar alarm. Like a ward's kryptonite."

I didn't recognize the last word but took her meaning. And I didn't like it, as the whole thing threatened to give me a migraine. Another migraine, I should say.

Licking some icing off his thumb, Seaton said, "What I'm hearing is that this boy is uncontrollable, his parents can't even keep him in check, and unless we have some flash of genius, he's likely to do it again."

Jamie shrugged, still sympathetic. "That's about the size of it."

More chocolate was called for. I bit into another and mourned my life.

Silence descended for a long minute while everyone thought. No one offered a suggestion. A flash of genius did not seem to be forthcoming. Darn the luck.

Seaton mimed picking something up and setting it off to the right. "Putting that aside, how goes the train robbery?"

"Ah. Well, that's kinda hard to judge at the moment." Jamie ticked things off on her fingers, closing each digit into her palm as she spoke. "We know they used Raskovnik to get through one of the locks, but have had no luck so far figuring out their source. Gibson and I tracked down one of the sources before you messaged me about Eddy. No one's reported any missing, and that's a highly controlled substance. For good reason. He's going to keep asking around. We did discover that the station employees get no advance warning about gold shipments, so whoever planned this had to be sticking pretty close by in order to move quickly enough."

That information pulled me from my peregrinations and I blinked at her. "Wouldn't it also mean they would need an inside source informing them the gold was onboard?"

She waffled a hand back and forth. "Gibs and I are still debating that. We're not sure about an inside source or not at this point. Maybe? But even if they had an inside source, the people at the yard don't know they have gold until about fifteen minutes before they load it up. Fifteen minutes is not a very long span of time to get your thieving friends a ticket and on board the train."

I nodded slowly, letting the logistics of that whirl about in my mind. Perhaps ten years ago, it would have been feasible for someone to be waiting at a nearby apartment or tavern, waiting on word to board. But now? With traffic conditions as they were? Sometimes it took fifteen minutes just to cross the blasted street.

Colette reached for another apple tart, encouraging Jamie, "What else?"

"Hmm, we have a theory that the thieves had to ride the train on a regular basis, a just-in-case measure. The gold is always shipped out in the evening, it turns out. There are no stops, so it's a more secure line. Our guess is the thieves rode the evening train for several days—maybe even a full week—in order to hedge their bets. The station manager is compiling a passenger list for the last two weeks for us. It might get us a suspect pool."

That sounded like a great deal of cross-checking, and I made a mental note to try and help with that. Most trains carried upward of a hundred and fifty passengers, after all. Still, this information gave us something more to go on, which was helpful. "That might explain a few matters. The lack of notification in advance, I mean. Like why they weren't able to take all the gold."

Jamie nodded at me. "Yeah, they didn't know how much to plan for. I had the same thought. It must have grated, actually, to be forced to leave some of it behind."

"I imagine it did." Seaton seemed much more replete with the two cinnamon rolls in his belly and sat back, a man once again at his leisure. "While you wait for those lists, I suppose you'll focus on the Raskovnik?"

"For today, at least. Mrs. Watts has our trial run set up for tomorrow. We're going to see if we can reenact the heist."

I raised my eyebrows. "I didn't realize she would have it ready so quickly."

Jamie nodded. "Maybe if we can figure out exactly how they did it, it'll give us a leg-up in the investigation. Henri, you never did answer me earlier. Do you think they had a magician or not?"

"I'm of two minds on that myself," I admitted frankly. "There were no spells in use that I could see. The vault had anti-theft spells on it, so unlocking spells wouldn't have been able to penetrate. Still, cleaning spells would have been safe to use. Silencing charms. Even the re-application of the wax and bands would be easily accomplished with a few spells. But none of those were in evidence."

"But they knew to use the Raskovnik," Colette protested.

I splayed a hand in acknowledgement. "And that's my issue. How would they even know what that is, much less how to use it, if they didn't have at least some magical training?"

Seaton shook his head. "I think you're all overthinking this. The first case you and Jamie worked was in all the papers. Everyone knew the details of how the thieves were getting into places, stealing things. Their theft of the Raskovnik from the Conservatory was headline news a year ago."

Jamie smacked her forehead with a palm, the meaty slap of skin loud in the small room. "I'm an idiot. I'd forgotten that completely."

She'd also not been able to read a newspaper at that point, but I charitably refrained from saying that aloud. Instead I mentally kicked myself. "Seaton, that's an excellent point. Jamie, I think that provides our answer. Everything they used is something a layman would know about—odds are likely there was no magician in the group. Or, if there was one, he was third-rate at best and his spellwork so unreliable they chose not to implement it."

"Fair enough. Also makes my life easier. I'm looking for good old-fashioned criminals this time." She rubbed her hands together briskly, anticipation lighting up her face. "I do love me some good heist."

My partner truly did enjoy a good intellectual challenge. I had no doubt that was the reason she made such an excellent detective. In this case, I was relieved she seemed to have things in hand for the moment. I had little time to spare to help her.

"Returning back to the wards," Jamie warned, glancing between Seaton and I. "Have you considered an alternative method for people getting in? I know you said certain personnel, like the kingsmen, have a seal on the back of their neck that allows the wards to recognize them."

"We can't put a magical seal on every single person who enters palace grounds," Seaton objected strenuously. "Those seals are simple to place, certainly, but the magical drain that would take to apply them on all the visitors—"

She held up a hand, staying him. "I'm not talking about anything so fancy. I mean, the palace grounds receive tourists daily. That would be an insane headache. No, I meant something easier. Like an ID chip—ah, crap. Uhhh...something like a card? And the bearer of the card would be able to pass through."

Seaton's mouth was still open on an objection that never seemed to quite form. He closed his mouth with a click, frowning absently at the wall dead ahead.

I personally saw her reasoning and worked through the logistics aloud. "The cards would be something we could re-issue over and over. Not something that had to be replaced every day. Short term, it would be a burden on the maker, but long-term it's feasible to sustain. But that doesn't prevent the possibility of someone nicking a card for their own use."

"It has its drawbacks," Jamie admitted, "but it might also help settle people's panic some. If you've got a possible solution, it looks better than, 'I got nothin',' if you catch my drift."

Seaton slouched into his chair. "That I do. I certainly can't think of anything better, and it might keep our wayward thief out. Especially since we're raising security levels at the same time. What do you say, Davenforth?"

"I say it can't hurt to try." I gave Jamie a nod of thanks. "We'll try it. Thank you for the suggestion. And breakfast."

"You're welcome. I'll let you guys get back to it. I've got to figure out where that Raskovnik came from. It's giving me grey hairs." She popped up, ready to leave, but I stayed her with an upright hand.

"I was contacted yesterday by the mage who created Clint," I informed her. "He wishes to visit and evaluate Clint. And I think he has many questions for you, as well. Are you amenable?"

"Sure? Is this a formal thing?"

"Not at all. But Clint is the first Felix to be out and about in the world, and you've put him to a use that Magus Felix didn't think of. I think he's very curious."

"Ah. Then sure, set it up. Dinner or something should work."

I nodded agreement. "I shall, then."

Jamie headed for the door, then paused in the doorway to address Colette. "You still on for Girls' Night this week?"

"Yes, of course," Colette answered readily. She had the most intrigued look about her, an expression I hadn't seen in years.

With a salute, Jamie was off, her usual long stride eating the distance quickly. Sometimes she forgot to move at the same pace as the rest of humanity. It was part of the reason I always huffed and puffed while trying to keep up with her.

Seaton asked the question I wondered. "Girls' Night?"

"She invited me over to her flat to meet some of the other ladies she's friends with," Colette explained, drifting back to the work she'd set aside. "Apparently she gets together with them a couple times a month. She cooks, then we all sit about and gossip and play board games. Sounds smashing."

Seaton looked dubious at this description so I further explained, "I can hear it play out whenever she has those nights. There's a great deal of giggling and thumps. I guarantee you they have the time of their lives. Usually until the wee hours of the morning."

"It must be interesting, living next to her."

"And fattening." I mournfully looked down at my vest that strained at the buttons. "She's entirely too good of a cook."

"Davenforth." Seaton's eyes twinkled in that devilish way that never boded well. "Not to tell you your business, old chap, but considering your occupation, and the very active partner you have—not to mention her cooking skills—have you considered regularly exercising?"

"Why do you say such hurtful things?"

Colette threw her head back and howled.

Some friends I have.

Henri, you really need to have <u>some</u> form of exercise. I know you don't like jogging along the streets, so how about if I get you a treadmill?

Excuse you very much. I will **NOT** get on some contraption invented for prison use!

wait, treadmills were seriously invented for prisoners?

Actually, they were. It's part of the reform program.

yeah, I can tell right now
I'm going to have to switch tactics

Report 08: Trial Run

Mrs. Watts was good to her word and had everything set up and ready to go. We were a short little train—an engine, passenger car, and baggage car. The passenger car was in case we chose to just ride back from Bristol. I had a feeling we wouldn't use it—I at least wanted to do two dry runs. I had the feeling a lot of fumbling would happen in the first one.

We'd assembled a four-man team, as we suspected our thieves had: me, Henri, Gibson, and Foster—a new kingsman. A werefox, he had no magic abilities, unlike most kingsmen, although I understood he'd aced the physical exam. Foster wasn't a typical red fox in looks, although he had some red fur. Mostly he was grey in the face and body, a bit of white fur peppering the dark, his ears tall and mobile. I liked the spark of intelligence in his golden-brown eyes. He came with five years of experience being a palace guardsman. I had an overall good vibe with him, and the suspicion I'd like him if we got the chance to know each other better.

Clint also accompanied us and chose to sit on top of the vaults and observe. We had dummy lead shot and bricks to substitute the gold, plus a bag full of the tools we guessed necessary to do this.

Lots of guesswork on this.

I stood at the side of the engine, greeting our engineer, a snappy young woman named Fotina. She had a quirky, almost genteel look to her face that did not match the strappy body lurking in her coveralls. And the voice really didn't match either, all smokey sounding, like a lounge singer. "Detective. Ready to go?"

Before I could answer, Gibson stopped me. "First let me introduce Henri to our colleague helping us out."

Gibson waved to Foster. "Foster Osborne, this is Dr. Henri Davenforth. He's both a magical examiner with the Kingston PD and Jamie's partner. Davenforth, our latest kingsmen recruit, Foster Osborne. I'm still training him, thought a bit of investigative work would do him good."

Foster gave Gibson a wry look. He clearly knew exactly why he was here, but he politely gave Henri a nod. "Pleasure, Doctor."

"Yes, quite, Kingsman." Henri signaled me with a nod and loaded in the car.

I smiled at the engineer. "Okay, we're ready now. Thanks for this, Ms. Fotina."

"My pleasure. Have to say, none of us have been happy about the recent theft. Paints our railroad in a bad light. If this will help, I'll take you as many times as you like."

"You're good people, Ms. Fotina, thanks." With a wave, I took myself back to the baggage car and hopped the short distance inside. Turning, I slid the door shut and secured it.

The inside was dim—with no windows, and only a small top skylight, no natural light could seep in. Two lanterns bracketed either end of the train car, illumination solely for the guard's and baggage carrier's convenience. It was also insanely crowded, with barely enough room for a single person to walk the breadth of the compartment. Put four grown adults and a curious cat in here, and there wasn't much room left to maneuver.

"I vote we assume they started the minute the door closed," Gibson stated.

I raised a hand. "Seconded. Let's get to it. We're also assuming they only had some of the keys necessary, so I've got a sprig of Raskovnik to get through the vault door."

Henri held out a hand for it, and I passed it along, as that was easier than trying to slip past everyone. As he worked on that, I pulled out a pocket watch and set it there, encouraging Clint to move over to the shelf. "Field cat, I need you to keep track of the time for us."

"Okay," he said seriously, hunkering around the watch so

he could look at its face and us.

Henri had a copy of the guard's keyring and used it to spring the padlock, then he inserted the sprig of Raskovnik into the keyhole of the vault. With that open, he used the ring of keys and opened the three compartment doors. Then he pulled out the safes containing our 'gold,' unlocking the top of each safe before passing two of them along to Foster and Gibson.

I could feel time ticking by in the back of my head with a loud tick-tick, because just doing that took five minutes. Wrestling that much weight in these tight quarters was not at all easy. With me in the very front of the car, I couldn't help during this process at all, either. In fact, I shouldn't—I was stronger than all the men, and me helping might throw things off.

I went with what I could do—get ready to get those bands off the boxes. The carpet bag of tools waited nearby, and I pulled that closer, bringing out the pliers to handle the bands.

Gibson put a safe on the shelf nearby with a grunt.

"Can't do that," I warned him. "The baggage car was full that night. Shelves wouldn't have been usable."

He let out a vile curse and then struggled to get it off again and onto the floor, letting it land the last two inches with a thump. "That is *not* as easy as it looks."

"It doesn't look easy at all. That's a lot of dead weight, and it's an awkward shape to boot."

The wooden boxes inside all had a rope handle along the top lid so it was easier to lift them in and out. Some frustrated person had probably thought that one up. Gibson used it to lift the box free and hand it to me.

I took it with an oof of effort. It wasn't so much the weight, as the awkwardness of it. Setting it down at my feet, I hunkered over it as I bent the iron bands off with the pliers. Which was a lot easier to say than it looked. It took a lot longer than I anticipated to wrestle them off, but I finally did. "Victory! First one free."

"Okay, give that to me. I'll swap things out while you work on the next one."

"So, I'm in charge of bands, huh." I shrugged, amenable to this.

We swapped boxes, Foster handing me the next one to work on. Henri, still in the padlock area, worked on yet a third safe.

It became something of an assembly line. As soon as I had the bands off, I found myself with the first box back, having to put new bands back on. And wax seals, of course, to top it off. I had trouble keeping the wax lit—going sideways like that, the flame kept trying to sputter out. I lit it three separate times just to get the one box done.

The men called out instructions to each other on how much lead shot they needed to switch out with each box. Gibson and I had requested that Mrs. Watts not mark which box had 'coins' or 'ingots' to make things as authentic as possible.

With so little clear floor space, we basically worked on top of each other, and things quickly got mixed up in the confusion. The rattle of the train as it went along the tracks didn't help, as the wax seal kept rolling underneath the baggage shelves. Clint had to fetch it for me twice, as it went out of our reach.

I was sweaty and huffing for breath by the time I got the last box re-banded and sealed. "Alright, go!"

Gibson took it from me and put it in its safe, and promptly closed the door. "Who has the key?"

Henri tossed it to him.

Trying it, Gibson made a face. "No, not this one. Where's the other one?"

"Maybe that's the one I need?" Foster offered, holding out a key to swap.

They swapped, growled when it still wasn't right, and went for the other keys lying in a pile. I stared at them and suppressed a sigh. Really? They couldn't keep the keys straight after wasting time figuring it out the first time?

Clint from his perch on the shelf lifted his head and announced, "Five minutes left."

Swearing, we all leapt into action. Nothing was put away yet. We crammed boxes back into the safes, and Henri shoved those back into the compartments. We still hadn't squirreled away all of the 'gold' yet, and we hastily started on that while Henri managed locking everything. For that matter, things had gotten so mixed up I wasn't sure if we'd stolen enough 'gold' out of the boxes or if some had been left over.

The train whistle sounded overhead and the train slowed, beginning to pull into the station. I held up a hand, calling a halt. "Stop, stop, we're done. We didn't make it."

"That is *unbelievably* tight," Foster exclaimed, staring around at the mess at our feet. Wax droppings, bent metal bands, and all the tools lay in disarray around us. "Look at this, we barely have the gold put in our pockets or bags. Never mind cleanup."

"There was too much fumbling about with the keys," Henri observed. "If not for that, we might have made it."

It was strange. When I'd first heard of this case, I thought forty minutes was challenging but plausible. But it hadn't really sunk in how much practice this took, how smoothly everything had to go, in order to make it. It wasn't just swapping out the gold for lead—it was cleaning everything up so precisely afterward that no one suspected anything was amiss. And the cleanup would take up quite a bit of time. "Guys, how about we do another dry run on the way back to Kingston?"

Foster nodded firmly. "I want to. I'm not satisfied with this."

That seemed to be the general consensus, as the other two nodded as well.

"First a cold beverage," Henri suggested, patting at his temples and cheeks. "And then we discuss what else we need to make this more feasible."

I could think of a few things, in fact, but... "I'm definitely up for a drink."

Our engineer, because she was amazeballs, did two more runs for us. It took three runs total before we finally had everything cleaned up before we pulled into station. The second time we were very close; however, the goal wasn't to just have it cleaned up but to be able to walk out the minute we pulled in. That's what the thieves had to do, after all. Immediately leave and vacate the area as quickly as possible before the theft was discovered and the station locked down.

On our way back to Kingston, we chose to use the passenger car instead. I, for one, was tired. I felt like I'd just marathoned a three-hour raid in some MMORPG and got my can kicked in the process. The feeling was a mutual one in the group. We slumped in our train seats, none of us exactly perky. Clint was the only one with energy, but then, for the most part, he'd just watched and enjoyed the show. Sometimes giving us an unnecessary countdown because he was evil like that.

I felt like it needed to be said, even though we were thinking the same thing. "I know we didn't precisely hit the mark on that last run, but we were close enough to make no difference. No tricks or magic was necessary to pull this off. This is doable."

Gibson nodded, although he didn't bother to open his eyes or change from his slouched position. "It is. They must have practiced many, many times to get the timing down smoothly. I almost wonder now if it wasn't a matter of weight so much as time."

"What do you mean?" Foster inquired.

"The gold they left behind," Gibson elaborated. "Why do so? We assumed it was a matter of weight—they didn't know how much to plan for so were caught short. They were forced to leave some of it behind. But it could have been timing, too. Maybe they just couldn't get all the boxes open and shut again before they ran out of time. Knowing that, they cut their losses."

I splayed my hands in a shrug. "Could be either. Or both. Who knows? It certainly was tight enough just managing what we did, and we're good at working with each other. This takes some phenomenal teamwork."

"The silencing charm was definitely a necessity," Henri observed, rolling his head back up to look at us. "It's impossible to move in those confines without creating quite a bit of racket."

"Yup. So, we're looking for people who know each other well, or at least work with each other often. I don't think you can pull together a group of strangers and get this to work well without a *lot* of practice. Maybe months."

Gibson nodded in agreement. "And they likely had some obscure place set up with a practice area. Not that we have any idea of how to look for that."

"It's probably dismantled by now, anyway." More's the pity. Lots of possible evidence was in that spot, wherever it was. "I'm saying this, too. Definitely four people to pull this off."

"Agreed." Gibson frowned, finally opening his eyes and focusing on us. "But I don't think it's possible it was any more. Five people would not have fit into that baggage car."

"If there's a fifth—or even sixth—person, then it's an informant," Foster agreed immediately. "There's no possible way to put another person in that baggage car and have the necessary room to maneuver. I'd almost say it would work with three people better rather than four, if it wasn't for the weight. The one time we tried to distribute the weight among only three people, it was very obvious."

I didn't quite agree there. "They may have found a clever way around that. We were making do with regular clothes. But a bulky coat would hide a multitude of sins. Or a specially designed briefcase, for instance. It still might be three. But the workload would make that challenging. We barely managed it all with four."

"And I feel like they would have two people working on the metal bands," Henri pitched in. "Having just one slowed us at times."

"Yes, I think so as well." Gibson slapped both knees. "Well! Good work today. When we get back, let's call it a night and go home. I'm not sure about the rest of you, but I could use the respite."

"I have a hot bubble bath and a good book calling my name." My calves were killing me from all the squatting. But we had done good work today, and I was proud of that. I felt like we had a firmer grasp on the mechanics of this.

Now to figure out whodunnit.

Jamie's Additional Report: Fanmail

Most of Friday—ahem, excuse me, Scribe Day—I spent doing background checks with Foster. Not because I didn't trust him to do a good job, but because he wasn't all that well versed in what to look for in investigations like this one. And it seemed a crappy thing to do, to throw all the legwork on his shoulders.

We started with alibis—that was the easiest way to knock people off the suspect list—and then moved on more intensely when someone couldn't offer a rock-solid alibi for the day in question. Of course, not every single person had been working that day. Some of the guards only had the morning shift, or weren't on schedule that day, or were out sick, etcetera, etcetera.

We fetched to a stop near the end of the work day and visited Gibson at his office.

Normally, Gibson's office was this paragon of organization and cleanliness. Today was not that day. His desk was cluttered, stacks of files covered both visitor chairs, and even the seascape painting behind his desk was crooked. My friend was bent over his own list of tasks, what looked like a re-arrangement of kingsmen, and I winced. Wards still wonky enough to call for double shifts, eh? Ouch.

Gibs looked up with relief from his desk as we entered. "Tell me you have good news."

"We have a narrower suspect list, at least." I decided against dropping into my usual chair and leaned up against his desk instead, the edge of it pressing against my hip. "All the clerks have solid alibis, as do the porters. Admin staff never went near the baggage car, so they're in the clear. Not all the guards were on-duty so unless we see evidence that they were at the station, I'm not inclined to think they're involved. We started background checks on all the guards. So far, no alarms."

Foster nodded along in support of this. "No one has any priors, or even skirted along the wrong side of the law. We'd have to pull warrants to look at people's finances, but there's nothing to indicate we need to do that."

"So, what you're saying is, we have no new leads."

I *tsked* him with a wagging finger. "'Once you eliminate the impossible, whatever remains, no matter how improbable, must be the truth.' We were just eliminating the impossible today."

"Sherlock again?" he asked wearily but with a slight upcurve of his mouth.

"Surely I don't quote him so often that you remember the source."

"You really, truly do. Alright, so you were eliminating the suspect pool. Who's still in it?"

"Hmm, right now Cain Innis, Marianna Rutherford, Jacob Swoles, Jodan Nichols, and Simon Biggs look iffy. But they only look iffy because they have access to the keys, worked the day of the heist, and I can't pinpoint where they were at all times. They say they were in certain places but can't seem to offer me a witness to prove it."

Gibson frowned and rubbed at his jaw. "But other than that, do they look suspicious?"

Foster answered with a shake of his head. "Not really. None of them have priors. None of them are acting out of character or have tremendous debt, as far as we can tell. Rutherford and Innis both guarded the train, but in different places, is all. Ezer Fagin was the engineer. Swoles was the one who accepted the gold and oversaw it loaded onto the train. Nichols guarded the baggage car as they off-loaded it in Bristol. Simon Biggs is actually a clerk, but he has access to all the keys to the station and is responsible for locking it up every night."

"So, it's more like they have opportunity and means but

the motive is a big fat question mark." Gibson sighed as he sank back into the chair. "Anyone else?"

"A few questionables, but that's my main list at the moment. I think I want to go through the passenger lists before we really start cracking down on people. It's something that can wait for another day, at least."

Wearily, he agreed with a nod. "Then good work. Thanks for updating me. I'll hopefully be free to join you once I get this shift re-scheduled."

"Better you than me." I gave him a casual salute and took myself off again. I had errands to run if I was to get my Girls' Night going on time in…. I took out my pocket watch from my vest and winced at the time. Wowzer, I had two hours.

I better get moving.

With a casual bye to Foster, I caught a taxi and headed to Ellie's lab. I had something in particular I needed her help with, and I'd prefer to get it done now, before I put it off any longer than I already had.

I'd received three letters that week, and even though I'd tried in vain to read them, it had proven impossible. It wasn't something I could shrug off, either, not with these letters. I had to respond, and I wanted to do it sooner rather than later. My Velars had improved rapidly in the almost three years I'd been on this planet, but people's handwriting sucked, and that could throw a crimp in my style.

With my usual helper (Henri) being busy and my other usual helper (Sherard) on the verge of a meltdown, I went with the saner option and asked for Ellie's help.

I went to her lab, partially to check on the upgrades to my bike, with a stack of letters in my hand. She was ratcheting away at something as I came in, a streak of grease on her fair cheeks, as usual. Her flaming red hair was caught up away from her face with a folded bandana, forehead dewed with sweat. She looked up as the door shut behind me, grinning. "There you are!"

"I'm not late," I pointed out laconically, weaving my way around piles of half-finished projects. "And what are you doing to my bike this time?"

"Improving the suspension," she reported, returning to her ratcheting. "I've almost got it, I think. You can have it back tonight."

"Sweet." I hopped up on the table behind her, as there wasn't a seat in sight available, idly swinging my legs.

"What did you need help reading, anyway?" Ellie inquired, still fiddling.

"Letters. I got in three this week that I haven't been able to fully decipher. A few words are throwing me off."

"Yeah? Who writes you letters?"

I scratched at a cheek, a little embarrassed. "It's, um, fanmail? Sorta?"

Ellie paused and gave me a look askance over her shoulder, brow raised. "Fanmail?"

"The people who survived Belladonna," I explained with an awkward shrug. "You know, the ones who lived through the cities she blasted apart, or the ones who lost a loved one due to her killing sprees. They reach out to me sometimes. They don't really know an address, but everyone knows I'm a detective, so they mail it to the precinct."

She put the ratchet down, turning to fully face me. Curiosity canted her head to the side. "And what do they say?"

"It varies. Sometimes it's a simple thank you. Sometimes they're looking for…I don't know, a sympathetic ear, or advice. A few people who write to me regularly are borderline suicidal because of what she did to them. They take some sort of comfort from the fact that I survived her too and am back to normal life."

"If she can do it, I can do it?" Ellie offered, expression pensive. "Is that their thinking?"

"Yeah, something like that. And one guy, he's seriously gotten so much better. I told him about having Clint, and how much that's helped me, so he went and adopted a dog. That dog's saved his life, no joke."

Ellie smiled at me, but the expression was sad more

than anything. "That's quite the burden you've shouldered, dearling."

I snorted. "It's not a burden. It's group therapy. We're just doing it long-distance, is all. So, can you help me read the letters? Some of the handwriting is bad, or the spelling, and I can't be sure I'm reading it right."

"Of course," Ellie assured me, smile softer now. "Of course I will."

Report 09: Stalkers Make Poor Life
Decisions aka Jamie has fun

After Ellie helped me, I went to the grocer's to pick up a few ingredients—I was making clam chowder, a hit with the Girls' Night crowd. I expected the usual suspects plus Colette. Ellie and Penny were very curious to really meet our new magical examiner, and I had a feeling Colette was starved for some quality female friends. I fully anticipated Colette and Ellie to get along like two peas in a pod. They had similar senses of humor, to start with. Penny was generally shyer making friends, so we'd have to see how that went.

I left the grocer's, and as I crossed an intersection, I spotted a familiar head of black braids ahead of me. Colette stood a good head above even most of the men, so it was easy to spot her in a crowd. "Colette!"

She turned, pausing under a lamppost, then spotted me and waved in greeting.

I stretched out my legs to catch up with her while she waited patiently. It was getting late in the evening, sunset falling, and the lampposts were yet to be lit. I imagined the crew who lit the gas lamps were still working toward this street. I was glad to run into her. Colette's formidable, and I didn't think many men would be stupid enough to cross her, but with women it was always safer to be in numbers.

"Fancy meeting you here," she joked with me, a grin lighting up her heart-shaped face.

"I know, right? Is that wine I see under your arm?"

"It is. I know you said to just bring what I wanted, but I've had this hanging about in my house for two years now. Someone needs to help me drink it."

"Fair enough." I started off again, leading the way, and she fell into step with me. I hadn't seen much of Colette this week, just the two times I'd stopped into the precinct. It was part politeness on my part, but mostly curiosity when I asked her, "How goes everything?"

"I'm still catching up with protocols," she answered, lighting up, free hand coming up to gesture as she spoke. "But I love the work. I can't approach it with any preconceptions. A few of the detectives aren't sure how to react to me yet, but the rest are just relieved to have a third magical examiner in house to shoulder the load. Poor Henri really was swamped."

"Yeah, he really was. We all recognized it, but unfortunately there wasn't much any of us could do about it."

"They've been patient explaining the rules to me as I get the gist of things. Good people to have as colleagues, that's been my impression. And that young officer you're training, Gerring? He's a delight. He escorted me to one crime scene and stayed right next to me as I worked. He said it was a bad area, and he wasn't leaving me alone out there."

"I do love Gerring. He's the sweetest guy, as you've learned. He's also one sharp cookie. I anticipate in another six months or so, he'll make detective as well."

"As Detective McSparrin did? I understand she's also one of your ducklings."

"She was, yeah. Detective in her own right now. I'm training a few other girls, but they work in other precincts. The Queen's a huge advocate of me training the women— I'm not going to patronize them, like some of their other trainers, and I'm a master in a fighting style that gives anyone the ability to take down a larger opponent. It gives the girls an edge they need."

"That right? Gerring mentioned you also know a way to revive someone who's stopped breathing, like a drowning victim."

"You have to get to them quick," I warned. "Within five minutes. But yes, I know a way to do it. I'll be happy to teach you. I'm trying to teach as many people as possible how to do CPR. It literally saves lives."

"I imagine so—" Colette stopped dead and peered at something across the street. "Hmm. Looks like trouble. Jamie, we might need to rescue a girl."

I followed her gaze and immediately saw the problem.

People get a certain expression when they're panicked and in trouble—part fear, part apprehension. Their eyes dart in all directions, they hunch in on themselves, and there's a scurrying quality to their gait, like a mouse trying to find a bolt hole before the cat catches up. This girl was definitely a mouse being stalked. She was a pretty thing—blonde curls, petite frame, dressed in some silky-lacy contraption of the latest fashion. Young, too. If she was in her twenties, I'd be surprised. She spied us staring at her and relief crossed her face before she darted across the street, ignoring the outraged honks of the drivers as she dodged cars.

I watched her, of course, but I also kept an eye on the opposite side of the street. She was running from something. I wanted to know what. I had a feeling I knew. A man stopped dead and watched her too. He eyed the traffic, as if gauging the right moment to follow her across.

Something about him felt off to me. He was dressed alright, in a plain suit like a young clerk would, but his hat hung low on his forehead, shielding his face. No call for that at this time of the evening. There was barely enough light to see by. My instincts said he was trouble. I was inclined to listen to them.

Blondie wasn't even fully across the street when she started talking, her soprano voice high with panic. "Please help me! He's been following me for five blocks now—I can't shake him!"

Colette didn't even look surprised. She held out an arm, and the girl nestled straight into it like Colette was some great oak that would shelter her from a storm. "Don't you worry, child. You've found the right women. I'm a magical examiner with the Kingston PD. This is Detective Edwards. You point that man out to us, we'll take care of it."

The girl looked outright relieved she'd happened into

two cops off duty. "He's the man with the hat low over his face, the one in the black coat and pin-striped pants."

"Thought so," I muttered grimly. "Colette, can you take my bag? I'll grab him."

"Sure thing."

I transferred the bag over to her and cracked my neck to either side, loosening up a bit. I hadn't had a good chase in ages. I saw a slight break in traffic and took off, going at full speed because why not? I could see the panic on his face as I went straight for him.

People in Kingston, they're used to all types. Weres, supernats, magicians, the works. Still, it always surprised them when I approached with superhuman speed. Probably because I looked fully human, so they didn't expect anything out of the norm with me. He turned to run, but of course it was too late by that point. I caught up to him before he got more than three feet.

Clamping down on his coat, I whirled him into the nearest storefront, his face meeting the brick with a not-so-kind smack. Fortunately, I had a pair of handcuffs on me and reached for them.

"You can't do this!" he protested. "I didn't do anything to her!"

"Way to confirm you were stalking her," I drawled, slapping the first cuff onto his wrist.

"I wasn't going to do anything to her. I just wanted to follow her."

"Woooow. You're a total douchebag. Dude, seriously, that just creeped me right out. You know what we women think of men like you? That it would be better to douse you in gasoline and light you on fire than let you roam around." I leaned in and breathed, "You scared her so bad she ran into the arms of complete strangers to get away from you. But it's not your day, sicko. I'm the Shinigami Detective."

He whined in the back of his throat, rolling his brown eyes at me, properly terrified now.

I grinned back at him. "And I don't like men like you. Up

you come. We're going to the precinct."

"I didn't do anything," he babbled at me, fighting me every step. "But I didn't do anything to her!"

"You stalked her for five blocks. I'm a witness. You're screwed, dude."

Colette and our scared victim caught up at this point, although the girl looked vindicated now that he had cuffs on. She looked at me with big blue eyes, and I could see the hint of elvish blood in her elongated ears and the slim lines of her face. She looked like a doll. Poor girl. She probably caught all sorts of wrong attention from her looks alone.

"I need you to come to the precinct with us, get a full report on him," I told her. "Then you can go. I'll put in a restraining order so he can't get anywhere near you."

She stayed planted in Colette's shadow but gave me a game smile. "Thank you so much, Detective."

"And the next time this happens, I don't want you to run. You stand your ground. Scream your head off. Tell everyone around you he's stalking you, that you don't know him. Someone will respond and help, if you don't feel like you can handle it yourself. Trust me, I've seen that play out several times. These guys, they pick on girls who are quiet by nature. They're cowards. You make enough noise, prove you won't go quietly, and they'll disappear rather than deal with you." I shook the guy in my grip, leaning in to snarl between my teeth, "Because real men don't get a kick out of scaring women. Sicko."

She bravely nodded. "I'll do that next time."

He glared back at me, which was an odd juxtaposition considering he was still shaking like a dog with its tail between its legs. Didn't like being called a sicko coward, huh? Tough luck. That's exactly what he was.

Colette didn't like him any better. She glared at him as if mentally calculating whether she could get by with hexing him or not. In the end, she seemed to reconsider and didn't. (Pity.)

We grimly marched the three blocks back to the precinct,

and I hauled him directly into a jail cell. He could rot there for the night. I didn't do more than get his name so I could process him. If he missed work, tough. I wasn't doing this man any favors.

It took more than a few minutes to process things, get the girl's statement, and all that. I was running late for my Girls' Night, so I sent off a quick message we'd start an hour later than planned. Fortunately, everyone was well aware crap just happened with me sometimes. I wasn't always able to be on time.

Colette soothed the girl and got her settled into a taxi, safely on her way home. We caught one ourselves, hoping to speed up the process of getting back on track to my apartment. As I settled into the seat, I said, "I find it interesting she went directly for you. That happen often?"

"Oh yes. Most women, they look at me and think: No man would cross her. I often look down and discover a woman's shown up in my shadow, evading some man's unwelcome attentions." Colette shrugged, resigned to her status as protector of strangers. "I've magic to help keep us all safe. And most men don't cross me, that's true enough. Does this happen with you too?"

"Hmm, sometimes. I think it's because I'm in a suit, they get the impression I'm capable of defending them. I usually flash a badge at some point, reassuring them I'm a cop, and then deal with whoever's hassling them. It's sad women have to do that. But it's also kind of funny if it happens when I'm out with Henri." Remembering the last incident, I couldn't help but laugh. "He's got this lecture he unleashes on any man scaring a woman. More like a rant."

"Oh, I've heard it," Colette assured me dryly. "He's said it more than a few times in my hearing. He's very much the gentlemen, our Henri. Doesn't understand why any man would be hateful to a woman. And he takes it as a personal affront when they do."

"I feel this urge to tell Henri all about tonight and point him in the direction of the idiot."

"I don't see why you shouldn't." Colette grinned at me like a co-conspirator.

I grinned back. Yup, it's official. I liked her.

Of course, that meant I had to properly corrupt her, right?

Oh heavens. I should have warned Colette first.

cackles tooooO00000 late

I was afraid of that.

Henri's Additional Report 9.5

Girls' Night, from what I could hear, was in full swing upstairs. The laughter, thumps, and occasional "whoops!" told heaps. Jamie always introduced some Earth game—sometimes drinking games, sometimes absurd things. Like that Twister game with people's limbs going everywhere. I'd nearly broken my neck playing that one with her.

I was ostensibly sitting in my chair, studying my notes on mine and Seaton's secret project, but in truth I couldn't focus on it very well. My attention kept being diverted upstairs to the sound of feminine laughter.

I heard a scratch at my window and turned to see purple fur pressed against the glass. I cast a spell to open it, as I was too lazy to get up and undo the latch myself. Clint squeezed in a second later, hopping lightly down to the sofa and regarding me with his bright gold eyes with something like desperation.

"Stay here?" he asked hopefully.

"All the attention was too much?" I asked in understanding. It wasn't the first time he'd ducked out mid-party.

He nodded fervently. Taking my question as tacit permission, he curled up at my side, stretched out along my thigh. I gave him a good belly rub, starting him purring.

Slitting open one eye, he reported to me, "Jamie happy."

That was the one thing uniting the two of us: the happiness and well-being of the woman upstairs. I'd forever be glad I'd gone to such trouble to acquire Clint for her. "Thank you, Clint."

With that reassurance given, he settled in, purring away. I idly stroked him as I returned to my notes. As long as Jamie was happy, we could both be at our ease.

And what's this secret mission you and Sherard are up to?

Believe it or not, it's a secret.

I'll get it out of you eventually.

No doubt.

Report 10: Magical Passes

Seaton and I were, lamentably, working on the wards once more in his study. We'd used Jamie's suggestion of physical passes and presented the idea to Queen Regina. She'd agreed it was an option worth trying and formally approved it, if only because she was tired of the heightened security and willing to take any possible solution offered. I was not, however, of the mind to question that.

The wards were very, very complex after so many generations of people tampering with them. We had to redesign them carefully. Any alterations we made might conflict with some other facet of them. In fact, we erected a mini-model of the palace in Seaton's study so we could try out the wards on a smaller scale, test them before performing alterations on the real thing.

Seaton frowned and poked at part of the design. "I think if we simply add the instruction of the card's recognition, it'll be fine. There's nothing that should conflict."

"I agree, but we have to design something much like the mark we use on everyone else. Otherwise we'll need more than a one-line adjustment." I grimaced. "Although I'm not sure if the marks will adhere to anything but skin."

"I don't think they will. They're not designed to." Seaton glared at the design of the mark in question, an innocent enough looking paper that sat between us on the table. "The question stands: Do we try to alter this just enough that it will adhere to something aside from skin? Or add another layer of complexity to the wards?"

"While we're asking questions that may not have a good answer," my partner intoned as she sailed into the room, "I've got one. Where can the non-magical people get their hands on Raskovnik?"

I hadn't seen much of Jamie in two days. I'd spent most of Scribe Day buried in the lab at the precinct with Colette helping her catch up on the workload. I'd heard her Girls' Night in full swing on Scribe Day, of course, but even at Colette's welcome party on Rest Day, we'd barely had a chance to talk. With so many cases weighing on me, I'd left early to work with Seaton on this blasted problem. We were at the start of an official work week now, so I wasn't surprised Jamie was back on the trail of the thieves. I was surprised to see her now, though, as it was barely mid-afternoon. We weren't supposed to meet and discuss the case until dinner this evening.

Seaton shook his head, shoving a lock of hair away from his face. "That's rather an oxymoron, Jamie. Oh, hello, Gibson."

"Gentlemen," Gibson responded with a nod as he followed Jamie in. "How goes it?"

"We're debating the merits of how to approach this, so, well enough, I suppose," I answered with a shrug. "But back to your query. You've still had no luck with the usual places that grow or sell Raskovnik?"

Jamie dropped into a chair, looking vexed. "Not a lick of luck. No one's missing any. People have kept a very tight control on it since the last case that used it. But the thieves got hold of it somehow."

"We took a trip into Bristol, thinking perhaps they'd gotten it from there," Gibson added. He took the only other available seat that didn't have a stack of papers in it, eyeing the mini-palace with keen interest. "But there's only two suppliers there, and one of them hasn't even had stock in it for the past three months.

We're at a dead end on this so far."

Jamie grumbled, sounding like a bear yanked early out of hibernation. "But there's not a lot of unique leads to follow, either."

I frowned in thought. I saw why they were so frustrated. One would think the Raskovnik would provide them with a vital clue, as it should be easy to track the theft of it. But that clearly wasn't proving to be the case.

Seaton abandoned the wards for a moment, leaning back with his hands comfortably folded over his stomach. "Hmm. What about the passenger list?"

"Ah, we got that this morning. None of us are really willing to compare lists, so we were trying to find an easier lead to follow through on." Jamie wilted in her chair. I think if we'd been in my lab, she'd have already started the hunt for chocolate. "We press-ganged Foster into helping."

"Menial tasks are good for the soul," Seaton said solemnly.

Gibson gave him an analyst's salute. "Truth."

A hunch stirred in the back of my mind. I edged my way toward it, as I wasn't quite able to frame it into words. "Have you decided yet either way if this was an inside job or not?"

"Meh, we're still sitting on the fence on that one." Jamie shrugged but her eyes were sharp on me. "Why?"

"So, there's enough evidence to suggest there was at least inside knowledge being passed to the thieves?"

"Yes," Gibson confirmed, interest also piqued. "I'm of the opinion that even if this person wasn't actively helping, they were at least passing on information. Why?"

"We know the thieves figured out a way to enter the baggage cars without raising suspicions," I pointed out. "Why limit that skill to only one occasion? It could very well be that someone shipped Raskovnik by train at one point. They could have stolen a strand or two at that time and bottled it."

Jamie's face lit up in a smile that unfolded in stages. "The shipment information on those declarations are never really detailed. No one would know a small amount was missing, not if the shipment changed hands in a different city. Henri, I could kiss you. Why didn't we think of that?"

I flushed. I hardly thought the suggestion was worth this much praise, although it was heartening to see her enthusiasm. "My question is only viable if someone did, in fact, ship Raskovnik in the week prior to the robbery."

Gibson snapped his fingers in realization. "Right. I'd almost forgotten that. The Raskovnik is only viable for about a week after it's been picked."

"It starts to lose effectiveness after seven days," Seaton corrected him, still at his ease. "It's viable to use for about nine days, it just won't open any serious locks. I'd say to be on the side of caution, look ten days prior."

Pulling out a slim notebook, Gibson made a note. "Looks like it's back to the precinct for us, Jamie. We need to pull some records."

"Yaaay," she deadpanned, heaving herself to her feet like an old woman with a bad hip. "I really wish more people had phones. It would save us all this running back and forth. Thanks, Henri. We'll look into it. Frankly, if this doesn't pan out, I don't know where else to look."

"I don't either," I admitted. She'd kept me abreast of the situation, so I knew where she had checked. I hope this worked. Neither she nor Gibson had much in the way of clues. As they left, my attention gravitated back to the problem at hand. Which would be easier: changing the wards' settings or the mark's design?

Jamie's head popped back in around the doorframe.

"Guys, just a thought. But wouldn't leather work? For putting the mark on a pass, I mean."

I stared at her, the question echoing through my brain like a lonely spoon dropped into a bucket. I turned to Seaton and found him copying my movement perfectly. In near sync, we both asked, "Why didn't we think of that?"

Laughing, Jamie winked at us. "You're welcome. Have fun, boys!" Her laughter carried down the stairwell as she exited.

"We've truly stared at this problem too long if the obvious doesn't occur to us," Seaton groused, glaring at the roof above him as if he could see the ward even through the shingles.

"Let's just get this done," I told him, fatigue pulling at me. "I'm tired of focusing on this problem. I want to investigate with Jamie."

"I know you've been chaffing at the restraints here," he said with some sympathy. "By all means, let's prove this will work, and then I can draft other magical help to craft all the necessary passes."

At least I wasn't beholden to do the grunt work in this situation. But there was one other task he and I needed to focus on. "What about Belladonna's research? You said you'd made it through all of Burtchell's notes."

"Ah. Yes, we got sidetracked from that conversation. In fact, I conferred with another colleague because Burtchell's notes didn't make much sense in the end. It was all numbers but no equations. It turns out they were three-point sequences."

"Three-point sequences," I repeated, voice rising as my incredulity doubled. "You mean locations?"

"In space, yes. Insane, isn't it? I felt the same way when she unraveled it. We all thought Belladonna wasn't keeping track of where she pulled her specimens. But in fact, she had. It was just so cryptically recorded we didn't recognize what we were seeing. It took Burtchell's genius to figure it out."

I rubbed at my eyes, buying myself a moment for this knowledge to sink in. That meant, theoretically, we knew where Jamie's home planet resided. That we could, in fact, possibly communicate with her home. But along with that possible hope came certain disappointment. I looked to Seaton and saw the same emotion reflected back at me.

"We can't send her home," he said in perfect agreement, as if I'd spoken the words aloud. "We know Belladonna used cosmic energy to power the portals, but harnessing it is madness, to say the least. I can't risk anyone trying it. If it fails, both the caster of the spell and the one attempting the portal will likely die an unpleasant death."

I nodded grimly. The power necessary to send someone to a different planet was immense. Cosmic energy made sense in that regard, but how had she harnessed it without burning out her own magical core? It was one of the great mysteries around Belladonna's brutal experiments. How had she managed to bring so many people through, when any other magician on the planet didn't even think it possible? I myself had tried calculating the power levels several times and came out with a truly staggering sum every time.

"But even if we could, we can't," Seaton continued with a long sigh. "Jamie said there's no magic on her world, not like we have here. It'll be suicidal to send her home."

"She's resigned to that. I know she misses her people terribly, but she's also content with the life she has here. I don't think she harbors any hope about returning to Earth. But..." I phrased this next bit carefully. "Seaton. If we could at least give her one opportunity to speak with her family, I think it would do her a world of good."

"I quite agree." Jaw set in a line of determination, he pointed at the ward design. "Let's get this done so we can focus on helping our friend."

"Indeed."

Why did you hide this? I had to do a seeking spell to locate it.

I hid the last few pages so Jamie wouldn't see it. I wish to surprise her. Besides, right now this is theoretical, contacting her home.

Excellent point. I'll hide this again, then.

Jamie's Additional Report 10.26

Monday started with us working on our next lead. The Raskovnik was a dead end as far as I was concerned. I couldn't find any report of it stolen or missing anywhere in the city or in Bristol. The stamp wasn't all that remarkable, true, but it gave us a possible lead to follow.

Gibson met me at the train station, looking better for having gotten some rest over the weekend. I greeted him with a wave as I crossed the street. "Morning!"

"May it be a good one," Gibson answered, holding his palms together in prayer fashion. "Morning, Clint."

Clint sat on my shoulder as usual and waved a paw. "Morning, Gibs!"

"Where do you want to tackle first?"

"There's a stationery shop here in the station and another across the street," Gibson said. "Surely they wouldn't have been so stupid to buy a stamp from their own station shop."

"I'd sure friggin' hope not. But let's try it first, just in case. I want to know if this is common or not. And I don't know where all the stationery shops in Kingston are."

"Me neither."

If neither panned out, I'd consult my Kingstonpedia (Henri).

"Just so you know, you've unduly tempted our queen."

I looked at him askance before stepping through the station doors. "You've got to be more specific than that, Gibs."

The man snorted. "I suppose you do that on a regular basis. What I meant was Clint." To the cat, he explained, "She's heard stories about you before, but now having met you and seen how charming you can be, she's enthralled with the idea of having her own."

Clint gave him a regal nod, as if this was only to be expected and was the proper response to his personage.

Gibson had to bite his bottom lip to keep from laughing. "She messaged me last night asking for an update and mentioned again that she wanted one."

Queen Regina really did get a lot of use out of that pad. "Well, RM Jules Felix is the one who creates them. I'm sure he'd give her one."

"Talk to her about it, won't you?" Gibson requested, looking both ways before crossing the very busy street. "She's hesitant about asking now and distracting you from the case."

"But she's willing to bend your ear about it?"

"I'm tried and true about multi-tasking," he deadpanned.

Chuckling, I gave him a pat on the arm. "I'll message her when we stop for lunch. Let's find out if our stamp impression is a helpful lead or not."

The stationery shop was not a large one, taking up only a narrow section of the interior of the station, opposite the ticket counters. It was more a glorified street stall than anything, although granted, larger than a street stall could ever be. A large white sign above the open doors proclaimed *Morter's Stationery Shop* in gold letters. Quite a few customers meandered up and down the aisles, shopping for pens and paper and the like, so we garnered no notice as we entered. I made a beeline for a person in a candy-striped shirt and brown apron.

"Excuse me, do you work here?"

The weredog's head came up, black ears flicking back and forth between settling. His nose flared at Clint, no doubt curious about this strange creature, but his response was professional. "Yes, I do. May I help you?"

"I've a question for you." I pulled out Henri's sketch and displayed it for him between both hands. "Is this something you recognize?"

The clerk bent to take a closer look, carefully not touching it. "Hmm, yes, this is something we carry. May I ask why?"

"It's part of a case we're investigating," Gibson explained. "Do you sell a lot of these?"

"Yes, they're quite common. In fact, almost any stationery store would carry this design. It's generic, you see, easy to blend with other markings."

Annnnd there went that idea. "I see. Thank you."

He gave us a sympathetic smile. "Sorry I can't be of more help. But these aren't unique enough to remark upon."

I nodded, giving him another smile as I slipped it back in my pocket. "That was the answer I feared. Thanks."

I bought one from him just in case, then led the way back out and sighed as I hit the sidewalk. Of course it couldn't be some amazing clue that would lead us to the culprit. Life was not that convenient.

I turned to Gibson, standing next to me. "Well, that was a bust."

"What next?"

"Hmm." I gave myself a second to think about it. "Henri wanted to run that experiment about creating the molds for the keys. I guess I'll meet him at the lab and do that."

Gibson gave a shrug of agreement. "If we're focusing on keys, then I'll go visit the clerks again and get a better idea of who all has access to them and lock down the alibis better."

"Sounds like a fair division of labor to me. Keep me posted." With an analyst's salute, I took myself back to the precinct. I only stopped along the way to get the necessary ingredients to make a mold with. Namely plaster, wood filling, glue, and clamps. As I jogged back to the station, I thought about the test we were about to conduct. I, of course, knew how to produce a mold for a new key. So did Henri. Would it be an accurate test if we tried to do this? We were testing both if you could create a mold for a key by just having the lock AND having access to the key, granted, but still. I could figure it out. I knew good and well Henri could, as that man seemingly knows everything.

If this was a crew of untrained thieves, not professionals (and yes, the odds were rather against that), wouldn't it be better to test this with someone who knew nothing about how to do this? This wasn't a land where you could just Google something and be an expert fifteen minutes later. Someone had to figure this out. How well could you do so?

Yeah, I needed a test dummy for this one.

As I walked through the side door into the precinct, I nearly ploughed right into Gerring. The Svartálfar jumped out of the way at the last second, using those excellent reflexes of his. The dark elf was unusually empty-handed, his uniform precisely pressed. He must have just arrived at work.

I grinned, the expression likely demented from the startled way he flinched back. "Gerring. Perfect timing. I need a little assistance with something."

He looked at me dubiously. "Am I going to like this?"

"I'm fairly sure it'll involve profanity before you're done. But it's a good thing to learn." Snagging him by the elbow, I hauled him along the hallway with me. "We're working on the train heist. I need to know how quickly a person can figure out how to duplicate a key if he only has the lock to work with. I also need to know how long it takes for a person to duplicate a key. I've got all the right materials right here. I'm going to sit you in Henri's lab and let you figure it out."

"That doesn't sound like fun," Gerring agreed wryly. "And why do I need to know this?"

"So that when you're working a theft, you'll recognize the signs if someone has duplicated a key."

"I take it you already know how to do this?"

"That I do. So does Henri. Now you understand why I need you."

Resigned to his fate, he gave a nod. "I guess I do."

My favorite partner was at his lab table, as usual, and I paused at the doorway. "Safe to enter?"

Henri looked up, goggles over his eyes, but waved me inside. "Abracadabra. Good morning, Gerring."

"Morning, Doctor. I'm here to do an experiment. My mentor said so." He smiled as he said the words, already taking the bag of supplies from me.

See? This was why I liked Gerring. He was a good sport. "Gerring, that safe on the table is the one in question. I don't have one of the keys that goes to it, but feel free to use any key. It's the process more than anything I'm testing with you."

"Alright." Gerring went to the far end of the table and sat down, already getting to work.

Henri put down the project in his hands and threw a stasis spell over it before moving around the table to greet me. "You're having him attempt to do it under the assumption that one of the employees pulled the heist?"

"Yeah. How well can a layman pull this off? I think we should do it too and time how long it takes. We're not as smooth as a professional, granted, but we know how it's done. It'll give us an idea of how much prep went into this. And an idea of how long the safes or the keys had to be unguarded to get duplicate copies of the keys."

Henri nodded, but he frowned in disagreement. "I think this won't be as easy as you assume. I took a look at the lock in question and it's not simple in design. It would take someone skilled to do what you suggest."

"If this fails, we go around and see if any locksmiths have gotten an unusual request recently." I splayed my hands to either side. "The keys had to come from *somewhere*. We just have to figure out where."

"Agreed. Alright, well, I hesitate to do this in front of Gerring and give him an idea of the process—"

Gerring looked up with a whine. "No, seriously, I have no idea how to do this. A hint would be lovely."

I crossed both arms in front of me, making an x. "Denied."

Whining again, Gerring slumped in his stool.

Henri, amused, poorly disguised a chuckle as a cough. "Then shall we work on something else in the meantime?"

A knock sounded at the door, and we all turned that direction.

A man in a dramatic half-cape of dark blue stood half-inside the doorway. He was a pretty man, slender and pale, blond hair worn in a gentle wave down to his shoulders. I didn't recognize him at all, but Henri immediately stepped forward with a hand outstretched in greeting.

"RM Felix, a pleasure to see you here," Henri greeted. "I'm a touch surprised, however. I thought we were meeting for dinner tonight?"

"Yes, my apologies," he said, seeming sincere, "but something has come up to utterly change my schedule. I won't be available for some time and barely have more than an hour or so today. I hope I'm not unduly interrupting, but I wished to chat for even a moment."

Henri cast a glance back at me, the question in his eyes.

I didn't mind. I needed a mental break from the case, in any respect. "Sure, that's fine."

"Come in," Henri invited. "This is Jamie Edwards, and our colleague in the corner is Gerring."

"A pleasure," Felix said with a sweet smile. He didn't shake my hand but lifted it to his lips and bowed over it.

One of those, eh? He wasn't like the other mages I'd met—but then, every mage seemed to be unique in their own rights. "Come, sit, we can talk for a bit here. Clint, off the stool, give him a place to sit."

Clint hopped up and into my arms to clear the way.

Royal Mage Jules Felix sat on the stool and stared at Clint as if he'd never seen him before. Which was patently ridiculous—the man had made him with his own magic.

Henri sat opposite him while I took the last stool at the head of the table. "I've no refreshments to offer, RM Felix."

"Jules, please," the mage responded in his soft tenor before finally tearing his gaze away from Clint. "And think nothing of it. I'm imposing, after all. Detective Edwards, I must say, of all the Felixes I have created, yours has by far surpassed every standard I set."

That was interesting and not at all what I expected him to say. I settled Clint into my lap. "In what ways?"

"In every sense. Physically, mentally, emotionally—I'm quite astonished. The Felix, you know, adapts to its environment. I made it that way specifically so it could be whatever the owner of it wished for." Jules reached out and stroked Clint's head. My cat obviously adored his creator, since he arched into the touch, purring. "I have released precisely thirteen of them to another's care, yours being the eighth to leave my hands. And yet, Clint far exceeds them in both affection and ability. I'm enormously pleased by this but also curious what you did that was so different than anyone else."

Clint opened his eyes and informed his maker, "I help Jamie."

"Do you?" Jules encouraged with a smile. "In what ways?"

"I field cat," he answered proudly.

Knowing Jules probably wouldn't understand what that meant, I pitched in. "And you're an excellent field cat. What he does, Jules, is both complex and simple. I use his heightened senses to help with investigations. Because he can reach areas a grown adult can't, we send him in. He detects anything out of the ordinary and reports back to us. He's proven to be very adept at this. When he's not at work with me, he chases mice for practically everyone on the block, which has made him many friends."

"And he sings," Henri added dryly.

Jules stared at Henri as if he'd announced something preposterous. Like the moon wouldn't rise tonight. "I'm sorry?"

"He sings," I repeated, amused at that poleaxed expression. "And reads, and sometimes writes when he's willing to put in the effort. It's one of our favorite things to do, learn songs and read stories. Ain't that right, buddy?"

Taking this as his cue, Clint promptly started singing. "Now I've...had...the time of my life~ No, I neeeever felt like this before~"

Swallowing a laugh, I joined in. "Yes, I swear it's the truuuuth~ And I owe it all to youuuuuu~"

Clint reached out and bumped his paw against my fist, mischief dancing in his golden eyes. "Yeah!"

"They do this often," Henri informed our guest laconically. "If you're looking for a reason to explain Clint's excellent development, you're looking at the answer. Unlike every other person you've given a Felix to, Jamie understands their nature. The creature you've created is much like the ones found on Earth."

If Jules was intrigued before, he was fascinated now. "Did I truly?! Tell me everything."

"Well, they're called cats—and they range wildly in size from a domestic house cat—Clint's size—to something about the size of a large dog. They're amazing animals in every sense. What you've created is incredibly close to the ones on my home planet, in fact. There's only minor differences here and there."

Jules sat on the edge of his seat. "Tell me precisely what differences."

"Well, color, for one. They're normally earth tones or calico shades. And most of them have tails, although some are bobtailed. Lynxes especially."

"What kind of tail?" he pressed. "Does that alter their body in any way?"

"Well, it alters their balance. Definitely does their body language, as a lot can be said with the tail." I sat back, a cat happily sprawled across my thighs. With such an invested, curious audience, I had a feeling this would take a while.

You realize that he's now enthralled with your knowledge and will be taking all your suggestions and incorporating them into the next generation.

Maybe not all, but yeah.

I think he was serious about giving you another one, too.

Two singing cats mean twice the fun!

Heaven preserve me.

Report 11: Where's a Computer When I Need One?

Comparing lists was, needless to say, tedious. Comparing lists that weren't alphabetized or organized in any fashion? Heart-rending. Comparing multiple lists that stretched out over a two-week period, with each list containing anywhere between a hundred and fifty to two hundred names?

Soul-destroying.

I did not have enough chocolate for this.

I prostrated over the desk in a dramatic fashion that would have done Sherard proud and whimpered loudly, "I want a computer. And a database system. Excel would work. I love Excel."

"Uh, Detective?" Despite having worked with us on our trial run, Foster's eyes scrunched nervously.

"Ignore her," Gibs advised, sitting at my side. "She's chocolate deprived. Jamie, I have someone fetching you sugar now."

"I will need a ton of it," I informed him, not at all kidding. "Isn't there some magical spell we can use to organize crap like this?"

"If there was, don't you think I would have used it by now?" he retorted.

"Yeah, okay, good point." I lifted my head, and of course one sheet wanted to stick to my face. I yanked it off, slamming it back down. I really hated lists.

The only saving grace was that I was now more or less conversational in the native language. I still ran into words and phrases that were new, and that would likely be the case for years yet, but I could read simple books now. So, lists like this didn't challenge my intellectual knowledge. Just my sanity.

We'd commandeered a room in the Kingsmen Offices on the palace grounds and basically turned it into our investigative HQ. Gibson had found a chalkboard on wheels from somewhere and rolled it in here so we could write down any names we saw pop up more than once. I'd gotten into the habit of keeping a list of any surname I saw multiple times. That helped me more than anything. I wasn't even trying to keep all this in my head.

The other men had come up with their own systems, which seemed to work for them. I honestly didn't know the best approach to this. I could only hope that whatever our approach, we didn't somehow bungle this and miss the people we needed to pinpoint. Whenever Henri got here, I hoped to have him do a magical search on the common names we had found, maybe speed this up a little.

It might have worked better if we'd been able to sit somewhere with a view. Or at least windows. But the only office space available was dead center in the building, enclosed on all sides. It really felt like I was being punished for some dreadful sin, locked in the room like this. I would have taken the lists outside to work instead, but we currently had a raging storm beating at the city. You could hear the rain pelting the roof in a loud tumult. I was stuck.

I really, really wanted a computer.

Our experiment two days before had taught us a great deal. Gerring had not been able to either create a key or create a mold from the lock. Granted, he'd only had four hours to work with, but it was a complete failure. Henri and I had taken a stab at it and hadn't had much better luck. The locks were indeed designed to be formidable, as locks on a safe should be. It meant we'd have to go hunting for locksmiths later and hopefully find whoever had made the keys. It was a good lead, assuming it panned out.

But before that—lists.

A quick series of steps carried toward the door, and I looked around, ears perking. I knew those footsteps. The indomitable magical examiner had arrived.

Henri stepped in with two gold chocolate boxes in his hands, a thermos in the crook of his elbow, and a crooked smile on his face. "I'm finally free to help. I've chocolates and sun tea to fortify us."

"You're my favorite," I informed him, reaching for the chocolate with gimme gimme hands.

Laughing, he handed the top box promptly over. "Gibson said you needed stimulating. Do have some tea and chocolates. Well, catch me up to speed."

I paused him, as I wanted to know if he was here for an hour or if I finally had my partner back. "The wards?"

"I am, hopefully, done with those. We're still not sure how Eddy slipped through, but the best we can come up with is another level of security to thwart him." He took a seat at the head of the table, looking over the stacks of lists with misgiving. He had only exchanged one problem for another, and his expression clearly stated he realized that. "We've re-structured the wards to accept our new development, and your suggestion of leather passes works admirably well. It's been tested, approved, and now some poor team of magicians gets to produce all the passes. More luck to them. Unless something else goes wrong, I am free of that responsibility."

Lifting my hands above my head, I clapped and cheered. "Alright! Then you get to join us."

"At apparently the wrong time," he drawled, still eyeing the lists. "I feel the sudden urge to go visit Colette."

"I will have Clint catch a mouse and release it in your pantry if you even think of abandoning me here," I threatened. I was mostly kidding. Mostly.

He blanched and glared at me. "Nothing I'd ever do to you deserves such a threat. And where is Clint, anyway?"

"You know he doesn't move on rainy days like this. He's snoozing away wrapped in a blanket, the fiend." I was admittedly jealous of my cat just then. "We're still waiting to see if your genius paid off or not. Train station's going through the records to see if any Raskovnik was shipped in the ten days or so prior to the heist."

"Ah. Then we'll see." He doffed hat and coat, settling in more comfortably, and reached for the nearest pile.

I popped a delicious morsel of cherry and chocolate into my mouth, drank a cup of the tea, and felt much better for it. Then again, the brain ran off of water and sugar, so that only made sense.

Henri dove in by looking at the names we'd already found and doing a search on the papers to see if the name appeared again anywhere else. When those pages separated themselves out, Gibson took over and started matching them up. Foster took it from there and wrote out the name and the times they were on the trains, whether working or passenger. It relieved me to have something to speed up the process, even if it was only by a little.

The room turned quiet again as we all focused on the paper in front of us. I normally liked a bit of noise when working—not anything obnoxious, but a steady background sound. Pure silence unsettled me. But today the heavens provided my white noise as the rain continued to pelt the roof in a steady thrum.

I made it most of the way through the passenger list for the evening train, marking a dozen or so possible names that looked familiar, when Foster asked uncertainly, "Should I mark it when the same employee rides the trains?"

That question brought all our heads up, although Gibson was the one to respond. "Yes, I think so. We're still not sure whether or not the employees played any part in this. Why, do you see someone consistent?"

"Two people, sir. Train engineer and the guard."

"Ah. Mark them. Just in case."

Since Foster looked a bit confused, I elaborated for his benefit. "We've got mixed signals on this case. We're almost a hundred percent sure an insider fed the thieves information. They knew too much. What we're not sure is how active this person was in the theft. For instance, they had to use the Raskovnik in order to get through one of the locks, but they had keys for the rest. You see?"

Foster nodded immediately. "Yes, that is odd. Alright, I'll mark employees as well."

We returned to the lists.

Have you ever reached that point when you're so focused on paying attention that you're more focused on focusing than the actual thing you should be concentrating on? I found myself sliding into that zone when thankfully Henri broke the silence again.

"I've now seen Jodan Nichols twice. Anyone else?"

I had Nichols written down as a possibility and quickly reviewed the sheet I'd checked Nichols on. "Huh. Me too."

Gibson lifted a hand. "Thirded. Foster, put that name on the board."

Belatedly, I thought to ask, "Can everyone double-check the engineer and guard's name too? Guard for me was Cain Innis. Engineer Ezer Fagin."

Henri shook his head. "Different engineer for me. But the guard's the same."

"Thirded on the guard as well. I do have the same engineer as Jamie," Gibson threw in.

"I have a different engineer—Kuper Seabrook?" Foster looked about but didn't see any nods. "No? Alright. But the guard's the same. I have Cain Innis for both evening trains on the sixth and seventh."

Dots started to connect in my head. "I have him for the ninth and tenth. Who's got the eighth?"

"Me," Henri volunteered. "Gibson, what days are you looking at?"

"Fourteenth and fifteenth. He's guarding the train for both days." Turning to me, Gibson inquired, "Didn't Mrs. Watts say the guard shifts are normally seven days on, seven off?"

"Yeah, because they guard all day. That's weird, right? It'll make sense if he's guarding the sixth through the thirteenth, that's a full shift for him. But he shouldn't be back to guarding by the fourteenth. Unless he was pulling extra shifts. Are they allowed to do that?"

"A good question for Mrs. Watts." Gibson made a note. "Alright, keep going."

Now that we were actually making some progress, I felt more energized. Having some payoff always soothes the brain.

I lost time while shuffling around lists and double-checking names. It could have been ten minutes or three hours before the door opened. Sherard swept inside with a disgruntled Clint held like a football in his arm. The feline perked up on seeing me and started squirming, silently demanding to be let down.

"Jamie, your creature just about caused cardiac arrest for every guard on duty," Sherard informed me tartly, thrusting the purple furball at me. "He waltzed through the wards as if they didn't even exist. He's not supposed to be able to do that."

Clint crawled into my lap and clung to me, giving me pitiful eyes that protested his innocence.

Henri made a squawking noise of protest. "Clint! How did you do that? Blast it, wait, I bet I know. Intent."

"He didn't have any intent except to find his person," Sherard confirmed, still glaring at Clint. "I *truly* wish we could somehow alter the wards to close out that clause. It's somehow circumventing the need for permission."

"You can't, not without turning the palace grounds into a prison and completely scrapping the wards we have now and rebuilding them from scratch," Henri denied wearily.

I looked down at the pitiful cat huddling in my arms and wasn't sure who to feel sorry for—the boys or the cat. "Sorry? Clint, I thought you were going to nap at home today. You told me you didn't want to get out in the rain."

"Lonely," he said mournfully.

"You must have been, to brave getting wet all the way here." I assumed Sherard had hit him with a drying spell since he wasn't damp. "Sorry, Sherard. Did he completely overturn all your efforts?"

"No," Sherard said on a long sigh. "I lied to them. I

managed to convince everyone that because you're in here, and you have right of passage, the wards recognized him as your familiar of sorts and granted him permission too. For all I know, that's actually what happened."

"That's probably it," Henri observed. "In fact, I'll bet it is."

Technically, he's not my familiar…yeah, you know, I was going to let sleeping dogs lie on this one. "Okay. Want some chocolate?"

He nodded, snagged two pieces, then reconsidered and grabbed a third before whirling dramatically for the door once more. I assumed he was returning to work on the wards and getting the new protocols set up.

I looked down at the cat in my arms and asked, "Are you going to help or nap?"

With a yawn, he curled himself about and settled into my lap, chin on his splayed legs.

"Of course you are." Shaking my head, I went back to the list. Or attempted to. Foster's nose kept twitching as he stared over the table at the bundle of fur in my lap. I got this reaction a lot with Clint. Most people had never seen a feline before. "Foster, this is my Felix. Have you heard of those?"

"Heard of them. Never seen one before now. It's interesting. To my nose, he's alive, but not mammal, if that makes sense."

"He's a construct of magic," Henri pointed out. "That makes perfect sense."

Clint opened an eye, looked at Foster with vague interest, then closed it again. Apparently nap took priority just then.

We returned again to the task at hand. It was definitely going faster now that Henri had joined us. He was good at fine detail work like this, no doubt a skill he'd learned in his occupation. Or maybe it was his talent that made him good at his job. Either way, with his help, I had high hopes we'd actually be done weeding through this pile sometime before the end of the century.

"Okay, everyone, stop. It's past quitting time. Mark

where you are, and we'll pick up tomorrow." Gibson looked around at us. "I think we've made good progress. Foster, how many names do we have?"

"Thirty at this point, sir." Foster had thankfully numbered the names to help us keep track. "Some of these are probably innocent, I'm sure. More than a few people commute into the city from Bristol for work."

"They'd have to be rather affluent to be able to afford it," Henri pointed out. "Bristol is quite expensive to live in. And the train fare isn't expensive, but if a person rode it daily, the fees would quickly add up."

"So they would," Gibson agreed. "We'll need to keep that in mind while pruning these names down. Either way, enough for today."

I was good with that. I stretched my arms out above my head, working out the kink in my shoulders, then hefted a boneless cat up. Clint went with a purr, settling in against my chest. No intention of walking by himself, eh.

Henri walked out with me, and that was nice. I'd not been able to just walk with him for a while. He'd been busy rushing from place to place for the past month.

"Did Colette seem to enjoy Girls' Night?"

"Are you kidding?" I paused so he could open the door and then paused again on the porch to dig out my umbrella. Clint was, of course, not helpful in this effort. "She had a blast. At one point, she had us all literally on the ground and rolling with laughter. I've told her it's mandatory from now on she come over on Girls' Night. She was happy to agree."

"Good. I didn't get to hear much—I passed out fairly quickly. But it seemed as if your evening was enjoyable."

"That it was. Colette said all her paperwork is now done. She's a legal eagle. How does it look like she's doing from your end?"

"Splendidly. I've spot checked her work and found that she's done it all according to procedure. But I knew that she'd be good at this. And truly, it's come in handy to have a female magical examiner when it's a case that requires discretion."

"Ah. I didn't think of that, but I bet it does." Then again, Kingston very much held to Victorian standards. I was still rolling my eyes at some of it. "Well. Here's hoping we've finally caught a break!"

He shot me a disgruntled look. "Please do not jinx us."

"Nah, that's not enough to jinx us. We'll be fine."

I totally jinxed us

Yes, yes you did. But your realization is far too late.
#mybad

Report 12: No Rest for the Weary

Seaton, do you know of an invisibility spell?

If I did, I would have already used it.

I need an invisibility cloak. Maybe then I could take a nap.

Henri! Good job on the Harry Potter reference.

I'd barely attained my flat when there came a call from my telephone. With such suspiciously impeccable timing, I wasn't enthused about answering it. In fact, I had severe misgivings as I picked up the receiver. "Hello?"

"*Ah, good, I timed it right. Davenforth, this is Gibson. Is your pad working? I couldn't reach you on it.*"

I pulled it free and looked at it with a sigh. "Apologies, I didn't hear it chime."

"*Quite alright. Snag Jamie and meet us at the train yard. There's been another robbery. Different line, same procedure.*"

I just knew I should have ignored the ringing phone. Although lamentably, people knew where I lived. "I'll fetch her."

"*Good. I've called a taxi, it'll pick you up at the door.*"

"I appreciate it." Although I had a feeling it was less about courtesy and more about efficiency. Hanging up, I did take a moment to change suits. Mine was rather done for after a full day of tromping about in the rain along muddy streets and the like. Cleaning spells can only do so much before it ruins the pressed lines. As it had finally stopped raining, I had hopes of being somewhat dry and presentable for the rest of the evening.

Feeling a little better with the new clothes, I went up a floor and knocked on Jamie's door. She opened it immediately, Clint in the crook of her elbow, and greeted me with, "Gibs just messaged me. Said he called you, there's been a robbery, he's got a taxi waiting. You know more than that?"

"That is, in fact, the extent of my knowledge. Are you ready?"

"Yeah, it's not like I got settled." Looking down at her Felix, she inquired, "Stay or go?"

"Go," Clint informed her seriously. He had what I thought of as his 'working face' on.

Since he'd found a vital clue the last time he came to the station with us, I wasn't inclined to argue. "Then let's go."

We tromped down the stairs and out to the somewhat shaded front door. As we did so, Jamie stopped and rapped on Mrs. Henderson's door. Our elderly landlady answered it, wrapped in a thick shawl. I didn't think it that cold, but the rain had made the foyer damp and chilly.

"Sorry to trouble you," Jamie said with a grimace. "We got called out on a case, but I just called in an order of groceries. Can you put them in my cold box for me?"

"Oh, bless you, dear, of course. But you're going out again tonight?" Mrs. Henderson peered doubtfully through the front windows. "It still looks like rain."

"No help for it," I informed her with a long sigh. "It's best if we see the scene fresh."

"If we're lucky, we'll be back tonight." Jamie shrugged, already resigned to the very real possibility that it would be morning before we came home again. "Thanks, Mrs. Henderson."

"Good luck, dears," she called to us as we left.

"I have a feeling we'll need it," Jamie grumbled. "Ah, there's our taxi."

Indeed, the driver had a very handsome set of matched bays that looked fresh from a stable. The day shift must have already ended. We climbed up into the carriage and Jamie knocked on the roof to get him going.

The taxi set off and I eyed my partner, judging her on many levels. Physically, Jamie's stamina and strength put most humans to shame. Only the weres could keep up with her. And the elves, of course. Magically speaking, her core was a mess and likely always would be. Magicians such as myself could take one look at her and see it. I used that sight now to gauge how she fared. Despite the insanity of the past several weeks, it seemed Seaton had found a moment to reset her magical core, as she seemed balanced. For her, at least.

This relieved me. While I technically knew how to reset her core now, I didn't have the magical strength to do it. I might well injure both of us even in the attempt. Bless Seaton for keeping her health a priority.

"What?" she asked. Of course she'd caught my study of her.

"I wondered how you fared. You've been jumping about just as much as I have of late."

"True. Life got a bit crazy there, and it doesn't seem interested in letting up anytime soon." She re-arranged the Felix sprawled over her lap with such ease it was clear she was accustomed to moving him about. Clint rolled where she dictated with a purr, not stirring himself to any effort. "You look more tired than I am, honestly. You changed suits?"

"The other needs a good ironing and a trip to the laundry. Although I now wonder if I shouldn't have packed an overnight bag. We'll need to go into Bristol, after all, and I doubt another train is running at this hour to bring us back."

"Oh, snap," Jamie said, body jerking upright. "I didn't think of that. Urgghhh my brain's too tired for this crap. Couldn't they have stolen something tomorrow?"

I snorted a laugh, which came out a touch black. I wasn't actually feeling humorous. "My sentiments exactly."

"We're going to be up all night, aren't we." It was clearly a rhetorical question, judging by the way she slumped sideways on the bench.

"I truly hope not. But my pessimism prophesies otherwise."

"What a coincidence. So does mine."

We grimaced at each other. The saying goes that misery likes company. I rather felt that if I must be miserable, I'd prefer her company over anyone else. Oh dear, that sounded maudlin.

The taxi pulled up to the station. It was nearly seven now, and the area wasn't nearly as crowded as before. Most had either arrived at their destination or were on the last evening trains to their destination. I did wonder where our crime scene was and how we'd get to it.

The young kingsman I'd met earlier greeted us at the front station door. Foster waved to us as we alighted from the carriage, then stepped forward to pay the driver.

"Come directly with me," Foster instructed, already heading inside the station. "They've got the night train waiting on us."

I caught up with his long legs, stretching my gait unnaturally to do so. Of course Jamie had no issue with it. "I thought the night trains were only for cargo?"

"Typically, you're correct, Doctor. They attached a passenger car for us. The railroad companies are going the extra mile to help us solve the case." Foster shot me a grin, revealing sharp canine teeth. "For obvious reasons. Through here."

The station was relatively quiet, only one train on the tracks, with steam leaking out of the smokestack of the engine. They were ready to go, alright. The passenger car was on the tail end, obviously a last-minute addition, and Gibson stood near the steps, waving us forward impatiently.

I ended up jogging the rest of the distance, praying something hot and strong featured in my near future. Alas, this train had no dining car, so that didn't look feasible.

We boarded without a word to each other, Gibson calling out to the conductor, "All aboard!"

The conductor waved to him, then lifted a whistle to his mouth, signaling the engineer. I heard it all play out through the windows as I found a likely bench seat and more or less fell into it. In the nick of time, too, as the train started moving a moment later. Jamie slid in next to me, Foster and Gibson sitting opposite. Clint was too busy exploring to do something so mundane as sit still.

"Alright, Gibs, shoot," Jamie invited wearily. "How much, where, when, how?"

"I wish I knew who as well." Gibson looked just as exhausted as the rest of us. He was half-slumped, his hands dangling over his knees. "I only know as much as the original report. It was the same as before. No one noticed anything odd until the train arrived in Bristol. The theft was discovered once they opened the crates at the station. This time it was around two-hundred-forty thousand stolen. Not quite as big of a payout."

"They stole a collective five-hundred-fifty thousand in under three weeks," I deadpanned. "I feel no pity for them not achieving the same goal this time."

Gibson grunted sourly. "Me neither. Anyway, what is different is that we're dealing with another train line. Bristol Oceanic is the railroad company stolen from this time."

I double-checked with the query, "Wasn't it Kingston Metropolitan the first time?"

"Correct," Gibson confirmed, slumping a bit more in the seat. "Also a different gold company: Kingold. They're already putting together a timeline for us."

I personally was of the opinion that if a different company's gold had been stolen, that put to rest any doubt the shipping clerks at Gold Limited had anything to do with the first theft.

Gibson sighed, showing his weariness for a moment. "Alright, you now know everything I do. Local police have shut the area down and are keeping everyone still until they can do a proper search. I've asked them to do a pat-down of everyone and get names. If they don't see anything suspicious, they're allowed to let people leave."

It saved us the effort of going through two hundred interviews, which I appreciated. I doubted the job would be done by the time we arrived, however.

"There's probably a million fingerprints inside the train car," Jamie muttered glumly.

"Yes, quite likely," I concurred, giving her a sympathetic pat on the knee. "We'll collect as many as we can and tackle it later. I hope, however, we can collect trace evidence. Gibson, I'm not sure if you're aware, but Seaton and I had something of a breakthrough last case. We were able to take a suspect's trace saliva on a cigarette and track him. The spell can be used for skin, hair, nails, or any bodily fluid."

For the first time since boarding, Gibson lifted his head with interest. "Is that right? Alright, we'll try that. There's still likely random hairs and such that will be mixed in with the thieves' leavings."

"Yes, I'm aware. But hopefully if we systematically go through them all, we'll be able to catch a break." I splayed my hands in a shrug. "Police work is often about eliminating possibilities."

"That's quite true. Alright, I'll leave that up to you."

I looked to the feline who jumped onto the bench next to me. "Clint, I expect your aid on that. Your nose can find things we might overlook."

Clint stopped grooming his ear to give me a serious

nod. "Okay."

"Actually, Foster..." Jamie canted her head. "I bet your nose is good for that kind of investigative work, too."

"My sniffer's pretty keen, Detective," he said politely. "I'd be interested in helping. It's a good learning experience for me."

"Then please do," I invited him.

With so few people on board—we were essentially the only ones except a guard and another man at the front—everyone stretched out. Clint started singing something about going off the rails on a crazy train, not a song I recognized at all.

Pointing to him, I inquired, "You have trains on Earth?"

Jamie gave me an odd look. "Of course we do."

"But not in current use, correct? If you can fly through the skies, why would you still use trains?"

She made that bzzzt sound she did when I gave a wrong answer. "Trains are still very much in use. Mostly for cargo, but passengers still use them too. Flying's fast but a little expensive. If you want to go a short distance, say from one town to another like we're doing now, then trains and subways are still a very good option."

"Subways?"

"Trains underground," she explained. "People discovered that train tracks and stations take up a lot of room, so they started digging out tunnels to put them underground instead. Save the surface area for things like buildings and parks."

"That seems a great deal of effort, building underground."

"Yeah. But that's how valuable real estate can be." Jamie shrugged, as if this was understandable.

It rather was, as I'd seen real estate's value double in the past year alone. "Is that why you're so comfortable with trains? I'd assumed it was because you'd ridden them here before this case."

"Well, and I had, but I took the subway all the time on Earth to get to work and back."

For as many conversations as we'd had, there was still so much I didn't know about her. "I thought you traveled all over your country?"

"Yup, did that too. But the first bit, say about a year after I joined the FBI, I was near main headquarters. I didn't get out into the field until later." In a nostalgic tone, she leaned back into the bench, her eyes going out to the window. "And I was in the same city for school, too. I left home at eighteen and basically didn't go back except for Christmas and the occasional quick weekend."

I didn't ask if she regretted it. The emotion was written all over her face. But then, we often regretted the things we didn't do more than the ones we did. If she'd known, if she'd possessed any inkling she'd be yanked into this world with no option of returning, I'm sure there were many things she'd do differently.

We didn't speak much beyond that. In fact, we napped as much as we could, anticipating a very long night. To that end, I awoke as we pulled into the station feeling not in the slightest refreshed. Taking a nap was like playing roulette—I'd either come out of it feeling energized or like roadkill. My gamble this time had not paid off. Then again, with such a short trip, I'd only managed about twenty minutes.

I tried to keep my craggy temper in check as I descended the train. My colleagues didn't deserve to bear the brunt of it.

The train yard was a cacophony of unhappy, tired people. I panned the area with a simple turn of the head and winced in anticipation. People were sitting or lying flat on their backs, their heads cushioned with coats or bags. Toddlers lay limp in their parents' laps or screamed their heads off. A few ignored their surroundings, choosing to bury their nose in a book to help pass the time. Others lifted their voices and fists in the air, demanding to be released. I glimpsed three policemen—wait, I retract that statement. Two policemen and one policewoman. Smart of them to have a female officer on hand to search the ladies.

I extended a hand to Jamie, giving her a hand off the train. It was a bit of a drop on the last step. She took it with a grateful smile that turned into a grimace as she caught sight of the station.

"Oh, that's not going to be fun," she muttered.

"Indeed not. The female officer, are you acquainted with her?"

Jamie squinted her eyes in the mellow lighting of the lamp posts and then brightened. "Yeah, that's Charlie. Charlotte Howell. I've done two seminars with her. She's good people."

"Excellent, I hoped that was the case." Jamie routinely held seminars and training camps with the female officers in Kingston, and I knew the outlying cities often shipped their officers in to have her train them. "Let's attend to the crime scene first."

"I'll help Charlie sort through the people afterward," Jamie agreed, in perfect accord.

Gibson had gone ahead for a moment, conferring with the yard supervisor, then came back to us with a ground-eating stride. "Everyone, this is Supervisor Wilson. He'll show us the car in question."

Wilson ducked his head in greeting, narrow face sour and pinched. I suspected him to have poor health. His pale skin had a distinctly sallow cast to it even in this poor lighting, and his uniform hung on his shoulders. "This way, gentlemen, ma'am."

We followed, and not for any long distance. The train in question still sat on the tracks along the station's platform, and we boarded the last car. I noted that someone had hung an extra lantern to provide more illumination, which I appreciated. I barely had a foot inside when I realized our plans to pick up trace evidence had been neatly foiled.

"Uh, Doctor?" Foster turned in place, his black nose twitching, whiskers bristling. "Correct me if I'm wrong, but I think a cleaning charm was used. I can't even smell any dust in here."

"You are not wrong," I confirmed for him darkly. "A charm or hex was indeed used. Curse their foul hides."

The train car was spotless. The bags were still in place, their tags hanging from the handles, but there wasn't even the faintest trace of smoke evident in the car. I stepped quickly through, my eyes looking for any trace of wall, somewhere a charm or hex could be attached. I found a silencing charm, like last time, and—ah. There it was. The remains of a cleaning charm fading even now from view. They'd taken the paper with them, of course, but the trace of magic remained.

Someone leaned over my back, and I knew immediately who. I directed my words to her without turning my head, "Cleaning charm. I can see the traces of its magic. It's too faint for me to be sure of the maker, but it looks of a garden variety. Rot their souls."

"They likely did it because it's easier to pack a cleaning charm than brooms and dusters," Jamie observed, sounding just as irate. "Clint, check the locks for us."

The Felix bounded immediately off, heading for the vaults dominating the far wall.

"I see the silencing charm, but like last time, I'm not seeing any traces of spells." Gibson grunted and thumped as he moved past us. "Same on the vaults. No spellwork I can detect. How is it, Clint, any sign of Raskovnik?"

Clint dropped down from sniffing and reported, "No."

"Now that's interesting," Jamie observed. "So, they didn't need it this time? Or they just didn't have it available?"

Foster also had his nose to the locks, and he observed each one in turn very carefully. "I don't see any signs a lockpick was used here. I know they've got magical protections on each lock to prevent it from being picked, but a skilled enough thief can get around those."

That sounded like experience to me. "Indeed, you're correct. Not that there's many thieves who can pull that off. This might be a rich enough prize to draw their attention, however. I suppose I shouldn't make assumptions in this case."

"Either way, no sense for us all to be bundled up in here. Foster, go out and start searching the area. We're looking for a tool bag that's been dropped or hidden nearby. The theft was discovered ten minutes after the train pulled in, which isn't much time. They had to put it somewhere nearby."

Foster nodded and bounded out the door.

"Clint, help him," Jamie directed. "Go in the opposite direction and search wide."

Clint looked delighted at this order even as he also bounded out the door.

"I don't think there's any answers to be had here," Jamie observed, already turning for the door. "Let's go look at the substitute crates, see if there's something to be had from there."

Thieves normally improve their skills with each job they completed. I doubted they'd make a mistake this time when they'd been so careful on the first one. But I knew better than to say so. That truly would jinx us.

Report 13: ~~Evidence!~~ But It Was Bad Mouse

Judging from that title, Clint somehow managed to find this, and offered a correction?

I was drafted as his scribe. Be thankful his handwriting is chicken scratch.

His excuses are improving.

The woman in question turned and brightened instantly—and not just in the usual sense. Part woodland fairy, Charlie had interesting biological reactions. She could light up like a firefly or go pitch dark and camouflage into her surroundings like a lizard. It had been very, very interesting training her. Normally she looked perfectly put together, green hair pulled back into a severe braid, navy blue uniform pressed just so, but tonight she was definitely frazzled.

She didn't reach out and hug me, although with the way she vibrated in place, that option was still open. "Jamie, what are you doing here?"

"I'm a kingsmen consultant," I informed her. "Recent thing. They pull me in for cases like this, where it's more investigation than political hamming. Read me in."

She nodded, pulling me a little aside from where everyone was sitting, and lowered her voice for good measure. "No one realized anything was off until they got the boxes into the station office and undid the metal bands. The boxes were filled with lead shot instead of gold coins. I was on duty nearby, so they grabbed me first, and then I locked the area down. Whether I was fast enough in doing that, I do not know. It was just me and my partner, and it took ten minutes for our backup to arrive."

I nodded in understanding. Even if she had been able to call this in with a phone, it took people time to get somewhere else. "Okay. Anything else odd to you?"

"The whole thing's odd to me." She splayed her hands in an open shrug. "The vaults were locked, there wasn't any sign of forced entry, and not even a single fingerprint except for the guard's. I checked that first thing."

"Bless you. I'd hoped to dust for prints, but after seeing they used a cleaning charm...."

"Yeah. The guard I discount, though. He opened the doors back up for us and he's *supposed* to be in there."

"Sure, sure." It was nice all those lectures had stuck. Charlie had applied what I'd taught. It wasn't her fault there was no payout for that on this case. "For the record, what's the guard's name?"

"Innis."

So, one of our suspects. Int-er-esting. "What else?"

"I didn't take a thorough look," Charlie admitted frankly. "I knew it would be a kingsmen case. My priority was locking the place down."

"Fair enough. We're searching the area for their tools. I know for a fact they had some very select tools to pull this off. You're looking for anyone carrying a lot of weight on them, and has wax, a seal, pliers, or anything else you can think of to carry this off."

She nodded, frown deepening the furrow between her eyes. "We'll keep a sharp lookout. Most of these people have nothing like that on them."

"And they're free to go. Just double-check their name on the passenger list."

"That we've been doing."

"I'll come back and help once I get a good look at the area," I promised.

Putting one hand up in prayer fashion, she said, "Please and bless you."

Snorting a laugh, I hopped back down off the platform and went hunting.

I found Gibson first, talking to a man I didn't recognize, and flagged him down. "Innis was the guard on duty tonight."

Gibson nodded, already ahead of me. "Just spoke with him. He says he locked and unlocked the baggage car, but otherwise didn't enter it. He did do a check once during the trip in and had a smoke break outside on the back of the passenger deck before coming in."

The man standing nearby piped up. "I'm service attendant on the train, ma'am. I can vouch that I saw him twice in the passenger car. Once as we were setting off, another time about five minutes before we pulled into station."

But that left a good thirty or forty minutes with him out of sight. The alibi wasn't as solid as this man was making it out to be. "I see. Does he normally take a smoke break on trips like this?"

"Sometimes, ma'am. I think he lingered back there longer this time because we had gold on board. Wanted to keep an eye on things." The man sighed. "Not that it did any good. Thieves still got on and off quick-smart despite that."

Yeah, my spidey sense was tingling. Something wasn't adding up there. I shared a look with Gibson and could tell he saw the hole as well. I mentally shrugged. We could always come back to Innis if my hunch was correct. "Okay. I'm searching the area first."

"Go," Gibs encouraged.

My senses were much better, of course, after Belladonna's modifications. I was of two minds still about everything she'd done to me, but I had to admit there were times when the superior speed came in handy. Or the strength. This was a moment when my heightened night vision was a good thing. I didn't need a torch in my hand as I walked through the area, searching intently for any nook or cranny someone could stuff a bag of tools into. Nothing leapt out at me.

The nose wasn't as helpful tonight. Maybe Foster or Clint would have better luck, but all mine could pick up was smoke, oil, people, and the strong tang of salt brine from the sea. We were near the coastline here, as Bristol sat right on the curve of the continent. I knew that from memory. Gibson and I had come out this direction before. Although with all the buildings in the way, I didn't have a prayer of seeing it.

We were spread out. I could see Henri and Gibson both at work, searching in different areas. I tried to think of the logistics. Assuming I had fifty plus pounds of gold coin on my body, and tools to get rid of, how far could I walk before dumping the load of tools? Or would I keep them? How far could anyone go, carrying that much weight, before the train station was locked down?

The rule of thumb on guesswork like this was to take your most feasible assumption and then double it, just in case. I assumed someone could at least gain the street outside, maybe even cross the street, before the alarm went up. So, I had to assume they could have gotten a block away.

Hopping back onto the platform, I moved out of the station's area. The side gates leading out directly onto the street were all locked of course, but the main doors were unlocked and guarded. I went through the rectangular building and out the main door, nodding to the policeman on watch, stepping free onto the street outside. Here it was calmer, most people at home or dinner at this time of night, and I breathed in deeply. It felt nice to get the scent of oil out of my nostrils, although I didn't pick up any clues in the process. Just the scent of water and brine from the sea, several streets over.

There were trash basins nearby, as well as narrow alleyways, so I started poking around in those. I ranged from one side of the street to the other, but no dice. I didn't see anything that even hinted at the robbery. Seriously, had they kept the tools? Ditched them somewhere else?

The pad in my pocket buzzed a little chime and I pulled it out, angling it a bit toward the lamplight to read Gibs' blocky writing better.

Foster found bag of tools. Go to waterfront.

I punched the air in victory before writing back a quick okay. Finally, a break. I lost no time in running there, hopping the low fence that separated the coastal road from the beach. At least it was a proper beach instead of a sheer drop. That was a plus for us, as it made things easier to search.

Right before I left the grassy area for sand, Henri threw up a hand to stall me. "Careful. We have foot prints I'm trying to preserve."

"Oooh, footprints too?" I peered over his shoulder. Henri was on his haunches, a camera in one hand, a diagnostic wand in the other. The footprints were in loose sand at this point, and I frowned at them. It apparently hadn't rained here, and there was nothing to form a footprint with. "You're barely able to tell size with these."

"Hmm, true. The ones closer to the water have more definition, but I'm taking a trail of photos to link them together. Just in case."

He's thorough that way. And often, that thoroughness pays off. "Okay. I'll be careful not to tread on them. Foster! You are the man of the hour."

The werefox gave me a smug grin, tail wagging happily behind his back. "I'm glad I checked. I almost didn't, as this is a bit of a jaunt from the trainyard."

"Yeah, I wouldn't have thought they'd come out quite this far either. What made you come out this way?"

"I kept thinking of places it's easy to lose something in. The ocean kept popping to mind and I thought it wouldn't hurt. When I got here, there was this neat set of footprints leading straight in and out, which looked odd to me. The beach is otherwise pretty clean."

True, it was. This wasn't really a beach-going spot. Too much gravel and dirt to make it pretty and picturesque. The harsh way the waves smacked against the jumbled stones lining the water also said it wasn't a peaceful place to take a dip. It smelled a little off, too, somehow a bit rank. Although that could have been my over-sensitive nose.

I looked about again, taking in the scene better. The moon wasn't especially bright tonight, and there were no streetlights nearby. Only the lights from the few businesses still open on this street shone on the water. A dark, murky place to go. It had taken me five minutes to run it. Fifteen or twenty minutes for a person to walk it, especially heavily burdened. Foster was correct, this was the perfect place to dump incriminating evidence.

Someone had thrown up some mage lights at some

point, and they hovered overhead like little round light bulbs, bobbing slightly in the breeze. Gibson had found a tarp from somewhere, and both kingsmen were carefully pulling out each tool from a carpet bag that looked soaked to the gills. Gibson photographed each item, then Foster placed it in a neat row, both of them wearing gloves. I made a note to get prints later even as I scooted closer to take a look from the side.

Clamps. Stick of red wax. Seal with a wooden handle. Three charms, now so sodden with sea water the ink was running, making it difficult to determine their purpose. Two linen bags turned out to contain lead shot.

Lifting his head, Gibson observed, "They were prepared to take more gold than they did. We'll have to double-check if they stole the full shipment of gold this time."

"Yeah. But it looks like they did. Foster, anything else in there?"

"A mallet. That's about it." Proving he was a sharp cookie, Foster sat back on his heels and asked, "Where's the keys? Or lockpicks? They kept those?"

"Probably. Why throw away something hard to attain and that would be useful later?" Gibson took the last photograph and set the camera down on the tarp before calling to Henri, "Any luck?"

"Shoe's a common size, looks like a workman's boot," Henri called back, head still bent over the footprints. "I'll have to run some tests to get anything more than that."

I looked over the array of clues again, not entirely satisfied. I didn't think they would help us much. "What this does tell me is that our thieves are long gone. If the one who had to carry gold *and* ditch the tools made it all the way here? They escaped the lock-down."

Gibson grimaced. "You're probably correct. But we've got to check them anyway."

"Yeah." I caught Foster's eye and waved him forward. "Come with me. Let's speed things up and release people. And if you spy Clint, call him for me. Henri, you good here?"

He waved me off. "Fine. I'll catch up momentarily."

I figured.

"Kingsman, a moment." Henri pointed a wand at Foster, his cadence quick and light. "Water and sand, be as you are, rest as you once were."

Foster's pants and shoes dried instantly, and the werefox gave Henri a thankful duck of the head. "My thanks, Doctor."

"Not at all." Henri flashed him a smile before his attention went back to the footprints.

Foster caught up with me and we crossed the mostly deserted coastal road at a quick jog before slowing to a brisk walk to cross the rest of the distance. I kept ears and eyes open for a certain mischievous cat. He hadn't gotten distracted by mice, had he?

"Is that typical?" Foster asked out of the blue.

"I'm sorry?" I pulled my attention back to him.

"Dr. Davenforth's kindness just now," Foster elaborated, a complex expression on his face. "Does he normally do things like that without prompting?"

"Generally speaking, yes. Henri's a gentle soul, and he's very thoughtful of the people around him—assuming his head isn't buried in some complex problem." I sensed something was amok here, although I couldn't put my finger on what. I decided to press the point subtly. "You know, it's the reason why I partnered with him to begin with? I had three bad partners in a row, stupid idiots who thought that because I was a woman, I'd be fine with casual deviant sex."

Foster choked and tripped over his own feet, eyes wide and appalled.

"Yes, quite," I intoned sarcastically. "Henri was just as livid when he learned of it. He was a gentleman with me from day one, by far one of the best partners I've ever had. And I include my homeland in that. He really shouldn't be my partner, technically, as a magical examiner."

"I did wonder about that," Foster admitted.

"I made a case for it because I trusted him. Captain Gregson was tired of me punching out fellow detectives. It worked out all around. But yes, Foster, Henri Davenforth is one of those delightful people who doesn't carry around silly prejudices and knows how to be thoughtful of the people around him."

He dwelt on that for a bit, walking at my side, then finally spit it out, "My previous supervisor was always on edge with me. Distrustful, quick to find fault. It was stressful, to say the least, working under her. Kingsman Gibson didn't hold being a werefox against me. He liked the work I did. He was the one who encouraged me to apply."

I did and didn't follow this. "I'm sorry, back up. There's a prejudice against werefoxes?"

"Yes, Detective, most weres are accepted by society, but there're a few who are…tolerated. I suppose that's the best word. Werefoxes are one of them. As a race, we tend toward mischief that often lands us in trouble. The prejudice proceeds us that we aren't reliable workers, even though we're not all like that."

"Stereotypes rarely fit an entire culture," I observed. "And if you got Gibs' approval, you're certainly not like that. I can positively say I've enjoyed having you with us. We're a bit shorthanded trying to manage this case and look—you've even found us our first real clue."

Foster brightened perceptibly at that. "I did, didn't I? That's heartening. I really want to stay with the kingsmen. I want for this post to work out well."

"I think it already is. At the very least, you're not going to have trouble on this case. Frankly, Henri and I don't care what race you are." I remembered being that young, that new to a field, and all the uncertainty it involved. I'd have to find subtle ways to shore up his confidence.

Out of the darkness barreled a purple furball, giving me zero warning before launching from the ground and into my arms. I gave an oomph as he landed, his whiskers quivering in delight. "You've been hunting mice, haven't you?"

He looked up at me with the supreme confidence only cats and queens could manage. "Only one."

"Only one, huh. Well, while you were out hunting, Foster actually found the bag of tools."

Clint's ears immediately went flat as he shot Foster a betrayed look. "You did?"

Foster had a fist up in front of his snout, manfully trying to stifle a chuckle and failing. "Sorry, Clint. I really did. Footprints, too."

Clint deflated a little more. "But was bad mouse?"

"The justification doesn't really help you," I informed him, also trying not to laugh. "Come on, we have a line of possible suspects to get through. Put your nose to work, see if anyone has lots of gold on them."

His ears popped back up at this possibility of redemption. "Okay!"

I didn't have the heart to tell him the possibility of that was slim to none. He'd figure it out on his own in due time.

The line was much thinner when we got back to the station. Perhaps eighty or so people were left, most of them looking exhausted and done in. I zeroed in on anyone who had children. They especially were the least suspicious and needed to go home more than anyone else. My cat got distracted two people in as the kids reached out to him in fascination. His purrs could be heard all over the platform as he got belly scratches. I'd have scolded him for once again getting distracted, but he was acting like a good therapy cat, and it calmed people down some.

With Foster and I helping, we got through the rest of the line before it hit nine o'clock, and people thankfully trudged off, complaining about the delay as they went. I hardly blamed them for that, especially as this whole thing turned out to be fruitless.

I met up with the other officers, giving the six men and women standing there a smile. "Thank you so much for your help. I'm glad to report we *did* catch a break here. We found footprints, as well as the tools they used. Hopefully, it'll help us figure out who these thieves are."

A ragged cheer went up among them.

I gave them a casual salute with two fingers. "Thanks for your hard work. Let's hope we catch the dastards before they strike again."

We spent the night at a local hotel, hard beds and all, and were up again with the sun. I did not feel exactly refreshed, and pulling on yesterday's clothes didn't do me any favors in that regard. Although Henri had done me the favor of hitting them with a cleaning spell the night before. Still. Principle of the thing.

Henri voted we split up, as he wanted to drag the baggage car back to Kingston so he could unleash all his diagnostic tools on it. In fact, he was out the door and on the morning train before I could even get breakfast, taking Clint with him. Foster went back to Kingston as well, leaving just me and Gibson.

Gibson looked over his coffee cup at me, both of us sitting in the hotel's dining room, and quirked an eyebrow. "Well, what do you want to do?"

"There's two things I want to follow up on here," I informed him as I slathered butter over my toast. "And then I think we can join the boys back home. First, I still have that burning question of how common it is for the guards to work multiple shifts. Innis doing so and working so many days in a row bothers me. Second, now that we have a wax stamp, I want to see if we can trace where it was bought. Is this a common, everyday thing, or was it made for this purpose?"

"Both good questions. I think the easiest one to tackle is the station schedule. The station master here is Josef. A helpful sort, I've found."

"Good. Makes this easier."

We finished up breakfast and crossed the street, as we'd taken the nearest hotel last night, and the station really was that close. The place was already busy, the early commuters on their way, the rest heading off to various destinations. Gibson led the way to the back of the main, square building. It was much quieter in here, although the din of the train whistles, voices, and padding feet were still audible, if muted, through the walls. It was also rather claustrophobic with the dark wood paneling and small hallway.

A small sign protruded over a door that read simply *Station Master*. Gibson stopped there and gave the door a rap.

"Enter!"

"Pardon us, Master Josef," Gibson stated as he swung himself inside. "We've got a question for you."

"Of course, please come in."

I came in behind Gibson and got my first look at the man. He was a were...mouse? Big grey ears, button pink nose, round face, and whiskers that twitched as I entered. I'd heard of weremice before but I had to admit this was definitely a first. They weren't exactly a common race.

Gibs waved a hand between us. "Master Josef, my colleague, Detective Edwards. She's a consultant for the kingsmen and handles the weird cases. Like this one. I've recently brought her on, and she's still catching up to full speed. She had a question for you."

"Please, do ask, Detective," Josef encouraged in his soft, squeaky voice. "We'd dearly like to put an end to all this nonsense."

"My sentiments exactly, sir. Just one question. We've been reviewing everyone's schedules and I noticed that guards sometimes work extra shifts. Sometimes several days in a row. Is that common?"

"It comes and goes in waves," Josef answered with a shrug. His round eyes were shrewd, though, and he clearly wondered what the question was about. "Sometimes, like now, we're shorthanded. We've had a few accidents with our guards or illnesses, so we ask our employees to help cover the gaps. Sometimes they trade shifts among themselves when one or the other needs the day off. We don't mind such. Is there a problem?"

"No, I'm questioning everything right now," I assured him half-truthfully. "I'm trying to wrap my head around exactly how it all works. Thank you, that was my only question."

"Please do let me know if I can be of further assistance."

"Thank you, I appreciate that."

Gibson and I left at that point, but the answer still whirled in my head. It explained things, of course, but it still felt off to me. That was a lot of days in a row for Innis to have worked that he didn't necessarily have to. Who covered for another for more than a shift at a time?

Ahhh, beach. Beach is calling me after this case is done.

But the sand gets in everything.

Your version of sand is heavier, not as invasive. I actually like your sand better. But fine, if you feel that way. Sherard! Beach with me!

With pleasure.

Report 14: Key Conundrum

I'd requested the baggage car be taken back to Kingston so I could bring all my tools and diagnostics to bear on it instead of what little fit into my black bag. Because the thieves had used a cleaning charm, much of the trace evidence that could be found at a crime scene had been wiped clean. Most, but not all.

I still had a few tricks up my sleeve.

Clint oddly chose to remain with me today. He was still somewhat embarrassed by his mouse moment last night and attempting to make up for it. Or so was my impression.

By the time everything got situated at the Kingston station, what with all the traveling back and forth, it was nearly noon now. I set the diagnostic wand to work, recording every inch of the car, watching the numbers and facts scroll out in the air in front of me. Nothing out of the ordinary, so far. Still, I'd hoped our thieves had overlooked *something*.

"Hello again, Doctor."

I turned my head at the greeting, keeping my hands steady, and found Foster approaching. The young werefox looked bright eyed and bushy tailed, his kingsman-red uniform pressed and neat. He must have taken advantage of being near home to change, like I had. He'd been very stiff with me since the beginning—not cold, but somehow on his guard. This open expression on his face was a welcome surprise, although I wasn't sure what had changed his attitude.

"Foster," I greeted in turn. "You've come to help me, I take it?"

"Kingsman Gibson is keen I learn proper evidence gathering, and he said following your example would be best. I've come to help and observe."

"Ah." The sideways compliment made me blush a bit. "Well, I'll welcome the help, assuming we find anything. So far there's nothing out of the ordinary, which worries me."

He came to stand at my elbow, looking over my shoulder and toward the interior, what he could see of it from that angle. "Because no evidence leads to no convictions?"

"And because it bodes ill for us. In my experience, thieves get better with practice, you see. Not all of them. Sometimes internal struggle in a group of thieves leads to discord and their work suffers from it. We quite enjoy it when that happens. Saves us some effort. But in this case, this group seems to work quite well together, and they're learning. Or perhaps I should say, they're evolving. This theft was smoother than their first one. I fear the next time they strike, it will be even more seamless."

"Practice makes perfect?" Foster offered with a worried frown.

"Yes, quite. At this rate, we'll learn more from their first strike than any other."

"Doctor, that's rather alarming. We didn't learn much from the first."

"You now understand my concerns." A blip showed on the letters and I noted to him, "I can see traces of any magic used in the car. I just saw the residue of a silencing charm."

"Like the first time."

I hummed in agreement, still focused. "Not unexpected. The cleaning charm has of course already registered. I do not see any sign of Raskovnik. Did we ever follow up on the possibility of shipment during the timeframe?"

"Kingsman Gibson looked into it. I don't know if he got an answer though."

"I'll follow up with him after this."

Clint sauntered over to the edge of the roof and peered down at us. "No holes or sniffies."

"Sniffies meaning anything that made his nose twitch," I translated for Foster's benefit. "Because a Felix is designed to aid magicians of all types, their nose is very sensitive to any trace of magic. Thank you, Clint."

Satisfied with his contribution, he started grooming his back-right leg, casually hoisting it above his head.

I finished the spell and closed it with an aggravated sigh. "Nothing here to report, magically speaking."

"Then can we assume from this that no one in this gang is a magician?"

"Yes, I think that's a safe assumption to make at this point. I've not seen any trace of spellwork, craft, or anything of that nature. Just charms, and those can be bought in most markets." I rocked back on my heels and thought for a moment. What to try next?

"Doctor, do you mind if I examine the locks?"

"No, please do."

Foster hefted himself up and moved toward the far end of the car. I followed him, hauling my black bag with me. Clint chose to ride in on my shoulder, then leapt off of me like a launching board to stand next to Foster. I cast him a dirty look he pretended not to notice.

We divided the locks between us, me using a variety of examining spells, Foster using his eyes, and went over every inch of the locks. They'd used six of the smaller interior safes. It was quiet between us as we worked, but a companionable silence, one shared instead of tolerated.

"As far as I can tell"—Foster sat back on his haunches and half-twisted to look back at me—"a lock pick wasn't used here. There're a few scrapes, but I've never seen a lock that was perfectly pristine when it was actively used."

I nodded, as he was correct; that was my experience as well. "I think they had a full set of keys here. Interesting, is it not, that they'd have all the keys necessary here but not for the first job?"

"Does that mean their contacts changed? They made a new friend that could get them the keys?"

"Quite possible. It could also mean we've failed to ask a question we should have." I rose to my feet, as my knees were protesting being on the ground in that position. "It occurs to me that multiple train companies all use the same station. Wouldn't the clerks all have copies of the keys for every company? They'd have to, wouldn't they?"

Foster opened his mouth, froze, then closed it, head canting as he thought. "But each company has their own offices in the stations, too. Would they keep them separate?"

"You see? Neither of us knows the answer to that. If these keys are kept in the same location, then one person with the right access could copy any of them. But if they're separate, then we're not looking at one possible employee but two or even three who are working with the thieves."

He immediately stood, scooping Clint up as he went. "Let's ask. Anything else you need to do here, Doctor?"

"No, just seal the scene. I might have more questions later. We might need to revisit."

Foster grabbed one of my bags as we hopped off, and I lifted the other two. The door sealed shut behind us, and I re-instated the ward to make sure no one entered without my approval. The forensic wagon waited nearby and we loaded everything into it, locking it for good measure, before continuing on to the

main station building. Clint shifted from Foster to my
shoulder somehow during this process. Why he chose
to perch on me, I did not understand, but something
about the train yard deterred him from moving under
his own locomotion.

Whoever had brought the car in had possessed the
good foresight to not put the baggage car anywhere
near the rest of the cars or on the main lines. This
one was parked at the far end of a line and near the
station building, giving me quick and easy access to it
and the road. It barely took us a minute to ascend to
the wooden platform and the crowd awaiting there for
their train. Bypassing them all, I made my way to the
baggage office that sat off to the side of the building.
A clerk stood in the window, looking rather bored, his
face young under the hard-rimmed black cap.

As I stopped at the window, he came readily
alert, his eyes wide on Foster's uniform. I didn't wish
to alarm him and put a smile on my face. "I'm Dr.
Davenforth. This is my colleague, Kingsman Foster.
We're investigating the thefts."

The abject relief in his expression was clear. "Oh.
Sure, sirs, what can I do for you?"

"A few questions for you," I continued, juggling the
cat on my shoulder to reach for a notepad. I wanted to
record this precisely. He did another double-take upon
seeing the Felix, eyes round, but I ignored the reaction.
"The keys to the vault, compartment, and safes, and
the outer padlock area, where are those kept?"

"Not in the same place, sir," the clerk answered
after a moment, pulling his attention back to me and
scratching at one cheek. "The guards and baggage
carriers, they all have keys to the baggage cars and
the outer padlock. Part of the same set so they can let
people in."

I shot Foster a look, which he returned, as that
was not what we'd been led to believe.

"So, every guard and baggage carrier can reach the vault? On every line? What about the safes?" Foster inquired, also taking notes now in his own slim notepad.

Leaning in, the clerk said in a confidential tone, "Everything but the safes. We're not really supposed to, tell you the truth. We're supposed to keep them separate. But it was cutting into station-time, us having to find the right man with the right key, or fetching them from the office every time. Delayed us ten minutes or so every train, and that adds up quick."

That it would. I'd heard of an accident last year because one train left the station four minutes late and collided with another on the tracks. They ran the trains with very little margin for error.

"And when the employee is off-duty, he turns those keys in?"

"No, sir, they've got their own sets, and they just keep them. The outer keys—that's what we call them— they never make it back here. Now, the safes, those are here." The clerk pointed to the wall next to him, and I craned my neck to see where he pointed.

There on the wall were different sets of keys, all hanging off the hooks, neatly labeled above each hook for the shipping company lines. With three main train lines, times the number of keys necessary to unlock all the safes, it came out to quite the number. It was a trifle alarming how in view those keys were. Not to mention how close to the window they were. "And they stay there at all times?"

"Well, yes sir, but we have a door to secure them." The clerk reached out to demonstrate, and a hitherto unseen cupboard door was extracted from the side and swung shut to cover them. "We lock them up at night, when the station closes down."

I looked at the flimsy construction of the cabinet with severe misgiving. That did not look a proper deterrent. "Foster, can you attempt to reach the keys from here?"

He stepped closer to the window, thrusting an arm inside, and reaching with all his might. The window, however, was quite narrow, and it limited his reach. He failed several inches away. "No, Doctor, no chance."

"I knew I couldn't. Thank you for trying. Young man, two more questions if you will. Have you seen or heard of any of these keys going missing?"

"Ahh...yes, sir, come to think of it." He was back to scratching his cheek. "About six months ago, one of the guards lost his key ring. We searched all over and couldn't find it. Company ordered new locks and keys, just in case, as a safety measure."

My 'spidey sense,' as Jamie called it, tingled. Something about that was important, although I failed to understand why in the moment. "Indeed, and who was in charge of ordering the new keys?"

"Biggs, sir. Simon Biggs. He's off duty rest of the week, but on next if you need to confer with him."

"I just might, thank you. Final question. Who has access to this room?"

"Only the clerks, sir, and there's a hefty bolt to the door here. Each of us have a key, but we turn that into the station master before we leave our shift. She keeps track of it."

"Who's the station master here?" Foster inquired.

"Shannon, sir, Libby Shannon. You'll find her office inside, next to the front desk."

"You've been amazingly helpful," I praised him, this time my smile more genuine. "Thank you."

"Not at all, sir, but do you mind if I ask a question?" The clerk pointed to the Felix still perched upon my shoulder like a pirate's pet monkey. "What is that?"

"I am Clint," the Felix informed him haughtily.

The clerk blinked at him. "Cor, it speaks!"

"Yes, so he does." I found the reaction amusing.

"He's a Felix, a magician's familiar. Not mine, but he chose to help us investigate today. Thank you for your time, sir."

"Ah, yes," the clerk answered, still staring strangely at Clint, as if he'd broken some universal law by being both odd looking *and* intelligent.

Foster and I disengaged from the conversation, walking away. Foster leaned in close to me to murmur, "Now why didn't anyone mention to us before that there had been a complete change of locks six months ago?"

"A very interesting question, and one I want an answer to. I'm not sure if this helps our investigation or not, but it is intriguing. Let's follow up with the station master first, see if she has had anything odd happen in the past few months."

"Then catch up with everyone else?"

"Indeed. The safes were not as secure as we were led to believe. I'm not sure if that was gaslighting or indignation on their part, but I do know that there're holes in this system and someone has very cleverly exploited them."

Foster had a bit of bounce in his stride, tail wagging happily. "I hope this is another break. We sure need one."

"You know, Foster, it occurs to me that every time we've had a break in the case, you were present. Perhaps your beginner's luck is paying off to our benefit."

"Now that's a nice thought, sir."

"Let's capitalize on it before it runs out," I suggested, half-teasing.

We met Jamie and Gibson at Annie's Pub and Brew—a regular haunt of mine—for an early dinner.

I was famished, and it was a good chance for us to compare notes and catch each other up to speed. At this early hour, the seats were largely empty, and we had a back corner-booth to ourselves. It felt later than it actually was because of the dim interior, the dark wood encouraging the feeling, and I had to guard myself against a sense of lassitude. We were not done with the work day yet.

Jamie ordered a fried onion appetizer for us all to share, and I guzzled a full glass of iced lemonade before ordering another. Only then did we settle enough to actually speak.

"What did you find?" Gibson inquired of Foster and I. "Anything?"

"In the actual car, no," I denied. "They were very thorough. No trace evidence to be had. But we did find some rather interesting information. Foster, if you'll do the honors?"

The young kingsman shot me a foxy smile. "With pleasure, Doctor. So, we discovered today that the initial explanation we had about the keys is not actually correct. And they failed to tell us something important. To start with, the keys to the safes are kept in two separate locations, that's true. But the employees actually carry the keys to all the company lines—the guards have keys to the padlock, vaults, and compartments. It's a timing thing—they don't have the time to go hunt down or fetch the keys from the office every time."

Jamie rubbed her forehead with one hand, appearing as if her head was threatening to split. "Of course they did. And didn't tell their bosses, because of course that's against the rules, and arghhhh. Okay. What about the inner safes?"

"Now those are kept at the clerks' office," Foster confirmed, his free hand floating out to the side to give Clint a good scratch along his back. The Felix flopped bonelessly, purring at the attention. "It makes sense, really. The safes are pulled from the baggage car and carried to the clerk's office for retrieval. They're not opened until the owner comes to claim it. Why carry the keys to them when you don't need them?"

Gibson grunted, not sold on this logic. "Still, the security is not as tight as we were led to believe. And the clerks' office itself?"

"Not as secure as we assumed," I agreed wryly. "The keys all hang on a rack in plain sight of the window, and while a cupboard door covers it at night, there's only one stout lock on the door. It would be easy enough, I think, to pick that lock and make an impression of the keys."

"The other thing we learned is that a key ring was lost six months ago," Foster added. "The train companies replaced all their keys and locks at that time as a security measure."

Jamie and Gibson shared a surprised look, then growled in vexation.

"They should have mentioned that before!" Jamie exclaimed in frustration. "That impacts our timing on this."

I nodded sourly. "Yes, I felt the same way about it. Now, the question stands: Did the thieves capitalize on the change of the locks and have an extra key made for their benefit? Or does it simply limit their planning of this heist to six months?"

"I'm inclined to think it only limits them." Gibson paused as our waiter returned with our orders, the plates set before us, and only continued once she had left again. "If they had a copy of all the keys, they wouldn't have used the Raskovnik."

"Or someone bungled the order and didn't get them all the keys they needed," Jamie pointed out. "They clearly have all the keys now so something changed."

I hummed in thought, my mind turning over the

facts. "Right now, we simply don't know enough to make any deductions. The other conclusion I reached is that there is not a magician in the group. There are still only charms in use."

Gibson had his mouth full of bread but nodded in agreement.

"What did you two discover in Bristol?" I prompted, in part so I could start on my own dinner.

"Found partial prints on the tools and wax," Jamie informed us, cutting into her steak. "If I have something to compare it to, we'll be set."

Foster looked intrigued by this. "Does that help us find suspects?"

"Yes and no," Gibson explained, passing a small water bowl down to Clint. "As we have few fingerprints on file, we have no one to really match them with at this point. But, once we have suspects to question, we can try to match their fingerprints to the ones we took off the tools."

"It also has the added benefit of telling us if we missed anyone," Jamie threw in happily. "If we still have fingerprints we can't match, then there's one loose."

It was the benefit of the system and part of the reason why I always supported searching for the prints. "If you were busy lifting prints, I don't suppose you followed up on any lead on the Raskovnik?"

Gibson settled back to his meal now that Clint was settled. "We confirmed there was a shipment from Bristol in the right time frame. So, someone could have snipped a sprig from it. My money is on it, at least."

While that was interesting, it didn't really further us along. I looked about the table, meeting each of their eyes for a brief moment. "So, are we all in agreement? At least one of the members is an employee of the station?"

"Yes," Jamie said firmly. "Has to be. No other way

around it. And I think it's either a guard or a clerk—probably a guard, considering which keys they had access to. We've got how many guards on the list of possible suspects?"

"Four," Foster supplied readily. "But that number's bound to change now that we have a whole other line to investigate. We'll have to compare lists and see. I've got one suspicion already, but I want to confirm who else overlaps before we move."

Jamie stared at him with dawning horror. "We'll have to compare lists with THIS line too. Heaven preserve me."

"Sadly, we can't assume that just because we find the right guard to question, he'll give up all his associates too." I patted her on the shoulder, fully sympathizing. "And we need to have multiple angles to approach this from."

Her head dropped on my shoulder as she gave a muffled cry. "Someone shoot me now."

"Absolutely not," I said tartly, although I couldn't stop a smile. "That means I'll have to do your work *and* mine. Eat your dinner. We have lists awaiting us."

"And to think I used to like you." She straightened up, glared, but went back to eating.

"Help too?" Clint offered from the opposite side of the table.

"I now understand why the Japanese have that idiom of 'busy enough to take a cat's paw,'" Jamie sighed. "Yes, Clint. Please do help."

We'd certainly take all the help we could get.

Report 15: Don't Tase Me, Bro

We broke for the weekend without any other breakthroughs or heists and, personally, I was glad for it. I had laundry and errands to run, and we all needed a mental break from the case. Or so I told myself, although I found myself thinking about it far too often. Oh Gods Day, I needed a distraction from the thoughts rambling in my head and some girl time. I also had an idea to run past Ellie, one that Colette would probably be invested in herself, so I organized a dinner get-together for the three of us.

We met closer to Ellie's neck of the woods, as it was her turn to pick a restaurant, and I had to approve of her choice. Northwoods Cuisine was all light woods and airy interiors, the lighting mellow and the scents divine. A dryad couple ran the place, according to Ellie, and they knew how to spice things.

Settling around a table near the front window, I looked at my ginger-haired inventor friend and tried not to laugh. "You've got grease on your cheek again."

"Grease happens," Ellie returned, not bothered by this. "Colette! Good to see you. I hoped we didn't scare you off last week."

Colette made a scoffing noise that sounded like train steam going off. "You've got to try harder than that. I'm glad Jamie invited me out. I've been stuck in that lab for fourteen-hour days since I started."

I had wondered about that. "Henri keeps popping in and staying for several hours, so I'd hoped he'd caught you up. Or is there just that much work?"

"There's that much work," Colette answered on a sigh, her eyes devouring the paper menu in her hands. "But we're a good team, always have been, and we're powering through it. Haven't gotten overwhelmed yet. Got close a time or two, though."

"I bet."

Our waitress, a slim dryad with liquid black eyes and platinum-blonde hair, came to the table. "What can I get for you?"

"Seared salmon, veggies, and can I have two orders of crab cakes?" Ellie informed me, "You'll adore their crab cakes."

"You haven't steered me wrong yet. Order of crab cakes and the clam chowder, please."

Colette nodded decisively. "Crab cakes and two seafood pancakes."

"Coming right up." The waitress sauntered away again, her gait smoother than a human could manage. Did she actually have hips?

Ellie reached toward me with gimme gimme hands. "Idea."

I informed Colette drolly, "You'll discover she's a very, very greedy woman. She expects the people around her to always supply her with ideas for inventions. I put up with it because she'll cut me in on any idea she successfully sells."

"That and I make you things you like," Ellie snarked, still making the hands. "Well?"

"Part of the reason why I wanted Colette here is because I have an idea, and I think she'll be able to contribute." I turned to my new friend, who stared blankly back at me, as if she hadn't the foggiest idea of what I could mean. "You said before that women are constantly coming to you for protection."

Colette lifted both hands in a gesture, as if she were praying for patience. "Seems like it's a weekly thing. Only getting worse as Kingston grows."

"Unfortunately, that's true of any city population. Now the thing is, in my country, they made devices so women could protect themselves. Well, really, it was self-protection for anyone who needed it, but women bought them most of the time." Ah-ha, I had both their attentions now. "The devices required no training to use and were remarkably effective. Ellie, I'm not sure if you can make one of them, but I'm pretty sure you can make the other. The first one is a taser. It's a handheld device"—I used my fingers to create a boxy shape in illustration—"that shoots out an electric bolt. Usually about 30,000 volts."

Ellie's eyes almost popped out of her face. *"Thirty thousand?"*

Colette, being no slouch in the sciences herself, spluttered, "But wouldn't that kill a man?!"

"No, but it'll knock him out for a good long while. Anything higher than that gets dicey, I grant you."

That engineer brain of Ellie's started turning. I could see the gears whirling in her eyes. "How many charges could this taser hold?"

"Usually enough for one, maybe two hits. Then you had to recharge it." I waffled my hand back and forth. "This one might be a bit outside your current technology. But the other one, I know for a fact you can make. It's called pepper spray. It's a small, hand-held canister with a pepper and chemical mix in it that will temporarily blind people. Burns like crazy, too, and takes forever to wash out. About twenty-four hours. It's enough to stun and deter most predators in their tracks, giving a chance for their potential victim to get away. That one's only good for one shot as well."

Ellie, proving once again she was a registered genius for a reason, asked, "Aerosol delivery?"

"Yup." I grinned at her. "In this climbing criminal hotbed, I think you have a market for it."

"You want me to help her make it," Colette said, her eyes on me. "Why me?"

"Two reasons. One, Ellie's okay with chemistry but it's not really her forte. And this might be hard for her to get down to a portable size without magic involved. I figure, you have both the magical and chemical know-how to partner with her on this."

Ellie nodded in fervent support. "Please, Colette. Oils, gasolines, solvents, I'm good with those. But this might be just outside my comfort zone."

"I've asked her to make things before, and she had to partner with either a doctor or magician to make it work," I added with a shrug. "She's a genius, but still, she can't know everything. Second reason is you have experience in these situations. You've been there—you know what these girls are facing. You know what they need to have and what won't work. Who better to help Ellie make it?"

"I'll cut you in on the proceeds, fifty-fifty," Ellie promised, her expression already in that sparkling zone that meant she was creating the blueprints in her head even now.

Colette still hesitated, staring at Ellie as if she wasn't sure what she was getting into. Which was fair. She didn't.

"Come on, Colette," Ellie whined. "Come play with me! I promise to only bite on request."

Snorting a laugh, Colette relaxed and threw out a hand. "Shake on it."

Ellie slapped her hand in, both of them shaking firmly. "Good girl. This will be so much *fun*. See why I demand ideas from Jamie? She always comes up with something I'd never have thought of and makes us all lots of money."

"In return, she makes me things that I miss from home," I drawled, pleased with myself for putting these two together in a collaboration. "It's a good deal that works for me."

Our food arrived, and the waitress set it all down professionally enough, but then she lingered. "Um, can I ask...? I overheard some of what you're saying. You want to make something we can use to protect ourselves from stalkers?"

Uh-oh. I knew that look. This girl herself was a victim of it. "We are. I'm Detective Jamie Edwards, Kingston PD. This is Ellie Warner, head of the Black Clover Artificers' Guild, and Doctor Colette Harper, Magical Examiner with Kingston PD. Why don't you sit and tell me who's bothering you?"

She seemed overwhelmed at who was at the table, but not enough to hesitate. She promptly took a chair and leaned in, whispering. "He's not done anything—not yet—but there's this man who keeps showing up just as we're closing. He keeps following us home and then he stays out near the front door. Sometimes for hours. We can't leave once we're home—we're afraid of what he'll do."

Good call. "You tried reporting this, I take it."

She shrugged, and her pale skin went translucent for a second. "I don't know his name. He's not done anything but follow us. No one would take us seriously."

There were days I seriously hated the restrictions of the law. "Yeah, I had a feeling. Don't worry, this ends tonight. I'll stick around until closing and help catch this douche."

"You and me both," Colette informed me, then smiled at the girl. "Don't worry. We've got experience at this. When do you close?"

"Another two hours," our waitress said shyly.

"Then I have time for dessert." Colette winked at her, which got a smile in return.

"Cecily!"

"Oh." Our waitress—Cecily—popped up. "I'll get back to work. Request anything you like, I'll get it for you." With that said, she scampered back toward the kitchens.

"I feel like the girls working here should be my first beta testers," Ellie mused.

"That's really not a bad idea," I encouraged. "We'll definitely want to check the records on this guy when we catch him, Colette. Odds are he's done this before. He's probably guilty of worse than stalking, for that matter. Most of the time, the guys bold enough to stalk that openly aren't new at this."

Colette nodded, her eyes on the street outside the window, as if looking for anyone suspicious. "I think we should have a word with whoever ignored her too."

"Oh, we will." I'd make sure of it. Stalking wasn't always taken seriously by policemen. I wasn't sure why. They considered it to be a 'lesser' crime, and it was often hard to prove, since it was his word against hers. But it rankled because stalking was a gateway—it often led to rape and murder. If a cop would just show up, prove the girl had protection, often the stalker could either be caught or dissuaded. And really, if this guy was wanted for something else, the cop would have had a chance to catch someone at large.

Our food arrived and we ate and talked and schemed. Our waitress found ways to linger nearby so we could pull her into the discussion sometimes, and her experience helped Ellie get a firmer grasp of the requirements for the pepper spray.

As they closed up shop, I walked Ellie to her car (just in case), then came back around. Colette was hitting the floor with cleaning spells, chattering to the other employees as she helped clean up. I got a better look and realized Cecily was a triplet. The parents popped in and out of view, mostly in the kitchen cooking. This was a family-owned operation, and the resemblance between them all showed.

Cecily's sister drifted up to stand next to me, wiping down the front counter. "I'm Trisha. Cecily said you'll protect us on the way home?"

"I'll shadow you, actually, and hopefully catch the man stalking you. Your parents don't walk with you?"

Shaking her head, she explained, "They live in an apartment above stairs. We wanted our own rooms and space, so we all moved out last year into an apartment complex down the street. It's really nice. It's just that the road there isn't always well lit at night."

"Yeah, I know the problem. They really have to find a more efficient way to light the streets. Do you know where he's watching from before you guys leave?"

"Not really. We've tried different ways of leaving the building, but he always catches up before we go more than a block."

Well that wasn't helpful.

It took several more minutes for them to be ready, and

Colette and I slipped out ahead of them, waiting in the alley. It was a bit smelly, granted, but it gave us a protected way of lurking without being visible. I peered out around the corner, spotted the girls leaving, then looked carefully around the street. At this hour of the night, there wasn't much traffic, so I had faith I'd spot the guy.

Even with my advanced eyes, I almost overlooked him. He wore a mix-match of brown and dark grey clothes, a match for the buildings around him, which allowed him to blend in rather well. He moved with eerie silence, his rubber soles not making much noise against the sidewalk pavement. I could see how that would unnerve whoever he was stalking.

"Man doesn't even move human," Colette muttered in disgust. "What is he, a wraith?"

"You can catch a wraith, right, Colette?"

"You bite your tongue."

I chuckled and moved off. "Alright, let's follow for a bit and make sure we have the right guy. He's plenty creepy, but I don't want to show our hand until we're sure."

Colette fell into step with me as we followed. Both Cecily and Trisha looked back uncertainly several times, and they kept their arms linked with each other. For comfort, I assumed. The other sister marched forward, as if determined to not let fears prey on her. Or maybe she was trying not to give the game away. I let this play out a few minutes, until I had the right timing to catch Cecily's eye. I pointed to the guy and she nodded fervently.

This was him, eh?

"You want to pounce on him like the last one?" Colette drawled in a knowing tone.

"Aww, Colette, you say nice things." I limbered my neck muscles up a bit, head tilting side to side. "On three. One, two, three!"

I took off like a panther, eating up ground in long strides. My boots were loud and echoing in the confines of the street, and the stalker turned sharply to see what was running up behind him. When he saw me, he tried to flatten himself against the building. I swerved to match that movement, and realization dawned on his face.

Yeah, that's right, sucker. I'm here for you.

Swearing, he broke and tried to run for it. Try being the operative word. I landed with both knees on his back, hands on his shoulders, and used him as a landing pad. He went down with a painful grunt and smack of the head against pavement. He was stunned enough I got cuffs on both of his wrists before he could get his scrambled brain together and get a word out.

"I—haven't done anything!" he gasped, fighting for breath.

"You stalked three girls for weeks. That's doing something." I got off and hauled him up. The girls came rushing back to us, and this time there was vindication on their faces when they looked at him. "You three need to come with me to the precinct so I can write up a witness statement for all of you."

"That's just fine," Trisha assured me, still glaring at the man.

He wasn't much to look at, face sort of battered—the broken nose he now had probably didn't help. My bad. He was well-dressed, though, even if the outfit was hodgepodge. The individual pieces were nice enough, so he wasn't a desperate soul. I reached into his jacket pocket and fished out a wallet, holding it up to the dim light coming from the streetlight. One look at the name, and I almost had a hissy fit right there. "Colette."

She leaned over my shoulder and got a good look, then double-checked his face and swore long, loud, and creatively. "Son of a fish-mongering eel!"

The guy had the nerve to grin at her, blood mingling in with his smile. "What's wrong, handsome lady?"

Colette glared at him, looking sorely tempted to hex his arse. "Girls, I'm really glad you said something to us. This man's wanted for the murder of his wife, two daughters, and is connected to the disappearance of three other girls."

I could see the color drain from all three of their faces. It really had been a close call on this one.

"Can't prove anything," he caroled to her.

I brought him in a little closer, so I could look him right in the eye. "I don't know who's in charge of investigating your case, but let me tell you something. We have a *warrant* for you. That means a judge thinks we have enough evidence to lock you away. You're not walking off scot-free."

He put up something of a fight as I hauled him along. "I'm only suspected!"

"You're very guilty of stalking tonight. Two policewomen are witnesses. That's reason alone for me to haul your arse in. And trust me, you're not getting out anytime soon."

He kept protesting, of course, but I ignored that. The nearest police box was two blocks away, and I physically lifted him inside, throwing him into the nearest counter and holding him there. The two on duty scrambled up out of their chairs, their card game laid abandoned.

"Gentlemen," Colette said crisply, marching in sharply to stand on his other side. "This is Roan Doddery."

To their credit, they recognized the name instantly. And they should, as there had been a warrant out for his arrest for a year and something of a manhunt when the case first got serialized in the newspapers.

"Detective." The young man with Landry on his name tag gave me an actual salute before reaching for the man. "I've got a holding cell I can put him into. Can you write me up a witness statement while I call this in to the main precinct?"

"Absolutely. We have stalking to add to his list of charges." I gratefully let them take him but then second-guessed that decision. "Colette?"

"Put a warding spell to keep him from breaking out until they can get here?" She was already moving to follow into the narrow confines of the cells beyond this front foyer room. "Way ahead of you."

I eyed the remaining officer and asked pointedly, "Were you the one who took the girls' initial complaint of stalking or was that your partner?"

He had the good grace to look embarrassed. "That was me, ma'am."

"We'll have words about that later."

Crestfallen, his eyes fell to the floor. "Yes, ma'am."

"For now, get their witness statements."

"Yes, ma'am."

Young, yes, but he apparently was trainable. Really, I couldn't believe he'd ignore a stalking complaint and choose to sit here and play cards instead. But after tonight, I'd bet he'd not repeat that mistake.

My pad blipped at me. I took it out and read the message from Henri with rising eyebrows. Oh, this night was just getting better and better. "Colette!"

"Yes?" She appeared in the doorway, looking satisfied with herself, as she should be.

I waved the pad. "Henri's got some trouble."

"Oh no. Palace again?"

"Looks like it. Can you handle things here?"

She waved me on. "Go, go. I can manage."

"I feel bad. Every time we have dinner, shenanigans happen."

"Makes life interesting," she informed me, not bothered.

As I headed for the door, I threw over my shoulder, "I want life to be less interesting. Just for a day. Is that too much to ask?"

Report 16: Impenetrable Wards Penetrated...Again

No. But I can devise an *Can we kill him?*
unfortunate accident.

I stared down at the very dirty young man and felt the irrational urge to kill him.

Eddy Jameson didn't look up at anyone. He sat hunched in on himself, arms wrapped around both knees, eyes fixated on the tile floor beneath him. Myself, Kingsman Wallace, Seaton, and one of the palace guardsmen surrounded him on all four points, glaring down at the dirty head. He looked as if he hadn't bathed in at least a week solid, covered in sooty grime from head to toe. Then again, there was good reason for that, as he'd been hiding up in the chimneys to avoid the guards.

"How," Seaton gritted out between clenched teeth, "did you get back in?"

The boy hunched in a little harder, impossibly drawing himself into a tighter ball. He did not, however, answer. That was no surprise—he'd barely said a word since his discovery in the Palace Library.

I heard the familiar stride of boots on the tile and turned with a sense of relief as my partner walked in. I met her halfway, speaking in a low voice. "Jamie. Apologies for the late hour summons."

She waved this off. "I was actually out with the girls. I'll tell you the story later."

"There's a story to be told?" Oh dear. Now what had they gotten into?

"Oh yes, but it can wait. I see our favorite trespasser has gotten in again. How?"

"That," I grumbled, shooting the boy a glare over my shoulder, "is an excellent question. We've no idea. He was found roughly a half-hour earlier, mostly because of the marks he's been leaving behind. He's perfectly filthy. I've questioned him, Seaton's questioned him, Wallace has threatened him, and the boy won't utter a peep. We've no idea how he got in or how long he's been here."

"And you've called me in because he actually talked to me last time?" Jamie nodded, as if this answered the question. "Alright. Let me take a stab at it. Hit him with a cleaning spell, will you?"

An excellent suggestion. Really, I should have thought to do so before. I turned to follow her, pulling my wand out and hitting him with two cleaning spells in quick succession. The boy looked—and smelled—much better afterward.

Jamie went straight to him, dropping onto her haunches, amusement rich in her voice. "Well, dude, you've landed yourself in a fine mess again. Came back in to read another book?"

Jameson lifted his head and said plaintively, "I just wanted to finish it!"

I dropped my head back, staring toward the heavens and praying for patience.

"Seriously? This must be one excellent book. Did you finish it this time?"

He nodded gingerly, giving the unhappy men surrounding him a woeful look before admitting, "I found another good one and started it."

Of course he had.

Jamie lifted a hand to cover her mouth. I was fairly certain she was disguising a smile. Of course this situation would amuse her. *She* wasn't the person designated to fix it.

"Eddy, if you had time to finish one book and start another, I have to assume you've been here a few days?"

"Three," he admitted in a tiny voice.

So all weekend then. Seaton let out a growl.

"I promise I won't let them kill you or ship you off to sea," Jamie swore, lifting a hand as if she were in a court of law. "But you need to tell me how you got in. Did you worm your way through, like last time?"

"Sorta," he hedged, still giving us uneasy looks. "I saw the leather passes, heard what people were saying. So, I waited until a guard was on break and jiggled the lock on the window. I reached through and snagged one. It worked fine for me. Then I walked the grounds until I found another window open and slipped inside."

Was this boy a natural thief or spy? He made it sound so simple, what he'd done. He made all of our hard work moot. I didn't know whether to laugh or cry. I felt the urge to do both.

"Gentlemen," Jamie addressed us all with a pointed look. "I know you're ready to strangle him, but in truth he's found a security weakness we need to plug. And I'd rather a curious teenager find it first."

"I have to agree," Seaton grumbled. "Wallace, see to it, will you?"

"Sir." Wallace agreed with a nod, lectures and swear words dancing in his eyes. Whoever had left the passes unguarded would have their ears ringing before the night was out.

"Come on, Eddy, up you go," Jamie encouraged. She put both hands under his arms and pulled him upright. "I'll take you home. You realize there's new legislation in the works because of you? That trespassing is now going to become illegal just because of you sneaking in here?"

Jameson came up, staring at her with wide eyes. "Does that mean I'll be a criminal if I get caught again?"

"Yes, and can you focus on not doing it again instead of not getting caught?" Jamie requested, far more patiently than I could have managed. "Because 'not getting caught' should not be your focus. You really need to find a different method of getting your kicks, kid."

"I just want to read the books!" he protested innocently, honestly confused why this was bringing so much trouble down on his head.

Seaton almost had steam coming out of his nostrils. "They're not your books. You know you don't have permission to get in here. We've made that very clear."

Jameson's face fell. I couldn't read everything he was thinking, of course, but I had the feeling he still didn't understand fully what was so wrong about wanting to read the books here. Was his morality so skewed? Or did his desires overcome his good judgment? People possessed an amazing ability to delude themselves sometimes.

Wrapping her hands around both of his elbows, Jamie frog-marched the young trespasser out. I watched him go, the words tumbling out of my mouth unchecked, "You know he'll do this again."

"Hopefully not. Hopefully the realization he'll be a criminal if he does it again will stay his hand. Or his parents will find a way to keep him in check." Seaton rubbed a hand over his face, looking weary. "I give it fair odds he'll break in again, however. We really should deport him on a ship. He'll cause less trouble in the Navy."

"I'm inclined to agree with you. He's a tad young for it, though."

"Unfortunately. Although I think the queen will grant an exception."

"I might yet," Queen Regina announced as she strode in. "Where is the young troublemaker?"

I gave her a bow before responding. "Your Majesty. Jamie came and fetched him just now. She's escorting him home."

The queen looked as if she'd been on the verge of retiring for the night. She was in a very casual ensemble of loose pants, a cardigan sweater, and slippers. Still, her eyes were sharp on my face as she inquired, "Why Jamie?"

"Because we're all ready to kill him," Seaton answered forthrightly. He had, in fact, been asleep when the alarms went off. Seaton did not wake up well. Bears coming out of hibernation were more pleasant in demeanor.

Regina's mouth pursed. "I see. And she didn't mind getting out of bed to clean up this mess?"

I sensed censorship in that question. "She was still up, in fact. I do feel bad about interrupting her Girls' Night. I believe one was in progress."

"It was either her or no one," Wallace pitched in to explain. "The kid will only talk to her now. She's the only one he trusts enough to speak to."

"Is that right. Girls' Night?"

Why ask about this of all things? And why was she so interested? "Yes, she arranges gatherings with some of her female colleagues and friends every two weeks or so. They get together, eat cuisine from her world, and share stories. Or so I hear. They can get quite rowdy sometimes."

She nodded slowly, brows still lifted in a gesture that showed this intrigued her. "Well. Gentlemen, I assume Jamie got it out of the boy how he snuck in this time?"

"Yes," Wallace answered forthrightly. "We'll plug the hole in security tonight, Your Majesty."

"Please do."

With all the madness of wards, reckless teenage boys, and impossible train heists, I was at my wit's end. I chose to ignore it all for a period of two days so I could get Colette fully established in her new lab. That was definitely a two-man task, and she could hardly do her job by constantly working in mine. It was a hazardous accomplishment, to say it lightly. Sanderson's incompetency had left many things half-done that should never, ever be dangling about incomplete. It was stressful in a different way than everything else I'd been juggling. I was beyond relieved to have it finished.

I tumbled into bed that night feeling both exhausted and accomplished. I slept deeply and awoke to a paw tapping at my cheek. Knowing who it was, I grumbled without opening my eyes, "I don't have to get up, Clint. Let me sleep a little longer."

"Breakfast burritos," the feline stated.

My stomach gave an answering rumble. Those did sound a good idea. I cracked open one eye to regard the purple fluff sitting next to my shoulder. "Is that a request or a demand?"

"Jamie make you," he relayed.

"Ah, it's an *offer*. Tell her I'll wash up and be upstairs presently."

Satisfied he had done his duties, he sauntered along the mattress and hopped off the bed, then let himself out the window. I'd left it cracked to combat the unseasonable heat, not intending it to be Clint's egress.

Getting up, I went about my morning ablutions, dressing in my most comfortable suit. Today would mean a great deal of sitting; we still had those passenger lists to get through. I did expect we would make headway on our suspect list. I knew Jamie was of the mind that we needed to hone in on the guards and clerks first, see if we could spot the insider. If we could interrogate the right person, it might lead us to the others.

And frankly, we were all deathly tired of going through those lists.

I sauntered upstairs and was barely in the stairwell when I could smell the sizzling meat and melting cheese. Ah, what a pleasant way to start the morning. Attaining her apartment, I found the door ajar and gave it a single rap of the knuckles before venturing inside. "Good morning."

"I'm trying to make it one," Jamie informed me, standing in front of her stove, stirring things up in the pan. She wore a white shirt with its sleeves rolled up, wine-red vest, and black slacks. Mostly prepared to face the work day was my impression.

Quite accustomed to her apartment now, I fetched plates and cutlery as I said, "That sounds ominous. What's irritated you so?"

"Meh, a mix of things. I'm still peeved with Eddy. I think his parents are about ready to kill him." She flicked the nob off and spooned contents into flat burrito shells as she spoke. "The story I got is that Eddy's basically been a sneak since he was out of the crib. Constantly poking his nose into places when he shouldn't. It's driving them insane."

I accepted her offering on my plate, and my vexation was severe enough that it almost put me off my food. "So the odds of them successfully corralling him?"

"Nil, zilch, nada." She plopped into the chair across from me, pouring herself some morning tea and making a face. "I talked to him extensively about this on the way home and when I got there. The problem is, he really doesn't get it. He's not stealing anything, not damaging anything, so he doesn't understand why it's freaking people out so bad. I think he's an adrenaline junkie."

"I'm sorry, a what?"

"A thrill seeker," Jamie translated.

"Ah. Yes, I agree. But if that's the case, then he

is, in essence, addicted. He'll continue to break in no matter what we tell him or what punishment awaits him." I stared glumly down at my burrito. That was a grossly morbid thought.

Jamie shrugged and bit into hers, chewing with a thoughtful expression.

When she didn't say what she was contemplating, I followed her example and changed subjects. "You said you were out last night when I called for you? What happened?"

"I'm not sure if you're aware, but the crimes against women are escalating, especially in the past six months."

"I'm, in fact, quite aware. My mother and sister have bent my ear on numerous occasions about it."

Jamie for some reason looked intrigued. "Have they? I bet they'll make good test subjects too."

"Test subjects?" I parroted blankly. I had an inkling she was up to something again. For good or ill was always in question with her.

"Sat down with Ellie and Colette on Gods Day," she explained, her manner lifting and becoming more cheerful. "Explained to them that there are self-defense weapons a woman with no training could use. One of them might be too far-fetched for this level of technology, but not the other. Ellie's intrigued, and Colette's already eager to get started on it. We're making a pepper spray, an aerosol spray that will temporarily blind and incapacitate an attacker."

I found myself intrigued by the idea. "How portable is it?"

"Handheld. It'll fit in most purses." She grinned at me smugly. "Good idea, right?"

"It'll certainly help cut down the dangers. I'm loath to think the situation has degraded down to that level, however."

"Yeah, I'm not happy about it either, but we can't

be everywhere. This gives people more of a fighting chance. Ellie swears up and down she'll make it affordable, even if it cuts into the profits. We want this thing in as many hands as possible."

"Warner's good about that sort of thing. So, I interrupted a planning session?"

"Nah, we were done at that point. You interrupted my processing of Roan Doddery."

I nearly swallowed the wrong direction and had to cough to clear my lungs. My head spun in a dizzy manner for a moment. Surely I'd not heard that right. "You caught Roan Doddery?!"

"The waitresses at the restaurant told us someone was stalking them, and they'd tried reporting it, but the cops weren't interested enough to do anything about it. Colette and I stayed after closing and followed them home." She shrugged, as if this wasn't anything worth bragging about. "Turns out their stalker was Roan Doddery. Don't worry, Colette stayed, and two detectives from the precinct came and collected him personally. I was free to help you by that point."

I was still flabbergasted. "To think he was bold enough to enact another crime while wanted for multiple murders."

"Yeah. Guy's not right in the head. Kept saying I couldn't prove he'd done it, so I had to let him go." She rolled her eyes expressively. "Like me catching him in the act of stalking three women somehow didn't count. Criminals, man."

"I'm surprised he didn't fight back?" I was in fact alarmed she'd taken him on with only Colette as backup. Colette was intimidating but not a trained fighter. And yes, I was quite aware my partner was formidable, but there was no sense in taking chances.

"I kind of pulled a Clint? Landed on him and smashed him into the sidewalk." Jamie shrugged unrepentantly, mischief lurking in the lift of her smile.

The corners of my mouth curled up. "In other words, he was too dizzy and in pain to put up a good fight."

"He made a very nice thump when he hit the ground."

I chuckled in a low, rumbling way. Of course I could find it funny. No one dear to me had suffered, and it was quite the coup, catching Roan Doddery. The whole of Kingston had been searching for him for months. "That's quite the accolade to add to your achievements. And Colette's. Although, really, how do your Girls' Nights always end in some outrageous fashion?"

"Hey now, it's not like we find trouble on purpose."

I shot her a look that conveyed I was not at all convinced of that. I was content to eat my breakfast and not argue the point.

We finished up, washing the dishes and stacking them to air dry, before leaving for work. It was a fair morning and I decided to enjoy the sunshine while I could. Odds were we'd be stuck inside for the rest of the day. Clint chose to not ride on his master's shoulder as was his usual wont, but instead bounded ahead, chasing various things along our path.

As we walked, Jamie asked, "Which do you bet on? Guard or clerk? My money is on clerk."

"Why, because the theft has now occurred on two different train lines?"

"Yup. Each company has their own guards and staff. Clerks are the only ones who share office space enough to have access to all the keys." She tilted her head in question as she looked at me, dodging pedestrians absently so she could match her stride with mine.

"I still think guard. But I suppose we'll see shortly, won't we?"

"From your lips to God's ears."

Report 17: Good Attack Kitty

Clint says, "I IS a good attack kitty."

Meaning, you need to throw him at people more often?

that was my take away

It was hardly an invigorating way to start the morning, going back to the dreaded lists. I sat there like a lump on a log, going through one name after another, crossing things off, correlating with other sheets, and felt my brain grow mushrooms. Not the fun kind, either.

In fact, I was well on the way to moldering when Foster got up and went to the board. I idly tracked his movement as he wrote out three names, and what lethargy I had abruptly left me.

I stared at the board where Foster had just written the names of Cain Innis, Marianna Rutherford, and Chuck Hatter in his neat script, and spluttered a protest while pointing to it. "Now wait a minute! I know Cain Innis was there, but no one mentioned Marianna Rutherford!"

We were four hours or so into the list processing and nearing the tail end of it. I'd been on the verge of suggesting lunch—Henri's stomach was rumbling hopefully for food—when Foster popped up to write on the board. Now food was the furthest thought from my mind.

The kingsman shrugged at me. "They're all listed as guards on the line this week. Each a different day."

Gibson sat back at the head of the table with a huff, staring at the board as well in a thoughtful fashion. "We were told they trade shifts. And didn't Mrs. Watts say she'd double on the guards?"

I groaned in realization. "She did say that. And then unwittingly put two of our suspects to guard the same train during a robbery. That's some sort of kismet, right there."

"It's not like she knew that," Gibson pointed out. "Although really, someone should have mentioned before that we had two guards that night."

"They really should have," Henri grumbled crossly. "We've not had a single witness statement mention Marianna's whereabouts."

"Unfortunately, upset people rarely think clearly." I threw my pencil down on the table in disgust. "Well, now I don't know which to bet on, guard or clerk. I mean, seriously, it could be either."

"My money's still on guard," Henri said slowly. "This skipping back and forth between train lines further cements my suspicions."

Because we'd talked about it on the way in, I knew what he referred to. Since the other two were clueless, I filled them in. "Henri thinks the timing is too tight for it to be anything other than a guard. Think about it. From the time the train leaves the station to the point it arrives, it's about forty minutes. The guard checks in on the baggage line throughout the trip. He's responsible for closing and opening the doors. No way to get around that."

"So, the guard had to be either part of it, or deliberately paid to turn a blind eye to them as they worked." Gibson tapped the end of his pencil on the table, staring at the list of names in a way that suggested he wasn't seeing them. "I have to agree, Davenforth, your logic makes sense. So, it has to be the guard?"

"That's my assumption, and I've yet to see any proof I'm wrong." Henri lifted a finger before cautioning, "Now, I still think we should question the clerks. The issue of the keys has not been solved. It's still quite probable that at least one clerk is involved in this enterprise."

Gibson gave a sharp nod, looking at us. "I think it's time to rope in suspects and ask some questions. Foster and I will take clerks. Why don't you take guards? This might take several days, depending on their schedules."

"True," I agreed, already planning out the logistics of this. "If they're working, no telling what city they're in at this time of the day. Yeah, this will be a fun nightmare to figure out.

Henri, lunch. Then let's get a work schedule from the station master. I bet she's got one."

"Lunch," Henri agreed in heartfelt tones.

Libby Shannon blinked at us from behind her large, wire-rimmed glasses exactly once before her mouth dropped and she whispered furiously, "One of ours is behind this?!"

I was grateful the office door was shut. I leaned forward in my chair, dangerously close to the edge of her rather packed desk, and answered in a low tone, "Unfortunately, someone here has to be involved. There's too many coincidences for how they got into the safes. We're not sure if it's a clerk or guards at this point. It could be a mix of both. But we've got several names to check, as they were working the evening trains."

"What about the shipping clerks at the gold companies?"

"They may or may not have a hand in it, but they're very low on the suspect pole. Two different companies had gold stolen—that says to me the odds aren't good for any other co-conspirators. If you have an inside source at the gold company, why not stick with just the one company? Why steal from another? You see my point?"

She nodded slowly. "Their information must be contained within the railway station, or that's at least likely the case. Very well, I think I follow your logic. Who are your suspects?"

"My main suspect at the moment is Cain Innis. He was the guard for both trains when they were hit."

"To be fair, Marianna Rutherford was also on the second train, which makes her a suspect as well," Henri pitched in. "We'd like the work schedule for both of them."

"Of course." Shannon popped up and went to the blackboard on her far wall. Neat white lines formed a graph with magnets, times, and names written in a clear hand.

Everything was written in initials, due to the lack of enough space, and some of it I swear was encrypted, as it didn't make a lot of sense to me. She traced a line and said, "Cain Innis is not on schedule this week, formally speaking. He's traded shifts today, however, and should be coming back from the morning line in twenty-five minutes. Marianna Rutherford is on the northbound to Scoffolds, and she won't be back today. I suggest trying her in the morning. She's due back in just before noon."

I made a note in my book. "Thank you. Our third suspect is Chuck Hatter."

"Ah. Now, that might be an issue. Chuck fell last week and was hurt rather badly." Shannon winced. "He came off wrong from the top of a car."

I winced as well in sympathetic reaction. "Ow. That sounds painful. How bad is he?"

"Still hospitalized. The doctors have him medically sedated to help him heal faster. I don't expect him to be really available for questioning. Not for several weeks." Shannon cocked her head, the wispy dark hair falling further out of her messy bun. "What makes him a suspect?"

"We're asking questions of any guard who consistently worked the line two weeks before the thefts," Henri clarified for her. "As a precaution. Even if they had no hand in it, they might have seen or heard something that is helpful to us."

"Oh. Well, I can assure you he had no hand in the latest theft. He fell from the train car the day before it happened."

That did rather scratch him off our potential suspects for the second theft, at least. The first one was still in question, but the probability was low. I truly believed that whoever was involved in the first one had done the second as well. It was too tightly run for them to bring in a different crew or hire on additional members.

Henri made a note, his pencil scratching on the paper, then gave her a cordial smile. "Thank you so much for your help, Station Master. We'll go and question everyone and hopefully get to the bottom of this. If we do clear someone, please don't treat them as if they are somehow involved. I promise you, we will be very thorough in our questioning, and we'll apprehend the correct people."

Shannon gave a firm nod. "Don't you worry, Doctor."

"Thank you for your time."

I got up with him, and only when we were several feet outside her office did I lean in and whisper, "You think she'll blow this out of proportion?"

"She seems highly infected with the drama of it all, shall we say."

"Ah. Yeah, I got that impression as well." I shrugged. There wasn't much we could do about that.

Since we knew which train Innis was coming in on, Henri and I chose to wait near the clerk's office for him to arrive. It shouldn't be hard to spot him, as he'd be in a guard's uniform for the Metro line, the unrelieved black on black easy to spot in the crowd.

We had twenty minutes to kill. I idly stroked the purple furball in my arms, his purrs filling the air around us as I scratched just the right spot.

Henri hummed a note, catching my attention; he did that when he was thinking hard about something. I bumped him with my elbow and he looked up, blinking. Prompting him, I asked, "What?"

"Hmm?"

"You're thinking hard about something. What?"

"A curiosity." He hesitated for a long second, studying me as if not sure if or how he should say it. When the words did come, they came slowly, as if he weighed each one before speaking. "You said once to me that because of your job on Earth you rarely saw your family face to face."

"Yeah, that's true. Why?"

"Were you satisfied with a long-distance relationship with them?"

"Well, I mean it got a little lonely sometimes, as I missed them. But I had a way to call them up, talk to them when I did. And text and emails and stuff. It helped me stay connected with them."

"If you had a means to do that here, would life be easier on you?"

"You make it sound like life here has been rough on me." I shrugged. The answer seemed obvious enough to me. "This world's been very welcoming, really. I can't complain. I'd like to talk to my family, of course, but I'm content here."

That seemed to answer some question for him. Henri routinely checked in on my emotional well-being. It was sweet of him, really, and part of the reason why I so utterly adored him.

I sometimes wondered if I was too much of a burden for this man. He had to do so much in order to accommodate me, and I knew I took him routinely out of his comfort zone. Henri's a man of creature comforts. Didn't it grate sometimes that I demanded so much of him?

Something of that must have reflected on my face. He gave me that sweet smile of his and said, "For the record, I'm very glad you chose me as a partner. I do wish I could physically keep up with you better."

"You could—and I know this is extreme—but you could exercise?"

He put a wounded hand over his heart. "Fiend!"

I chuckled. I'd more or less expected that response. "The point of a partnership is so we can cover each other's weaknesses. Don't worry about that. You're the only man I'd have for a partner, Henri."

His smile widened. "I'm yours. Sorry, no refunds."

Head thrown back, I cracked up laughing.

The train pulled into the station, the whistle loud enough to cut off the conversation. It was a rude pull back into reality. Really, I'd prefer to banter with Henri for a while.

Clint moved so he had his front paws on top of my head. The better to see over the crowd with, apparently. I suffered it in silence even though I really didn't need an additional eleven pounds on top of my head, thank you. Still, he had a better vantage point than we did. After a moment, he informed us, "See him."

"Yeah? Where?"

"Baggage car."

Made sense. That's where he was supposed to be. We walked toward the back of the train, going against the crowd still off-loading. Sidling along the wall of the station was the only way to make any sort of headway. Eventually, we reached the last passenger car, and the crowd abruptly died. I spied the uniform before the man himself as he backed out of the car with a bag in each hand, which he handed down to a porter. He wasn't much to look at, with a bulbous nose, thinning brown hair, and a body sliding slowly into fat. Not ugly, not handsome, a sort of plain guy.

Some instinct made him look up, and he spotted us. Realization flooded his face. We weren't here for a casual chat, and something about our body language or facial expressions said so. Whatever it was, Innis took one look at us and bolted, hitting the station platform with both feet and sprinting away from it, toward the warehouse housing all of the trains.

"Why do they always *run*," Henri lamented.

I didn't bother to answer him. I grabbed the cat off my head and launched him from both arms. "Clint, attack!"

Clint hit the ground running, and let me tell you, outrunning a Felix was much like trying to outrun a cat on Earth. In a word? Impossible. In seconds, Clint was on Innis's back, tearing at it with claws and causing Innis to fight him off with both hands, screeching as he did so. Looked rather like Don Quixote fighting a windmill, not going to lie.

I caught up quickly enough and snagged one of those flailing arms, locking it in behind his back. "Good job, Clint. You're such a good attack kitty."

Clint hopped down and purred at me, satisfied as he licked the blood from his claws.

"You can't prove anything!" Innis gasped out, flinching as I wrenched his other arm around and cuffed him.

"See, when you say things like that, it just confirms you're guilty. Not helping your case, dude. Henri!"

Henri puffed up to us, red in the face from the exertion. He glared at Innis, no doubt for the indignity of making him run. "Really, man, do be sensible. You're facing the Shinigami Detective *and* her magical familiar. Of course running isn't going to do any good."

"He who runs only dies tired," I joked. "Come on, Innis. We have lots and lots of questions for you. You're going to give us all the lovely answers."

Innis's eyes were wide, like saucers that consumed his face, and he looked pale under the sweat dewing his temples. "Are you really the Shinigami Detective?"

Henri had dropped that on purpose to start the psychological warfare and, by golly, it seemed to be working. Good job, partner. "I really am. March."

Do you really do that? Tell people she's the Shinigami Detective just to make them afraid?

Gives us an edge in interrogation.

It works splendidly on some people.

He doesn't do it all the time, just sometimes. And sometimes I dress up pretty and act like an airhead. You won't believe what men tell me when they're being blow-hards.

As stupid as that sounds, they're so prideful and condescending towards women they end up boasting about everything they did.

One of these days, I want to watch that in action.

It is quite the show.

Report 18: Interview With A Thief

Innis looked extremely dejected as he slouched in the interrogation room, his hands in his lap, his eyes glued to the scarred table surface. He did not at any point look up, nothing more than quick glances to see who had entered the room. Jamie and I let him be. We'd get his full attention soon enough.

Our main issue was we had little idea just how tightly bound this ring was. Sometimes there was no loyalty among thieves, but sometimes there was. Sometimes it was a family affair and they'd die rather than sell someone else out. It would help our cause considerably if we could approach this from the right angle.

I held out a chair for Jamie and took the last one available for myself. Clint hopped onto the table's surface near Jamie's elbow, with both Foster and Gibson leaning against the walls behind us. They'd agreed to let us lead the interrogation—too many interrogators just confused the issue—but they wanted to listen in.

Excitement tingled at my fingertips. Finally, finally, we had a suspect. We had the possibility of answers. But the excitement tangled with nerves—ultimately, we had no way of proving anything right now. We'd built a very circumstantial house of cards. A confession would go a long way to prove Innis's involvement.

Jamie opened a folder and set it in front of her. It was a prop, nothing more. But Innis's eyes flickered up to it nervously.

"Did you know, Mr. Innis, that this is the greatest gold heist in history? The fact you pulled it off on a train is what makes it even more impressive. That was a very fine timeline you had to work off of. We tried it ourselves and barely managed it. When Gibson first told me about the case, I got a headache trying to figure out what you did. I can't imagine how much planning went into this."

So, we were going with the friendly tactic, eh? One glance at Jamie's face proved wrong. She sounded friendly. The smile on her face was challenging.

Innis's instincts were finely honed, as he heard the threat under the words, and a fine sweat dewed his temples. Despite his nerves, he said nothing.

"Of course, not everything went smoothly the first round, did it?" Jamie pulled out a photograph of the crumpled Raskovnik. "The keys got messed up the first go around. You had to improvise with the Raskovnik because the lock picks wouldn't reliably work on such complex safe locks. And you didn't know about fingerprints, so your team left those all over the tools, the safes, the crates—everywhere." Jamie waved to his ink-smudged digits in illustration. It was quite the bluff she was playing, and she did it admirably with a straight face. "I'll match yours up shortly. But that wasn't the only thing that didn't go quite right, was it? You left so much gold behind, that must have been frustrating."

Innis's set face twitched. That was a palpable hit.

"Didn't bring enough lead shot with you? That's our guess. Or you couldn't haul that much weight away with the crew you had. Could be that too, huh? It's not like you could carry much yourself, as you were still 'on duty.' Isn't that right? You could get rid of the tools, maybe put some gold in your pockets, but not enough to clink or have much of a bulge. Nothing noticeable. It had to grate, to still be guarding that much gold all the way to the Receiving Office and not be able to pinch even a bit more of it."

Innis hunched further in on himself, nostrils flaring. Scared or angry? Remembered frustration? His face was so firmly set into a mask it was impossible to completely read him.

"You know what makes no sense to me whatsoever? Is that you went for a second score." Jamie's hands rifled through the folder again, pulling out the missing totals reported by the gold and train companies. "Three hundred eleven thousand crowns is a crap ton of money, man. Even divided up, surely that's enough to buy a modest house somewhere on the coast and retire. You could probably live twenty years on that and not have to work. Why go again? Why take the risk?"

Innis impossibly hunched in even further, and he was sweating in earnest now.

"Walk me through this, eh? What was the money for?"

Silence.

Jamie pursed her lips and shot me a look. It was a common tactic from suspects to say absolutely nothing. If they were silent, they couldn't incriminate themselves, after all. Innis was the type of man who could not afford an attorney—well, he could, assuming he had the ability to lay hands on his portion of the money. With the gold marked and so famous at the moment, it would be very hard to move it. They likely would have to sit on it a while and wait for a future payout.

I decided to step in. "If you won't tell us anything, we'll need to question your family next."

"You can't bring my family into this!" he burst out, panicked and half-lurching out of his chair.

Ho. Now we had a reaction. I pushed him. "Innis, we must have answers. If you won't supply them, then we'll talk to every relative and acquaintance you have until we find them."

"My wife—" Innis choked, struggling to breathe. "My wife's already miscarried three of our children. She's bedridden right now with our fourth. You can't stress her. Please, you can't talk to her, she'll lose the baby—"

The light dawned. I possessed no idea what might be the motivation for everyone on the crew, but Innis's seemed clear enough. "We won't say a word to her, Innis, but you must talk to us. The second heist—was it because there wasn't enough money to go around for everyone?"

Innis's jaw flexed and his eyes dropped back on the table. He gave a shallow nod. Swallowing audibly, he whispered, "In part. In part because we hadn't been caught. When the kingsmen came in it was clear they had no clue how we'd managed it. They were lost entirely. Even the cops didn't seem to know who to suspect." Innis jerked a chin toward Jamie. "Not until she came in, anyway."

"So, you thought if it was that successful the first time, why not do it again once more."

"Yeah. And we were short, a little. At first, it seemed such a big score, y'know? So much money. But split up four ways like that, it's not really as much."

I carefully concealed a hiss of victory. The number of people in the crew was now confirmed. "Your cut of the first heist would have still bought you a respectable house somewhere and set you up financially for years."

Innis looked up. The fight slowly drained out of him, leaving him the scared and nervous man again. "It sounded good. We'd get out of that apartment, my wife and I. But I wanted enough that we could just live off of. So I wouldn't have to work so much anymore."

In a sense, I understood his stance. How often do we lament that we don't have enough time to spend with our loved ones? Especially for him, with his wife struggling, it was only natural for a husband to wish he could spend more time with her. In his shoes, I no doubt would wish the same. It wasn't often I felt sympathy for a criminal.

"A hundred and thirty-seven thousand crowns is how much you earned from both heists," Jamie noted, tone idle. "That's a pretty hefty sum. That would have been enough to set you up nicely for years, alright. If you worked part-time with the station, you could have lived on that for the rest of your life. Assuming you're good at staying inside of a budget. Or were you going to do one more, just to make sure you never had to work again?"

Innis grimaced. "They planned to. I told them after the last one I was out. It would draw too much suspicion if I quit altogether. I could use the excuse of looking after my wife to take fewer hours, no one would think oddly of that. We could buy a house, something good for her and the baby, and we'd be fine. But they weren't satisfied. They needed one more, they said. They kept trying to talk me into it. I threw the bag away, all our tools, to make my point."

"But you were too worried about your wife to agree?"

"We'd already gotten by with it twice. Three was pushing our luck." Innis let loose a laugh that sounded mad and despairing. "Only we hadn't gotten by with it at all. You just hadn't caught up with us yet. I could tell from the way Kingsman Gibson asked me questions he suspected me. I couldn't figure out what I'd done wrong. I made sure people saw me on the second heist so you wouldn't place me in the baggage car. What made you suspect me, anyway?"

"The schedule." Jamie drew yet another paper out and flipped it with a flick of her fingers to rest in front of him. "You're one of the few people working the evening train during both hits. And yes, people saw you, but only at the beginning and end of the trip. It was too much of a time gap. You had to be part of it somehow."

"Thrice-cursed schedule." Innis slouched in his chair, like a marionette with its strings cut. He was just an exhausted, resigned man now. "I was always afraid of that. But I couldn't work out any other way to do it."

"Yeah, I bet. Everyone knew you were anxious to get home to your wife every day. They'd think it odd if you rode as a passenger to Bristol." Jamie canted her head to the side. "How did you get recruited? Was it Jodan Nichols or Simon Biggs who first approached you?"

My partner was fishing. It was a good lure, though. I held my breath, waiting to see if he took it.

Innis rubbed both hands wearily over his face. "So, you've caught them too, huh? It was Biggs. Biggs approached all of us. He was the one to figure it out first."

I channeled my excitement into my fists, clenching them, although it was all I could do not to jump up and down.

Belatedly, Innis realized his mistake and looked sharply up at Jamie. "Why do you not know that?"

"Oh, we know they're involved," Jamie told the white lie with a pleasant smile. "But they haven't divulged every detail. Biggs figured it out when he had to re-order the keys, right? He was in charge of that, and he realized he could easily order another set of keys and no one would be the wiser. But he screwed up the order, you were a key short."

Again, fishing. It made sense, though. It was the only way it made sense—why would they need the Raskovnik the first time to get through that last lock? Because someone had made an error and not gathered all the appropriate keys. If Biggs hadn't ordered all the correct keys, then of course it would leave them in that predicament.

Innis grimaced. "Stupid idiot got all nervous when placing the order and accidentally ordered two of the padlock key. Like I needed two of those. He was able to fix the order later, get the right one in, but it meant missing that first shipment if we'd waited. I saw the Raskovnik come through six days before and grabbed it, just in case. It was tight—the stuff barely worked to spring the lock—but we managed."

He was chatty now, and I wished to capitalize on that before we lost this amiability. "I'm bemused on a few points, Innis. Why switch to a cleaning charm the second time? Was it a matter of weight?"

"Yeah, basically. We already had to carry so much in, and anything we could leave behind or switch out was for the better. I should have thought of it the first time, really. Biggs couldn't carry much in—he's too small a man to disguise an extra fifty pounds of weight well—and of course Marianna—" Innis clamped his mouth shut immediately.

"Marianna Rutherford was already a suspect, don't worry," I soothed him. "Keep going. Marianna couldn't carry much either?"

Innis's tongue darted out to wet chapped lips. "I really didn't give her away?"

The man was loyal, at least. Misguided and desperate, but loyal. "She was already on our suspect list, I promise you. The schedule gave her away too."

That relieved him, and he didn't question the way I'd worded the reassurance. "Oh. Oh, I see. Yeah, you probably found Jodan the same way, huh. Schedules were the death of us, I knew they would be. But Jodan and Biggs weren't working both nights."

"No, they were passengers sometimes," Jamie agreed, nodding. "We did check passenger lists too."

Another half-mad chuckle escaped Innis. "Of course you did. Of course you did. But yeah, Marianna can carry quite a bit of weight. She was under a tighter schedule though. She had to get back to the house before her husband suspected anything, and she had to stash the money first."

"You did dry runs of that, to get the timing down."

"More than a few." Innis's head lolled on his shoulder listlessly as he looked out the single small window in the room. From this angle, all he could see was a narrow patch of blue sky. "I'm going to jail. For a long time, aren't I?"

He was no doubt thinking of his wife and unborn child. I was again stirred to pity but in truth, the man had dug his own grave with such a poor life decision.

Gibson cleared his throat behind us. I turned and arched an eyebrow at him. He silently indicated he wanted to step in and I waved him forward. I had no idea what possessed him to do so, but trusted he had adequate reason.

Taking two steps forward, Gibson joined us at the table. "Mr. Innis, I'm authorized to speak with the Queen's Voice in matters such as this. Would you like to shorten your sentence?"

Innis's head snapped back around so quickly I heard vertebrae pop. "Yes. Can I?"

"You have that option, here and now, yes. No one else has told us where the money is."

For the simple matter we hadn't asked. But I wasn't about to interrupt him. Gibson's ploy looked viable for success.

"Tell us where you stashed it all," Gibson encouraged. "I can cut your sentence in half. Wouldn't you rather be home to your wife in two years instead of four?"

Innis's head bobbed in agreement, much like a puppet's when pulled on a string. Still, he hesitated a long moment before he spoke, as if weighing all his options first. In the end, desperation won out. "I'll tell you precisely where it is. But I only know Marianna's and Simons' locations. Jodan had to change where he put everything. He said it was in danger of discovery, and he wouldn't tell us precisely where it was. Just an approximation."

I suspected Jodan was attempting a double-cross, but we'd properly get to the bottom of that later.

"Tell us everything you know," Gibson encouraged in a gentle tone. "In fact, walk us there. As we collect the gold, it'll prove good faith to Her Majesty. After she hears your story, she'll be more inclined to sympathy. I promise you I'll stand at your trial and speak for you."

Relief washed over Innis, mitigated as it was by the disappointment of failure. "There's that, at least. Thank you, Kingsman, for the offer. I'll accept it. Take me out. I'll show you where all the gold is."

I do love it when we can troll them like this.

Troll? There were no Trolls in the room.

yeah, ok, wrong word choice here

Report 19: Wrapping Things Up

With Innis's confession on who all was involved, I was able to get warrants drawn up and authorized for the other three. Because they were working different train lines, we had to send the notification to other police precincts to grab them, then arrange for transportation back to our precinct. It was a bit of a logistical headache, but all was made easier because our fellow officers were happy to help. I think part of it was that they wanted to be part of the greatest gold heist in history, but I wasn't about to question their willing attitude.

It sounded simple to list out, but that took me five solid hours to orchestrate. While I did that, Henri slipped off to the lab to get caught up on fingerprints for this case, further solidifying our evidence of Innis's involvement. Gibson and Foster had the fun job of taking Innis to collect the gold.

With all that in motion, I stood from my desk and stretched. It felt good to get the blood moving again, a few joints popping. This had been such an interesting case, but good gravy, the legwork on this one. Geez.

From across the bullpen, the officer at the front desk belted out, "EDWARDS!"

Now what? Sighing, I headed that direction. I'd intended to go and help Henri with the fingerprints, but looked like that had to wait.

A tall, well-dressed dwarf stood just inside the front door. Well, tall for a dwarf—he probably hit chest height on me. He was impeccable in a three-piece grey suit, his red beard braided along the edges with small gold beads entwined. It took me a moment to place him, as we'd never spoken directly, but this was the owner of Gold Limited, the first company robbed. What was his name...?

Lawson, bless him, did the introductions for us. "Edwards, this is Mr. Elwood of Gold Limited. Said it's his gold we found. Mr. Elwood, Detective Jamie Edwards. She'll be the one to talk to, as it's her case."

Elwood held out a hand. "Pleasure, Detective."

I took it, felt the calluses, and was surprised by them. The man had his hands on something on a regular basis to give him such a rough surface on his palms. "Mr. Elwood. Come in, come take a seat at my desk. I assume you got our notification about the gold?"

"Yes, quite. I came here directly. You've really found it?"

"We believe so. Right now, we want verification to make sure there isn't any mix-up later." I escorted him back to my desk, gesturing him into the single chair that sat right next to it. Hardly tosh, but he didn't even blink, just hopped right into it. I settled into my chair and leaned across the surface to speak in a more confidential tone. "Here's the facts as we have them now. We have a confession from one of the thieves. The other three are being rounded up as we speak. The thief who confessed agreed to lead us to the gold in order to get a reduction in sentence. But he doesn't know where all of it was stashed. One of the partners changed where he hid it."

Elwood was a mixed bag of happy and peeved. "So we can't recover absolutely everything?"

"That's why I called you in. It wasn't just your gold stolen—we have no way of knowing which gold will show back up here. My colleagues are collecting it, and I expect them in the next half-hour or so. When they arrive, can you verify what is yours and what belongs to the other company? The markings of the gold ingots are so similar I don't want any mistakes on that."

"Yes, it's a point that has peeved us for quite some time. I think, after this especially, we'll change our seal." Elwood gave me a firm nod, his beard bobbing on his chest. "I'll be pleased to assist. It does irritate me one of the thieves will not receive a full sentence for this, but I do understand why you made the offer."

I splayed my hands in a shrug. "It was either that or tear the city apart. Or trust some honest citizen to find it and turn it in. I don't give either of those good odds."

"Quite." His blue eyes became very penetrating. "I understand you are a kingsmen consultant. They were struggling with this case before they brought you in."

"Theft is a little outside their comfort zone. In truth, the combined efforts of several people helped crack this case open." My pad beeped and I lifted it immediately to see the message. "Ah. My colleagues are at the back door. If you'll wait here a moment? We'll bring the gold into the lab and have you go through it for us."

"Of course."

I went back toward Henri's lab and found Gerring shuffling under the weight of a box of gold. He puffed and huffed, like the Little Engine That Could, but still managed a smile at me. "We've found most of it. Innis did his part."

"Good show! Put it in with Henri. The Gold Limited boss is here to double-check inventory for us."

"That's awfully nice of him."

"Isn't it, though?" I went sideways in the hallway to give him room to pass before going through the doors, intending to help unload whatever else they'd found.

I barely got my feet out into the yard when a prisoner transport van pulled in next to Gibson, blocking my view of them. The officer popped his head out of the open door and called out, "You Edwards?"

"That's me! Who've you got?"

"Two for you: Marianna Rutherford and Simon Biggs."

I hissed in a breath of victory. That meant we had three of the four. Only Jodan Nichols was left abroad. Well, they might have caught him and I just didn't know it yet. I hoped that was the case. Nichols would run for sure if he learned we'd caught the rest of the team. Which would be a rotten shame—he was the only one who knew where the rest of that gold was.

With some help, I got the two processed to wait in the cells. Marianna Rutherford was a large woman, and she used her weight to pull at people, her attitude belligerent. I had to step in and manhandle her into the cell, which she didn't appreciate. For that matter, neither did I. Biggs went so quietly I mistook him for a zombie. The man just shuffled along, skin grey, expression petrified.

That was three down, but where was Jodan Nichols?

I stepped back to my desk and made a phone call to Bristol Station. "This is Detective Edwards. I requested a suspect be detained and shipped to me."

The other side was crackly and scratchy but audible enough. "*Jamie, it's Charlie.*"

"Charlie, hey. What are you up to?"

"*Currently trying to wrangle an answer from your suspect, actually. I just stepped away from my desk to answer the call. You've got good timing. Turns out, Jodan hid the gold here in Bristol, but that's about all he'll confess to.*"

I groaned. It made logistical sense. Of course hiding it in Bristol was easier than carting it back to Kingston. "Yeah, we have confirmation that not all the gold was stashed in the same place. We've recovered the section hidden in Kingston."

"*So, he's not yanking my chain.*"

"Nope."

"*Well don't that beat all. Alright, how do you want to play this?*"

"I've got the CEO of Gold Limited up here double-checking things..." I trailed off, thinking of the logistics. "Let me get someone to babysit him. I'll grab Henri and we'll head down on the next train. It'll be faster than driving down." Mostly because a curvy highway led down to Bristol and Henri would insist I drive at a snail's pace.

"*Alright, I'll put him in holding for now.*"

"Thanks, Charlie." I hung up and went toward Henri's lab. As always, I stopped just behind the yellow line at his door, even though I was relatively sure it was safe.

Elwood was bent over an ingot, a magnifying glass held up to his eye, but he lifted his head as I came in. Henri sat opposite him with an inventory sheet on the table, marking things off, but he too looked up.

"Abracadabra," he said without prompting.

That still made me smile, no matter how many times he did it. Part of the fun with Henri was that he always played along. "Gentlemen, I've got a lead on the rest of the missing gold. Jodan Nichols has been detained, but he's only saying it's in Bristol somewhere. Mr. Elwood, I need my partner. Can another officer help you?"

"Please, Detective," he encouraged cordially. "I've no wish to hold up the process. I believe all my property is here, I'm just inspecting things to make sure no one tried to shave a bit off."

Ah. Probably a smart precaution. "I understand. I'll grab one of my trusted colleagues and be right back."

Henri stood, reaching for his coat hanging on the wall and sliding into it even as he moved. "Who do you want to fetch?"

"Gerring, if he's available. He's already pinch-hit for us once."

"Pinch-hit?"

"The baseball terms are the hardest to explain," I noted rhetorically. "Already helped, I meant. I'll grab Gerring, you update the captain?"

Henri gave me a nod and headed toward the front of the building. I headed for the back. I'd seen Gerring pass me a few minutes ago, headed this direction.

I was correct and found him in a few minutes. Gerring promptly agreed to my request, which reinforced once again that I really had to focus on getting him completely trained. He had the right attitude to make a great detective, he was just short on the know-how. If I focused on him like I had Penny, he'd be detective in six months. Easy.

Mental note to me: Gerring.

I introduced him and Elwood, and they cordially shook

hands before settling back in. I also poked my head into Colette's lab—which looked leagues different from when Sanderson occupied it. It looked (gasp! surprise!) organized— and gave her a head's up just in case the two next door needed help. Then I belatedly realized who I had not updated and fired off a quick message to Gibson.

Henri met up with me at the front door, a taxi already waiting on us. He'd always been good about anticipating things. He held the door open for me as I slid inside, settling on the bench. Henri joined me a second later, double tapping the roof to get the driver going.

"We know nothing about where the gold is, other than Bristol?"

"Nope, no clue. And even that might be a lie. I think Nichols is trying to hedge his bets, maybe get time off for being cooperative." It was a ploy most criminals tried. We sometimes played along, depending, as it did save time and aggravation on our end too. "Charlie didn't say as much, but that was the vibe I got."

"I see." Henri frowned, lips pursed. "I do wonder if we should perhaps stop by the apartment and pack an overnight bag. I have a notion this might run well into the night. And we're short on daylight as it stands."

Considering it was late afternoon now? "It's not a bad idea. I'd rather find a hotel tonight in Bristol than hang out at the station waiting on the morning train."

"Precisely." Henri grimaced. "The one time I did that was a notable memory that doesn't bear repeating."

"Oooh, I sense a story."

"One I'll regale you with later. Let me divert the driver." Henri shifted to the other seat and opened the pass-through window up front, giving instructions to stop by our apartment building first.

I asked Clint if he wanted to come or stay home and chase mice. His decision was quick and unanimous. Train.

I was an old hand at packing in a hurry, thanks to my FBI days. I was in and out in five minutes flat, a carpet bag holding the essentials. (I missed duffle bags and backpacks, but the old-fashioned carpet bags were charming.) Clint rode along my shoulders like the pirate parrot he was in a previous life, beyond excited to ride a train again.

Henri once again met up with me at the door and when he saw Clint on my shoulder, he arched an eyebrow in question.

"Trains apparently trump mice," I informed him drolly.

"Ah."

We loaded back into the taxi, my cat so excited he kept bouncing from window to window. If he'd possessed a tail, he'd have been wagging it furiously like a dog, I will swear to this.

"I meant to tell you," Henri stated in a by-the-by manner, "RM Felix sent me another message requesting a follow up interview with the two of you. He's quite excited you've agreed to work with him in perfecting the Felix."

I turned to face him, a little surprised by this. "Really?"

"Clint is, in a sense, a prototype," Henri explained patiently. "I was able to acquire him through connections. It wasn't because he was commercially available. He is, in fact, only the third generation of Felixes. You're one of the few aside from Jules who truly understands the Felix."

Now that was interesting. It didn't surprise me Henri knew the right people to acquire something that was still a prototype. The man seemed to know everyone in Kingston. "So he views me as...what? A consulting expert?"

"Quite so. If you're amenable, I can respond and set up a meeting?"

"Sure. I personally think it'll be fun. And he did mention he wanted to give me another kitten."

"Kitten?" Henri repeated blankly. "I thought that was in jest."

"Pretty sure he was serious. I think he wants to see if another cat I raise will perform better than the standard, like Clint has done. A repeat experiment on his part, or something."

"When put that way, it does make sense." Henri nodded firmly. "I'm definitely sitting in on that meeting when you two do talk."

I snorted in amusement. Of course he would.

We arrived at the station without fanfare and quickly got out, Henri paying the driver. He'd gotten better about letting me occasionally pay for things, but the bulk of the time he did so, even if it was an expense (like now) the department would reimburse us for.

Libby Shannon had somehow been alerted, as the station master met us at the front door. She kept her voice semi-confidential as she demanded, "I've heard the news, is any of it true?"

"Depends on what you've heard." With rumor mills, the sky was the limit on that. "We've arrested Jodan Nichols, Cain Innis, Simon Biggs, and Marianna Rutherford. Innis and Nichols have confessed. We've recovered most of the gold from the first heist and we're going through it now. We need passage to Bristol. That's where Nichols is—and supposedly the rest of the gold from the first and second heists."

Her mouth went flat with displeasure, eyes spitting fire. "So, it was some of my own employees. Curse their hides. Detectives, you'll get free passage. I'll get you tickets immediately. Whatever we can do to aid you, inform me immediately."

"With pleasure, Station Master, thank you," Henri responded politely.

When Shannon decided to move, she certainly did. She had us on the next train in ten minutes, one of the nicer first-class coaches—with snacks, no less. I appreciated the snacks. I'd missed lunch entirely, what with all the running back and forth.

As we settled in, the train took off in a slow chug, the whistle announcing our departure from the station. I mixed up a cup of hot chocolate and eyed the petite sandwiches, deciding which of them would grace my stomach first.

"Jamie." Henri was mixing up his own drink, lips pursed

thoughtfully. "How much would you care to wager Nichols has done something remarkably stupid, hence his hesitation to speak frankly with us?"

A dark, unamused chuckle tumbled free. "Yeah, no bet."

Report 20: Thief for Hire

I take partial credit for all his future brilliance

Gibson, somehow, beat us there. By probably five minutes, but that was still rather amazing considering how efficiently we'd moved to Bristol. He must have driven and put the pedal to the metal to manage it. He kept bouncing on his toes, like a child waiting for some highly anticipated present.

"You're a little too perky," I informed him.

"We're about to solve *and* recover the stolen property from the biggest gold heist in history," he informed me, still bouncing on his toes. "Of course I'm excited. Here, throw your bags under Charlie's desk. That's where she put mine."

"Alright." I took Henri's too, passing it along, as there wasn't much room to maneuver in this area of the room. "Is Foster here?"

"He is. Currently shadowing Nichols in the interrogation room."

"Good." I'd feel bad if Foster was left out. He'd done so much good work he deserved to help us close this one.

We threw bags under Charlie's desk, and I tucked Clint under one arm as we headed into interrogation. Foster let us in, a smirk on that foxy face of his, and I smirked back before sailing through the door. It did feel good being this close to having a resolution. It's what made this line of work so addictive.

Nichols did not share our excitement. Which was to be expected. He was an odd mix of his fellow thieves—he had Innis' resignation, Rutherford's belligerence, and the grey, ill skin tone of Biggs. That was quite the cocktail of emotions rumbling around in him. As I came in, his head snapped up, and he stared at me with flat brown eyes. I stared back, taking his measure. He wasn't a particularly handsome man, too thin for that, with his hair standing up at weird angles as if he'd been tugging at it. Maybe, under different conditions, he'd be considered attractive.

Right now, I kinda just wanted to shake answers out of him.

"Jodan Nichols." I smiled pleasantly as I sat opposite him at the table. "Let me introduce you. This is Kingsman Foster, Kingsman Gibson, and Dr. Davenforth, Magical Examiner and my partner. I'm Detective Edwards."

Nichols showed no reaction other than to stare fixedly at Clint, still in my lap. "And what's that?"

"A lie detector," I deadpanned, ignoring the chokes behind me. "Now. Where did you hide the rest of the gold?"

"I want immunity from the charges," Nichols said quickly, words tripping over each other.

"No," Gibson answered flatly. "You don't get off completely free from this. We can talk about a reduction of sentence—Innis made that deal—but you *will* pay for this crime."

Nichols shook his head, the argument building, but his eyes kept darting from face to face. Finally he seemed to realize the futility of it, and his shoulders slumped as he deflated. "Fine. Fine. How much of a reduction?"

"Half." Gibson's tone brooked no disagreement. "You serve two years instead of four if you help us recover it."

"Two years," Nichols mouthed, almost silently.

It was a short time, in the long scheme of things. But it was also two years in a place no one sane wanted to live, two years with people who were hardened criminals and had no mercy, two years of not having the freedom to do anything. Two years without family or friends. It was a lot, from that perspective.

"What if I lead you right to it, fetch it myself?" Nichols offered desperately.

"Innis did exactly that. He's still getting two years."

Nichols deflated even further. After a long, stuffy minute

of silence, he finally acquiesced. "You guarantee the two years?"

"I do. I speak with Her Majesty's Voice. I can overturn a jury's sentence."

"Oh. Then fine, I agree. I'll show you."

I stared at the site and whistled low. "Well. This will be problematic."

Nichols stood at my side, wringing his hands and looking (if possible) even paler than before. "It wasn't like this last week! I swear to you, I put the gold in a safe and secured it just inside. No one's worked on this site for months, almost a year. It shouldn't be like this!"

My eyes roved over the half-formed apartment building in question. The brick outer shell was done, but the windows were still tacked over. Even the door looked very makeshift. I could see how Nichols had easily gained access inside. I was still puzzled why he'd thought a half-constructed building was a good idea to hide approximately one hundred thirty-seven thousand in gold, but that was beside the point.

The point was that it was definitely a live construction site now. With protective wards around it.

Henri and Gibson sighed in unison, both of them sounding completely and utterly done. Turning to them, I requested, "Talk to me, guys."

"The wards here work on the same principle as any other," Henri explained, still staring at the wards as if they'd personally offended his mother. "They are couched in such a way that nothing can be taken from the site. Because the gold was there when the wards were set, they're now part of the property, and the wards will prevent its removal. I would guess this builder has had trouble with tools walking away and put the ward up as a deterrent."

I could possibly get through the wards just fine, thanks to Belladonna, but I wasn't really willing to risk it. If I was wrong, I'd end up with possible broken ribs, which was a fat no-thank-you in my book. I could hear banging and general construction noises coming from inside and pointed toward the door. "Someone's working in there."

Brightening, Gibson immediately went to the door and pounded on it. It took a second before the hammering inside stopped. Another minute later, the front door opened and a dusky looking fellow poked his head out, nose scrunching up in query. Werebeaver, eh? Didn't surprise me. They tended to make up most construction crews.

"Can I help you, Kingsman?" the man asked politely.

"I hope so. We're informed there's a great deal of gold hidden on this property. We need to extract it. Can you lower the ward?"

The brown-gold eyes went wide in his round face. "Gold? HERE?"

"Yes, from the train heist that occurred this month," Gibson explained patiently.

"Wow. No, sir, I know nothing about that. That said, we're still tearing into the building. Re-doing the frame and such, you understand. Could be here and we haven't found it yet." Rubbing at the back of his head, he looked doubtfully at the ward, the shimmering transparent gold layer that lay over the building like a finely crafted spiderweb. "And honestly, don't think you can bring anything out. I'd call the boss, but he's on vacation. I was just finishing up a task before quitting for the day. I'm the only one here."

Gibson bit off a curse. "Davenforth, what's your opinion?"

"The ward is very tightly anchored into the building. If we try to force anything, it will either injure the person trying to carry the gold out, or it will warp the building's frame." Henri looked as if he were biting into a rotten fish wrapped in moldy seaweed saying the words.

The construction worker shook his head frantically. "Please don't. Framing's only half-up as it is, and we've got things shored up, but it'll come down hard."

"All for avoiding getting magically eviscerated or having a building collapse on top of us?" I lifted a hand to vote.

Everyone immediately lifted hands to agree, even Clint with a purple paw.

"Let's verify the gold is truly here first," Foster suggested. A truly reasonable suggestion. "Nichols hasn't laid eyes on it for six days. Who knows what's happened in that time."

It was diplomatically phrased to not implicate that Nichols could be lying his face off. Even though we were all thinking it. The thief heard the unspoken words and was stiff as he marched ahead of us, leading us not up, but down into the basement area.

The area down here was crowded with leftover lumber, buckets of scraps, nails, and the odd collection of junk that amassed during construction. Nichols maneuvered around it all without any issue, heading for the furthest corner. He knelt in front of a stack of bricks, what looked to make up most of the foundation wall. Lifting sections of it out with his hands, he revealed a dully finished safe. Not something from the train yard, so he must have bought it for this purpose and stashed it here ahead of time. Still without a word to us, he ran through the combination of it, opening the door without a flourish and standing back.

One look inside confirmed all the missing gold was there. The ingots were stacked neatly and the bag of coins still bore the company's logo.

Foster immediately knelt in front of it and carefully moved things about. "Looks like it's all here. Now what?"

Henri and Gibson immediately put their heads together, magical terms and lingo flying thick in the air and mostly sailing right over my head. I let them talk for a while, listening, not for the words but the tone. It was clear they had ideas but didn't think any of them were viable.

I, on the other hand, did have a viable idea.

Clearing my throat, I got their attention. "Gentlemen. I have an idea."

They stopped and looked to me.

Smiling, I continued. "We do, in fact, know someone who can easily get past this ward. I'll bet you anything you care to name he can get the gold back out, too."

Henri groaned first in realization. "Him?"

"Him," I agreed, smile widening. "I know you don't like the kid, Henri, but he's got the skills to pull this job off."

Gibson's eyebrows went straight into his hairline. "You mean Eddy Jameson?"

"The very one."

Pursing his lips in a soundless whistle, Gibson stared at the safe for a long moment. "You really think he can? But he's only broken *in* before."

"Well, he's managed to breach every possible ward I know of in Kingston. If I tell him he'll get books for bringing the gold out to me, it'll bypass the security on the wards. After all, he's not stealing. He's retrieving. I think it'll work."

"That's a very fine line..." Henri cut himself off, frown deepening. "Technically, we could do the same."

"Do you trust the wards to stay benign?"

"No," he sighed. "After all, I have no nefarious intentions toward the royal family, and the wards still won't let me pass without invitation. I'm not sure what it is about Jameson's mentality that gives him the necessary loophole, but he possesses an ability the rest of us do not. Fine. Let's call him in."

It would mean a two-hour trip, at least, to Kingston and back if I were to fetch Eddy myself. I had a better idea and pulled out my pad, calling Sherard. "Hey, Sherard, I need the kid."

"*Which kid?*"

"The one driving you crazy for most of the month. Eddy Jameson. I need him to retrieve something beyond a ward for me."

"*If you're contacting me, then you want me to get him and portal him to you?*" His voice sounded less than enthused.

"You're so quick on the uptake."

"You realize you owe me for this."

"Yes, yes." I ended the call and put the pad away. "Sherard's portaling the kid to us. Henri, can you give him a precise location?"

With a deep, exasperated sigh, he acquiesced and headed back upstairs.

I knew they didn't like it, but in truth, I had another idea. And if Eddy could pull through here, then it made my idea all the easier to argue.

Because we had nothing else better to do, and I wanted to make this as easy as possible, we unloaded the gold from the safe and hauled it upstairs. We had it all stacked on a makeshift worktable by the time Sherard landed with Eddy, standing on the sidewalk just outside.

My friend looked as if he'd swallowed nails and chased it with lye, but he'd still brought Eddy for me. I really did owe him.

Eddy looked beyond nervous. Considering how many times Sherard had threatened to ship him off to sea, it made sense. He probably felt like he'd been kidnapped. I hastily went to him to put his fears to rest.

"Hey, Eddy," I greeted with a smile, bending a little to put us more at eye level. "I need your help on something. There's something in this building I need retrieved, but the wards on the building are giving us some trouble. So, here's the deal. I think you can get in. If you can retrieve it all for me, I'll pay you in books."

You'd thought I'd offered him all the gold in India. "How many books?"

"I will personally take you to a bookstore and you can pick out any book you want," I promised, my arm to the square as if we were in a courtroom. "Twenty's your limit. How about it? Deal?"

Eddy thrust out a hand immediately and we shook on it.

"Good man." Taking him by the shoulders, I pulled him around so he could see through the open door. "Okay, what I need is right inside the door. This is stolen property, okay?

We're trying to put it back in the right hands. The two gold ingots and all those sacks of coins on the table is what I need, nothing else."

Nodding, he left my hands and marched directly inside. He didn't hesitate to grab one ingot, turn about smartly, and march right back out.

Henri and Gibson both hissed in shock as the wards let him through without even a ripple. I had to bite down on my tongue to keep a cackle behind my teeth. I just knew Eddy could do this. The kid definitely operated in a grey moral area.

Eddy put the ingot directly into my hands, beaming at me. I took it and grinned back. "You just earned yourself two books, kid. Go get 'em."

Giggling, he skipped right back inside.

Yeah, this will be easy peasy lemon squeezy with him doing the legwork.

"Watching this is making my head hurt," Sherard complained to Henri under his breath.

"Tell me about it," Henri grumbled.

Since Eddy was still out of earshot, I took a moment to start my campaign. "But gentlemen, just think. What if we could use that natural ability? What if we could turn it to good instead of mischief? If we hired him to routinely test the defenses of different buildings, wouldn't that be a better use of his talent?"

Henri and Sherard looked at me as if I'd just suggested befriending the devil. But then, little love lost there. Gibson, however, looked intrigued. He at least saw the benefit of it.

Eddy must have overheard enough to get the gist, because as he handed the next ingot of gold over, he asked hopefully, "You need me to break in somewhere else?"

"One job at a time, kid," I encouraged him, shooing him back inside. "Let's focus on this job first. I, for one, want this case completely put to bed."

"But later?"

We really had to give him a legitimate way to use his

talents. He'd be in prison for the next century otherwise. "Later is bookstore, remember?"

Happy at the reminder, he dove back for another armful of gold.

Nichols took issue with this. He hissed at me, "Why is he rewarded for stealing something, and I'm punished?"

"First of all, he's never stolen anything. Second, it's about intent." I glared at him. "There's not a malicious bone in that kid's body. I can't say the same for you. Not only did you steal, but you were attempting to double-cross your partners."

Nichols went ashen white. Seriously, corpses had better color.

I wasn't even surprised. "Foster, we're done with him. Haul him back to the precinct and arrange for prisoner transport, would you?"

"Sure thing, Detective." Foster hauled him away, Gibson going with him just in case.

As for me, I kept standing there, accepting the gold Eddy handed to me, and packaging it up for transport as well.

It really was a heady feeling, solving a case.

Can I have my nap now?   I'll take one with you.

Together? Ooh-la-la

Oh, stop. It's not what Seaton meant.

Or was it?

DO NOT ENCOURAGE HER.

Final Report: My Girls Are the Best!

Girls' Night, for once, started on time.

I'd started out tonight a little differently than usual, mostly because of my additional company. The girls had been understandably a little nervous with having such an august guest, and I'd anticipated that. So, we'd started out with a drinking game, Quavers.

In theory, it was a simple rhythmic game. Move the cup to the right, left, then pass it to the person on your right. But as the rhythm picked up and got faster, drinks started spilling, and the first person to spill had to chug a shot—while still keeping the rhythm. Needless to say, it got messy fast.

After a full round, my guests were a little drunk, definitely giggly, and snorting the fruit tray like it was cocaine. Even my esteemed guest had gotten into the swing of things pretty quickly.

I stood behind my stove now, checking on the jambalaya. Everything looked and tasted right—it was about ready to serve. I had a mild and a spicy version, as I wasn't sure in this crowd who was good with spice. As I retrieved bowls, Colette fetched up against the other end of the bar.

Leaning in, she whispered, "Did you invite her?"

"She sort of invited herself," I admitted. "I didn't dissuade her, though. Everyone needs girl time."

Colette nodded sagely. (She was more than a little drunk at this point. She kept weaving and the head bobbing wasn't helping.) "She's fun. I've decided I like her."

The woman in question joined her at the bar, leaning into Colette's side and beaming up at her in return. "I like you too. I want to come play with you more often. Jamie, I have to play with her. And Ellie. And Penny."

I had to bite my lip to keep from laughing at these two. "You can do that. We're not stopping you."

I got beaming smiles all around. Maybe I should hide the rice wine while they were eating. They'd quite possibly had a bit too much at this point.

There was a respectful knock on the door in a rhythm I knew well. I opened the door and to my complete lack of surprise, there stood Henri. He was in shirt sleeves, rolled up to the elbows, and still in leather slippers, so he'd clearly been home relaxing. In his hands was a bowl, which he held hopefully in front of him like a beggar looking for alms.

"Is that jambalaya?"

I waved him in. "I should have known you'd show up. You were a bloodhound in a previous life, I will swear to this. Come on, come get a bowlful."

"Hi, Henri!" the girls still leaning against the bar chirped at him.

Henri came to an abrupt stop, eyes wide enough to fall out of his skull. "Uh...good evening, Your Majesty, Colette."

Yeah, he was about one second from bolting. Girls' Night was too peopley for him most of the time anyway. Throw a queen in the mix and he had no idea what to do next. I handed him a full bowl so he could escape.

Henri flashed me a grateful smile before cordially wishing everyone, "Enjoy your evening." He disappeared with alacrity for the sanctity of his own apartment, where sanity likely reigned.

My apartment did not fit that criteria right now and likely wouldn't for the next twelve hours. At least. I'd noticed Clint had already escaped.

Without hesitation, Regina took the next bowl and immediately popped a bite into her mouth. She chewed, swallowed, then looked me dead in the eye. "For the good of this country, I require the recipe."

Why was she adorable like this? And if I had to hold back any more laughter, my sides would ache the next day. "I'll make sure it happens. Now come sit down before you spill your bowl. Colette, Ellie, Penny, Charlie, all of you too."

Penny came for a bowl, but even as I ladled it in, she demanded of me, "You didn't really make that kid a professional thief?"

"The term you're looking for is security specialist," I told her, then steadied her bowl as she wobbled her way onto the bar stool. Definitely had to hide that rice wine. "And I didn't do it."

Regina threw her hand up like a child in a grade school class. "I did! I have a professional thief on my payroll. I pay him in books." She giggled, eyes sparkling. "Easiest person to pay. Jamie's to blame, though."

"Yes, yes." I shook my head, amused at the lot of them. "And when it all goes south, I suppose I get the blame for that too?"

"Of course!" Regina caroled. She went a little off key at the end.

Ellie slung an arm around Regina's shoulders. (It was supposed to look affectionate but Regina listed to the right, fetching up against Colette, and it was obvious Ellie's balance was long gone.) "After this, we'll go ride motorcycles. You'll like my motorcycle. It goes vrooooOOOOOOOoooooom."

Regina perked up. "Does it go really, really fast?"

"The fastest! Jamie told me how to design the engine. It goes too fast." Ellie was proudest of that last bit.

"Then let's ride it after the yummy jambalaya."

Guys. We may have corrupted the queen. My bad?

You didn't really take her on a motorcycle ride, did you?

I can neither confirm nor deny such an incident.

They came in about three o'clock in the morning, high on fumes.
I had to help carry Ellie in. She wanted to sleep on the
bike. They then proceeded to drink even more and played
something called "strip poker."

Jamie, you throw the best parties.
cackles

Jamie's Notes to Herself:

- Sampni – it's a fruit, kinda a mix between mango and passionfruit. Really yummy. I can drink my weight in this tea, no kidding.

- Cold tea – is not a thing here. Kingston views cold tea the way the Brits back home think of cold tea. America, WHAT ARE YOU DOING kind of outrage. I think I might have to give this one up as a lost cause.

- FINALLY FOUND SOY SAUCE. It comes from a tree, oddly enough. Kinda like a maple extract.

Air quality in Kingston is starting to get bad. I remember reading that the air quality around the major cities during the Industrial Revolution was really awful. I now see what they mean. I've got a bug in Ellie's ear about putting an air purifier on the mufflers of the cars. Maybe I can put another bug in Queen Regina's ear too?

I have found the equivalent of IKEA. Only it's a magical store. It is APPALLING how that place is laid out. I was lost in there for hours until Sherard rescued me. I learned very quickly that you cannot trust the arrows painted on the floor; that if you mispronounce any of the product names, you can accidentally summon demons; and worse, walls shift and appear out of nowhere! I refuse to go back in there again.

I found a treadmill! Henri's right, it was developed for prisoners and it's really kind of scary looking. Like, it has cuffs on the top handlebar? Not sure I want to get on it, to be honest with you.

Kingstonisms:
- At a rate of knots – to go at top speed, or driving very fast
- Dead on end – when something is lined up perfectly with something else
- Don't hand me a line – when someone is too busy talking and not actually doing the work
- Dragging your anchor – being impeded by something or acting in a tired manner
- Flogging the glass – leaving your watch ahead of schedule, originated by shaking an hour glass to make time go by faster
- A fluky – light wind that doesn't blow steadily from any direction, variable
- In the drink – someone that has fallen into the water
- Leading light – someone who marks the way or is a leader; comes from it being customary to mark the entry to a port with a line of leading lights to show the way
- Coddiwomple – to travel purposefully to an as of yet unknown destination

Fusty – rigidly old-fashioned or reactionary Scurryfunge – a hasty tiding of the house when a last-minute guest is coming to visit

A priori – formed or conceived beforehand, something presupposed by experience

Days of the Week

Earth – Draiocht

Sunday – Gods Day

Monday – Gather Day

Tuesday – Brew Day

Wednesday – Bind Day

Thursday – Hex Day

Friday – Scribe Day

Saturday – Rest Day

Months

Earth – Draiocht

January – Old Moon

February – Snow Moon

March – Crow Moon

April – Seed Moon

May – Hare Moon

June – Rose Moon

July – Hay Moon

August – Corn Moon

September – Harvest Moon

October – Hunter's Moon

November – Frost Moon

December – Blue Moon

Werespecies: werehorses,   wereowls,   weremules, werefoxes, weredogs, werebadger, weremouse, werewolf, werebeavers, wereelephants

Thanks for reading *Breaking and Entering 101*! Ready for their next adventure?

Three Charms for Murder

Other books by Honor Raconteur
Published by Raconteur House
♫ Available in Audiobook! ♫

THE ADVENT MAGE CYCLE
Jaunten ♫
Magus ♫
Advent ♫
Balancer ♫

ADVENT MAGE NOVELS
Advent Mage Compendium
The Dragon's Mage ♫
The Lost Mage

WARLORDS (ADVENT MAGE
Warlords Rising
Warlords Ascending
Warlords Reigning

ANCIENT MAGICKS
Rise of the Catalyst ♫

THE ARTIFACTOR SERIES
The Child Prince ♫
The Dreamer's Curse ♫
The Scofflaw Magician ♫
The Canard Case ♫
The Fae Artifactor ♫

THE CASE FILES OF HENRI DAVENFORTH
Magic and the Shinigami Detective ♫
Charms and Death and Explosions (oh my) ♫
Magic Outside the Box ♫
Breaking and Entering 101 ♫
Three Charms for Murder
Grimoires and Where to Find Them
Death Over the Garden Wall
This Potion is Da Bomb
All in a Name
A Matter of Secrets and Spies

DEEPWOODS SAGA
Deepwoods ♪
Blackstone
Fallen Ward
Origins
Crossroads
Jioni

FAMILIAR AND THE MAGE
The Human Familiar
The Void Mage
Remnants
Echoes

GÆLDORCRÆFT FORCES
Call to Quarters

IMAGINEERS
Imagineer
Excantation

KINGMAKERS
Arrows of Change ♪
Arrows of Promise
Arrows of Revolution

KINGSLAYER
Kingslayer ♪
Sovran at War ♪

SINGLE TITLES
Special Forces 01
Midnight Quest

THE TOMES OF KALERIA
Tomes Apprentice ♪
First of Tomes ♪
Master of Tomes ♪

File X: Author

Honor Raconteur was born loving books. Her mother read her fairy tales and her father read her technical manuals, so was it any wonder she grew up thinking all books were wonderful? At five, she wrote and illustrated her first book.

At *mumbles age* she's lost count of how many books she's written and has no intention of stopping before she climbs into a grave. Right now, she lives in Michigan in a wonderful old Craftsman house with two dogs, three cats, and a fish.

For more information about her books, to be notified when books are released, or get behind the scenes info about upcoming books, sign up for her newsletter at honorraconteur.news@raconteurhouse.com

www.honorraconteur.com
FB: Honor Raconteur's Book Portal
Patreon

Made in United States
Troutdale, OR
09/09/2023

12768271R00136